Charlene and Molley
I hope you enjoy Edie
stories as much as I do
God bless you
Annie Hyde

SMACK DAB IN DOG CROSSING

AND OTHER STORIES

By Ed Grisamore
Author of "True Gris" and "More Gris"

P.O. Box 4491
Macon, Ga. 31208

Library of Congress Control Number: 2005920058

Cover photographs by Joel Edward Grisamore
Cover dog: Jerry Grisamore
Cover design by Julianne Gleaton

ISBN: 0976287560

To Delinda, Ed, Grant and Jake

TABLE OF CONTENTS

INTRODUCTION

The title of my first book came to me in a vision. Well, maybe not a vision, but a mirage on the side of the road.

I was somewhere along Highway 41 near Perry, Ga. It was almost as if a billboard leaned over and slapped me.

True Gris.

My second book, which was co-authored with Bill Buckley, was about the 1973-74 Macon Whoopee hockey team. It was a fun book to write, and we hope a fun book to read.

The title came rather easily on that one — *Once Upon a Whoopee.* I still love to watch the expression on people's faces when I tell them the name of the book.

My third book, another collection of columns and stories, was even easier. Everybody loved *True Gris,* so I just flipped my last name and came up with *More Gris.*

When it came time to name this collection of columns, my friend, George, was ready to roll out the Gris wit.

George suggested *Gris and That* and *Gris is My Country.* He also tried me with *Gris Land is Your Land* and *Who Moved My Gris?*

Nice efforts. I didn't exactly reject any of those titles, but I'll admit I didn't want to wear out the Gris theme.

So I started looking. And looking. And looking.

I wanted it to reflect something Southern. I have lived in the South my entire life, and all but four years in Georgia. I went to my local library and opened a dictionary of Southern sayings.

I was about ready to give up when I landed on "S." And there it was.

Smack Dab.

Then came my next challenge.

Smack dab in the middle of what?

I've been smack dab in lots of places. Trouble. Love. Nowhere.

What about geography? I work in Macon. I have a home in what we call LB— Lower Bolingbroke. I was born in Atlanta.

It was time to settle on being smack dab in something.

Then I got to thinking about all the small towns I've visited in my years at *The Telegraph*. I've been to places so far off the beaten path they're off the beaten path's beaten path.

I could name a few. But one stands out.

I've been to Dog Crossing, and not many people can claim that. It's not on too many maps.

It's a crossroads in Upson County, not far from Thomaston. You can get there through Barnesville, and it's just a stone's throw from a community known as The Rock.

Only about two dozen folks and a few dogs live in Dog Crossing. They didn't even have a sign until I wrote a column a few years back and suggested they ought to put one up so people could at least know when they got there.

I also befriended Ed McHargue, Dog Crossing's best friend. He was the town historian, caretaker and ambassador. He and his son, Roy, had a cabinet shop.

Mr. Ed's father, John Henry McHargue, used to tell him the place got its name when a mule wagon ran over a dog crossing the road.

Mr. Ed died in December 2001, and I went to his funeral. I wrote a column about him I have included in this book. It is his story, and others, I want to share with you.

So please come with me to Dog Crossing.

You can get there from here. You'll be smack dab in the middle of stories you'll never forget.

Foreword

Several years after Ed Grisamore and I quit working together, I discovered Ed's secret.

The best stories are back-porch stories.

Somehow, some way, Ed makes it to the back porch of every home he visits.

OK, maybe he never gets past the living room or the kitchen. But it's in Ed's demeanor to accept the glass of tea, to sample a slice of cake, and listen long enough for people to get in a back-porch mood.

It's on the back porch where people relax in a rocking chair, enjoy a summer breeze, and start telling the stories of their hearts.

At that point, it's easy to do what Ed does. He simply retells the story to the rest of us.

Now this is remarkable. I'm convinced God has a call on each of our lives, and when Ed and I parted ways a few years back, I left journalism for the ministry. Ed simply found his ministry in journalism.

Have you noticed this? Column after column, story after story, Ed Grisamore has become the leading goodwill ambassador for Middle Georgia.

If the rest of the newspaper is filled with accounts of crime, political shenanigans and obituaries, you can count on Ed's stories to be the bright spot of the paper.

If the entire community seems to be in a bad mood, Ed's in a good mood. If the headlines ruin our breakfast, Ed gives us a reason to get on with the morning, anyway.

Through his column, he has introduced us to the best people in our communities. Some are unsung heroes. Some have shown great courage in the face of great adversity. Some have helped us smile. Many have reminded us how important it is to have a strong faith in God, and in one another.

It's a rare thing to make it to the back porch these days, but Ed takes us there over and over again.

You hold a real gift in your hands. The stories that follow are read much faster than they were first told. So maybe it would be a good idea if you grabbed a glass of ice tea, a slice of cake, and found a rocking chair.

Don't rush the reading.

Hear the screen door swinging on rusty hinges? That would be Ed, coming in to tell us another story or two.

I'm proud to call him my friend, and ready for a good, long break on the back porch.

Andy Cook, Pastor
Shirley Hills Baptist Church
Warner Robins, Ga.

FAMILY
MATTERS

A Father's Greatest Gift Is His Children
June 20, 2004

Dear Ed, Grant and Jake:

No, this isn't going to be another lecture. I'm not glaring at you over the top of my glasses.

I'm not going to ride your tail and remind you it's time for a haircut or to tuck in your shirt.

This is a thank-you note from a father to his three sons.

Thanks, guys.

Last week, another writer asked me to describe how I felt when I published my first book in 1997.

"I picked it up, held it in my arms and cried," I said. "It was like becoming a father for the first time."

Of all my life experiences, there has been no greater joy than my children.

I don't expect you to fully understand that now. One day, when you become fathers, I hope you will.

I remember each of those trips to the hospital to bring you into the world. Once, our car raced through the dark streets at 2 a.m. with your mother's contractions getting closer together. In the delivery room, I realized it's possible to be exhilarated and terrified at the same time.

In Lamaze classes, we had learned how expectant mothers should breathe.

Fathers could use some breathing lessons, too.

Those childbirth classes also emphasized the importance of having a "focal point" during the delivery.

Since the moment each of you arrived, you have been our focal point.

You've probably heard other men talking about the day they became fathers. The stork showed up. Cigars were passed around. Tears were dabbed at the windows of the hospital nursery.

But birth is only the opening act on the stage of happiness. "Proud father" is a permanent badge.

Fatherhood does not come with an instruction manual. There is no toll-free number to call for technical support, as there is with computers and lawn mowers.

Much of it is trial and error. OK, I'll admit sometimes it has been your trial and my error. But, for the most part, father knows best.

Don't ever forget it.

Parenting brings its share of splinters. There have been days when

you have gotten on my last nerve. You have sent my blood pressure higher than the Dow Jones average. At times, I've wanted to pull out my hair with one hand and wring your neck with the other.

But the rewards have been a trip to bountiful. I've popped so many buttons, I should keep a needle and thread with me at all times.

On a wall at home there are three framed sets of footprints. I can no longer keep pace with those feet. They won't stay still. You're off to theater camp. Or a job. Or a concert in Indiana. Or to Europe with a girlfriend.

I guess my job has become to throw down the anchor and be here when you return to port.

If there has been a character trait that has been constant in your lives, it is that you never forget to tell people you love them. You tell me every time you hang up the phone or walk out the door.

That's why, as my own father says, every day is Father's Day.

You are my greatest gift.

Love, Dad.

Hospitals Are a Part of Life

July 20, 2003

By the end of the day, I had been to five different floors at The Medical Center of Central Georgia.

I was following a woman with wheels on her bed. They kept moving her around until she finally spent the night on the fourth floor.

That woman was my mother, who had her second heart procedure in a week.

She kept insisting we didn't need to come to the hospital. It was just a catheterization, not surgery. They were only keeping her overnight for observation.

Ten days ago, the doctor pulled out detailed pictures of her heart. He showed us parts he had fixed and areas that required further mending.

I then realized I was looking at my mother's heart for the first time — the heart that has loved me all these years and swells with pride every time I see her.

But when she told me not to come to the hospital, I ignored her. How could I not be there?

On the day of the procedure, we were walking the labyrinth of hallways and pushing elevator buttons from floor to floor when my father asked me how many times I had been to the hospital.

I didn't know how to answer. I have visited the Medical Center and

the other hospitals in Macon so often I could qualify for my own reserved parking place.

I've gone countless times to see family and friends, made deacon visits and written hundreds of stories from hospital bedsides.

I've even been a patient myself. I know the cling of a hospital gown, the sight of blood being drawn from my arm and those final moments before the anesthesia whisks me from the conscious world.

I've been around hospitals my entire life. Dad is a retired physician. As a child, I remember tagging along to the emergency room one Saturday night, watching the skilled hands of a surgeon put accident victims back together.

A hospital is an institution where the life cycle is played under one roof. It is where first breaths and last breaths are taken. It is where lives are extended, last rites are issued and perhaps more prayers are said than in church.

As I walked the hospital hallways this past week, I thought about babies being born on the third floor while cancer patients were battling for their lives six floors above them.

I passed countless waiting rooms where people from all walks of life kept vigil in chairs. I saw doctors and ministers making their daily rounds, each healing in their own way. In the parking deck, I noticed cars from almost every surrounding county.

I overheard a man on his cell phone on the pedestrian bridge expressing the joyful news about his wife's successful operation. And a woman weeping softly at the foot of a bed as family members tried to comfort her.

I saw patients with tremendous support from their families. And others sadly having to brave it alone.

My mother is home now and doing fine.

I'm sure I'll be back at the hospital soon. It's not something we ever plan.

It's a part of life.

Thanks, Dad, for All Life's Lessons

June 16, 2002

Dear Dad:

I wasn't surprised when you wrote what you wanted for Father's Day from your five children.

It can't be bought in a store or ordered from a catalog.

You asked for a letter from each of us.

So I'm writing to say thank you.

Again.

Thanks for encouraging me to be whatever I wanted to be in life, not what someone else wanted me to be.

In doing so, you taught me to follow my heart.

Thanks for taking me places when I was growing up. From the family vacations at Jekyll Island to a glacier in Canada to the top of the Eiffel Tower in Paris.

In doing so, you opened my eyes to the world.

And thanks for showing me how to buy a car, too. You are a champion at playing hardball. I've seen you walk out of a showroom in a dispute over a few dollars.

In doing so, you taught me that you've got to make the dealer want to sell you the car more than you want to buy it.

Thanks for keeping me at arm's length at the supper table. You used to pop me when I was out of line. I usually deserved it. But you were always close enough to pat me on the back, too.

In doing so, you taught me that, either way, there is always love in a father's hands.

Thanks for emphasizing the benefits of drinking plenty of water. Or, as you call it, "nature's soft drink." And the importance of exercise, a low-fat diet, seat belts and sunscreen.

In doing so, you taught me the value of good health.

Thanks for taking me to see Phil Niekro throw his knuckleball in Atlanta Stadium and the Harlem Globetrotters entertain the crowd at the civic center in Jacksonville, Fla. Thanks for the tickets to watch Gale Sayers run like the wind in an exhibition football game in Norfolk, Va. Even though you weren't a big sports fan, you took me because you knew I wanted to go.

In doing so, you taught me the importance of spending time with your children.

Thanks for instilling in me a work ethic. I learned how to lay bricks and shovel the earth. It wasn't until later that I understood why you "tortured" me by making me help you in the yard on Saturday afternoons.

In doing so, you taught me the satisfaction of a job well done.

Thanks for letting me ride my new mini-bike before Christmas in the ninth grade. Better yet, thanks for insisting that I put it under the tree on Christmas morning, bent handlebars and all, after I had wrecked it.

In doing so, you taught me to be more careful.

Thanks for those pep talks to "slay my dragons." That always has

been your way of recognizing that every day is going to have its obstacles, so you might as well have your sword drawn.

In doing so, you taught me that opportunities are often disguised as challenges.

Thanks for all your advice about politics, gardening, photography and bread making. You have truly broadened my horizons.

In doing so, you taught me an appreciation for some of the finest things in life.

And you're one of them.

Thanks, Dad.

Love, Ed

Summers Before the Mouse

June 28, 2002

Thanks to those family vacations of my youth, I know the difference between a stalagmite and a stalactite.

I've been to the top of Lookout Mountain and cooled in the recesses of Luray Caverns. I memorized my state capitals in the back seat of a 1966 Buick station wagon.

Those were among the greatest adventures of my life, even if one of my sisters got car sick every time we weaved through the Smoky Mountains.

It was a generation ago, when gas was 29 cents a gallon — not $1.29 — and they pumped it for you.

If the neighbors asked about your SUV, they meant Summer's Unbelievable Vacation.

See Rock City. The glass bottom boats at Silver Springs. Lion Country Safari. Stuckey's: 10 Miles.

Vacations have changed. Sometimes I long for a return trip to the days before cruise control and vanilla voyages down the interstate.

I guess I should consider myself fortunate to have experienced summer before a mouse became mayor of Orlando.

All this came rushing back after a friend, Steve Cohen, brought by a book titled *Dixie Before Disney.*

Much of it is based on the recollections and research of author Tim Hollis. He pays tribute to the tourist attractions, pit stops and natural wonders that defined the South before Walt Disney World opened in 1971 and changed touring habits across Dixie.

Believe me, old times there are not forgotten.

I've aged enough to remember when folks paddled back roads

splashed with Burma Shave signs. And when barely a barn in the South didn't have "See Rock City" painted on the roof.

The book brought back happy memories of family vacations. Life marched to a different rhythm back then.

There was magic everywhere. You didn't have to go to the Magic Kingdom to find it.

Families now lump their vacation plans into an unimaginative response:

We're going to Disney.

OK, so the billboards tell us we can exit and save on Disney tickets from as far away as North Carolina.

But raise your hands if you remember planning entire trips around going to Marineland, home of the world's first trained porpoise show.

You tend to date yourself when you recall that they filmed Tarzan movies and the TV series "Sea Hunt" at Silver Springs in Ocala.

Or if you can mentally redial Tombstone Territory in Panama City Beach, now buried beneath the parking lot of a Super Wal-Mart and a string of fast-foot restaurants.

I still have strong memories of riding the incline to Ghost Town in the Sky in Maggie Valley, N.C. I've toured the Cyclorama and Castillo de San Marcos. I remember those pecan log rolls and rubber alligators at Stuckey's.

Sadly, some of the South's unique attractions have disappeared. Others are simply hanging on.

Many were a combination of wacky and tacky, proving the theory folks will spend their vacation money on just about anything.

A time. A place. Add a little glitter. The flicker of an 8mm home movie.

Dixie before Disney.

Sigh.

Back Porch People

The Whole World in Her Hands
September 27, 1998

REYNOLDS — Hazel Lane does not reach to shake hands. Instead, she wraps her arms around your neck and gives you a big hug.

She gives the best hugs in Taylor County. When you hear her remarkable story, you will want to hug her, too.

Not only is she the best hugger anywhere between Butler and Potterville, she also may be the best cook. They call her the "Dumpling Lady" around Reynolds. Her biscuits are dropped straight out of heaven's oven. Folks have been known to travel for miles to beg for her banana pudding recipe.

She cooks, sews, hugs and can tie a pretty Christmas bow. She once pinned diapers on three children. She has beautiful handwriting. An avid golfer, she has two career holes-in-one. But what's so special about all that?

Hazel Lane has lived 77 of her 78 years without hands. And, if you're looking for a hero this morning, may I suggest a dear woman whose courage and determination once inspired a Sunday sermon?

"To me, I'm just normal," she said. "The Lord helped me believe I was as good as anyone else."

Bruce Goddard, the local undertaker, has admired Miss Hazel since he was a young boy. Although he now towers three heads above her, he never has stopped looking up to her.

"It was a long time before I ever noticed her hands," he said. "She doesn't think: Why did the world do me this way? Her attitude has been to do the best with what she's got."

Lane doesn't remember tumbling into the fireplace when she was 14 months old. Her mother was in the back yard with the laundry and did not hear the screams.

By the time her mother found her, she was unconscious. The burned skin from her hands to her elbows fell to the floor. Doctors said she probably would not live. She had more than 30 convulsions.

But her father, who was studying for the ministry at Norman Park, huddled around the crib with other preachers and prayed. His daughter stood and reached up to him with her hands.

The accident left her with the stubs of three fingers on her left hand and three tiny appendages and a thumb on her right. She learned to turn the pages of the Sears Roebuck catalog with her toes. The other children were cruel and called her "Nubby." She became so self-conscious about her deformity that she even hid her hands from her husband until after

they were married.

"I would kiss him, but we never held hands," she said. Married at 16, she never could wear a wedding ring.

With three kids in tow, the family moved to Reynolds in 1948, where the late Wade Lane worked for Georgia Power. His wife would not walk downtown. She was afraid people would whisper and stare.

One day, though, she took her hands out of her pockets.

"I just got tired of living like that," she said. "I decided to let out the person inside of me. I was determined to be like everyone else."

So she went to work at a clothing store. She taught Sunday School for 40 years. Her golf handicap wasn't a handicap, either. She strapped on her trusty 3-wood, Old Betsy, and hit golf balls until her arms were black and blue.

Sure, children still stare. Adults sometimes give her strange looks, too. She wishes she could wear a sign. Or at least stop and tell her story. And she still believes hands are the most beautiful part of the body.

Chuck Byrd grew up in Taylor County as the son of former Lt. Gov. Garland Byrd and is a lifetime member of Hazel Lane's fan club.

Said Byrd: "She holds her hands to pray, just like everyone else."

Toast of the Town

July 6, 2003

MCRAE — The shoe polish has started to fade on the window of the 1978 blue Malibu parked on Corinth Avenue.

When you notice it from the corner of Andrews Street or coming across the railroad tracks downtown, you might assume someone just got married or was headed to the state baseball tournament.

Until now, nobody in McRae ever has been able to claim the words someone wrote on the rear window of Quinton Lampkin's car. Nobody from Georgia has, either.

This car belongs to the National Beta Club president.

Although the polish may be starting to wear thin, the thrill will never lose its luster.

Quinton Lampkin, a rising senior at Telfair County High School, is the toast of this town.

In the past week, he has spoken to the local Rotary Club, read a poem on the Fourth of July at the Chamber of Commerce, and will be honored at a City Hall reception Monday.

He is one of those young people you meet and don't ever forget. Bright. Articulate. Enthusiastic.

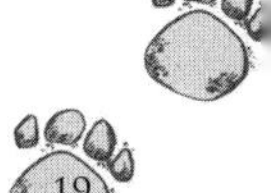

To appreciate where he is going, you must understand where he has been.

He has lived two very different lives.

Four years ago, that proverbial fork in the road was shaped more like a dagger.

The youngest of 10 children, he came from a broken home. He was a troublemaker at school. He had a few brushes with the law.

"I had to learn to be independent because I couldn't depend on my parents to look after me for everything I needed," he said. "I didn't care about life or care about people."

When he was in the eighth grade, social workers begged his grandmother to take him under her roof.

Teressa Blackshear wasn't sure she could handle Quinton, one of her 15 grandchildren. She was in her late 70s and had undergone a double mastectomy. She had suffered a heart attack and had two knee replacements.

"I didn't think I could take on a teenager," she said. "But I prayed about it, and he came to live with me. He has never been a minute's trouble."

From the day he arrived, Quinton has been an exemplary young man. He has made straight A's on his report cards, carrying a 98 average in the classroom. He has been class president every year in high school and is drum major of the Trojans' marching band.

He serves as youth minister at Corinth CME Church. He helps support himself and his grandmother by working behind a cash register at McDonald's.

It wasn't fairy dust or miracle water that transformed Quinton's life.

It was the strong embrace of a grandmother's love and the worn pages of a family Bible.

"This child has come a long way," Blackshear said. "God has his hands on him, and he is going to show the world what he can do."

Quinton has many people to thank along the way. There is his grandmother, of course. And a friend, Kashay Moring, who has pushed him academically. (He has pushed her back.) There is his cousin, SaJuana Wilson, now an assistant principal in Moultrie, who stayed on him about his grades, bought him clothes and showed him unconditional love.

His teachers have been there for him, too, and made sure he was a child who didn't slip through society's cracks.

"My teachers saw my potential even when I did not see it," Quinton said.

"They believed in me and helped me believe in myself."

As president of the Senior Beta Club at Telfair, Quinton won his campaign for state president in January at the convention at the Hyatt Regency in Atlanta.

Two weeks ago, he was one of 2,520 high school students who attended the national convention at the Gaylord Opryland Nashville Resort Hotel and The Grand Ole Opry House in Nashville, Tenn. He was one of seven candidates running for national president. After the first round of voting, he found himself one of three finalists. He was running against candidates from Texas and Missouri, places that had larger delegations than Georgia.

But his message resonated with other students at the convention. For his campaign slogan, he borrowed the title of a sermon he preached in his church a few months ago.

He turned the phrase "Don't Miss Your Cue" into "Don't Miss Your Q."

"The sermon was about Moses and the burning bush," he said. "When God does something to get your attention, don't miss the signal."

When the announcement came that he had been elected as the organization's 23rd national president — the first-ever from Georgia — he jumped in the air, then fell to the floor in tears of joy.

"Next to becoming a Christian, it was the highlight of my life," he said.

There is something else you should know about Quinton. When he ordered his senior class ring, the one with "Q" embedded in a blue stone, he had the word "President" engraved on the side.

No, it was not to celebrate being president of Telfair's Class of 2004.

Or even an omen to being named the top officer in the state and national Beta clubs.

It was a dream. A reminder. A challenge. An inspiration.

The young man who lives in the white house on Corinth Avenue wants to live in another White House one day.

"I want to be President of the United States," he said.

When the early polls come in, he already will have my vote.

A High School's Special Ambassador

January 18, 2004

THOMASTON — Justin Craft is Mr. Upson-Lee High School.

He is not the star quarterback on the football team. He won't be the class valedictorian. He does not drive the coolest car in the parking lot.

But you could search from Silvertown to Lincoln Park and not find anyone more deserving.

Justin isn't your typical high school senior. He doesn't worry about algebra tests or getting a pimple before a date on Friday night.

Justin is mentally challenged. Everything in his life has to be reduced to the simplest terms.

But, while his mental capacity is limited, he makes up for it with a size XXXL heart. Justin will give out more hugs in 12 minutes than most of us do in 12 months.

"It's unconditional love," said his father, Jim Craft. "He doesn't care what color you are, what kind of vehicle you drive, what kind of tennis shoes you wear or what kind of house you live in."

Jim Craft remembers when a stranger once visited their church. The man obviously had fallen on hard times, and was sitting alone. When Justin went over and put his arm around him to comfort him, the man started crying.

But Justin isn't the only hero of this story. The senior class at Upson-Lee is pretty special, too.

These seniors elected Justin as Mr. Upson-Lee last fall. It wasn't a joke or a publicity stunt. They went looking for a worthy ambassador, and their depth of understanding led them to Justin.

Senior Patrick Larson can't recall a time when he has seen Justin without a smile on his face. Another senior, Amy Blount, said Justin's loving personality is contagious.

"When I first met him, I think I pitied him," said senior Matt Peek. "But that quickly changed to admiration. He has this sweet innocence about him."

Upson principal Bill Aplin said the students' heartfelt decision to elect Justin "restored my faith in young people."

It didn't simply make Justin's day, Aplin said. "It made his ... life."

Jim Craft is a distribution manager at the Yamaha plant less than a mile from the school. His wife died of cancer in September 2000. (He has since remarried.)

He will never forget the phone call from Justin's special education teacher, Patty Gilleland, the day of Justin's selection. She was crying, and Jim thought something had happened to his oldest son.

When she told him, the tears flowed on both ends. "I couldn't even talk," he said.

Justin went to Wal-Mart, where he works as a greeter, and filled a buggy with candy. He tossed it out while riding in a convertible during the homecoming parade last October, a parade he still believes

was meant just for him.

Justin will wear his badge of honor in the coming months. He will sport a tuxedo at the prom on April 24. (He danced so much at last year's prom he got blisters on his feet.)

On May 22, Justin will take part in graduation exercises.

Said Peek: "When Justin gets his diploma, there's not going to be a dry eye in the place."

There's probably not too many reading this, either.

Butterbeans and Sunshine

June 7, 1997

He enjoys this time of the day, in the early morning before the sun comes up. The world lies so still he can almost hear his heart beating above the hum of the Chevy pickup truck.

"It's peaceful and quiet," said Oscar Whisby. "Sometimes, I can drive down Second Street at four o'clock in the morning and never meet another car."

His friends and family have called him "Sun" since he was a youngster growing up in Jones County 66 years ago. On most mornings, he gets to see his namesake make its appointed appearance in the sky.

Whisby then grins and flashes the only tooth in his mouth for all the world to see.

"I just thank God I'm here for another day," he said.

He has been delivering fruits and vegetables to local schools and businesses for almost 50 years. If you've ever topped your hot dog with onions at Nu-Way, had a sliced tomato on your salad at Len Berg's or plopped a banana on your cereal at Denny's, you can almost bet Oscar Whisby delivered it there for you.

Most of his career was spent in delivery at Mulberry Provision, where he began working in 1948. He retired in 1992, but Johnny Walsh of Stokes-Shaheen Produce soon brought him on board.

"He asked me what I planned to do when I retired, and I said: 'Nothing,' " said Whisby.

Trouble was, that's about what his Social Security benefits amounted to — nothing. So he returned to work out of necessity.

Mulberry Provision closed in 1996, but Whisby sometimes still wears his old uniform to work at Stokes-Shaheen.

"Sometimes I'll be walking down the street, and someone will say: 'Hey, Mulberry,' and I know they're talking about me," Whisby said, laughing.

Whisby's mother, Kate, died of a stroke when he was only a month old, and his father, Abe, passed away when Whisby was 14. He had wanted to enlist in the Navy when he was 17, but his older brother, Willie, refused to sign the guardian-release papers.

As a teenager, he got his start in the business by helping a local man go door-to-door selling fruits and vegetables.

"We would ride around town in his truck," Whisby said. "He would honk his horn, and people would come out to buy things like watermelons, cantaloupes, snap beans and butterbeans. If they needed help carrying it all back to their house, we would help them."

Whisby has become somewhat of an institution on his route. He knows all his customers, and they know him. His co-workers like to tease him about having a light foot behind the steering wheel.

"I do drive kind of slow," he admitted. "But I've never had an accident. I even got a 'safety' pin when I was at Mulberry."

That makes him almost as proud as his service as a deacon at St. Mark Missionary Baptist Church, the only church he has attended in his life.

He's in bed every night by 8 and up at 2:45 a.m. He begins his routes at 4 a.m. and finishes in the early afternoon.

"Sometimes, I sing hymns to myself while I'm making my deliveries," he said.

No doubt, "Bringing in the Sheaves" must be one of them.

Faith Lights Way for Blind Man

December 6, 1997

GRAY — Deacon Huff sits and watches the world go by on his own terms.

He hears the big trucks roll along, turning their 18 wheels toward Macon. Instinct lets him know when the nearby schools are dismissed every afternoon. That's when he can expect to hear children walking past his fruit and vegetable stand.

He senses when a customer has stopped by. A car door opens, and often the voice is familiar.

If he does not recognize the voice, Deacon Huff will reach to shake hands.

And maybe tell them he is blind.

But usually only if they ask.

Sometimes business is slow. Other times he gets so busy he must move quickly to keep up with the fruits of his labor. The vegetables, too.

"Between me and the Lord, I do real good," he said. "He watches over me. I have to give him all the thanks, because I'm out here by myself a lot of days."

His real name is Leonard Huff, but folks call him Deacon because that's his title over at Mount Salem Baptist Church. His wife, Alma, often stays with him under the tent awning. Other times, friends come by to keep him company.

Many days, though, he is alone with his collards and the sound of the radio in the cab of his pickup truck. If it gets real quiet, he may even take a nap.

"I meet a lot of good people," he said. "Some folks who come by want to pray for me, or have me pray for them. I meet a lot of bad people, too. I've had people steal my stuff. We live in a world where people will do anything. It doesn't happen often, but it has happened. What do I do? I just pray for them."

He has plenty of eyes watching over him, including the eyes of the law. Jones County Sheriff Butch Reece and his deputies regularly pass Huff's tent in front of the old Jones County High School when they pull into the driveway to the sheriff's office.

"I enjoy seeing him over there," Reece said. "He's a hard worker who doesn't give up. He's out there when it's cold. He's out there when it's raining. I sometimes see people from out of state who have stopped to buy from him. By being there, he helps give Gray that small-town atmosphere."

Growing up in Macon, Huff once knew a blind man, Walter Pitts, who ran a small store in his south Macon neighborhood. But he never dreamed he would have to deal with the condition himself. He lived a normal life, working at Keebler until glaucoma robbed him of his sight in 1981.

Within a year, he had slipped into darkness. At first, he began to feel sorry for himself. Then, he learned to accept it.

Six years ago, he began selling fruits and vegetables along Clinton Street in downtown Gray. He now pitches his tent just a stone's throw from the courthouse on Gray's main thoroughfare.

James Farlar, who lives in Clinton, sometimes will stop by on windy days and help Huff readjust the tent stakes.

"He gets out here and does this almost every day," Farlar said. "I think a lot of him. He's an inspiration."

Said Huff: "I have a lot of people who support me, because they know I'm out here trying to do something and not just waiting on a (Social Security) check every month," he said. "I enjoy getting out of

the house. I enjoy meeting people. Sometimes, people will stop and they don't realize I'm blind. They just stand there with the money in their hand until I tell them."

Because he cannot distinguish the denomination of bills, Huff said he has to trust his customers and rely on the honor system.

And while there may be a few bad apples trying to buy his oranges, he likes to think most people in the world are trustworthy.

That's just the way he lives.

"The Bible teaches us to walk by faith, not by sight," said The Deacon.

Like a New Pair of Shoes

May 2, 1999

The father called his son to let him know he had sent "something" in the mail. The postman was bringing it across four state lines.

The son waited for the mail, but he also stayed busy. After all, he owns a Ford dealership in Highland Park, Ill., a suburb of Chicago.

When he recognized the postmark from Macon, he knew "something" had arrived, so he reached to open the envelope.

It was a letter from Dad.

He closed the door to his office. And cried.

"Dear Son: I hope this note finds you well of the cold you have. I am learning how to write. I am in class at the time. We have been reading the Holy Bible. My tutor Amanda does not tell me what a word is. I am learning to sound out the words. This is the first letter I have written in my life. Love, Dad. P.S. Pray for me. I love you."

Carl Statham Sr. is 81 years old. For the past two-and-a-half years, he has been learning to read through the adult literacy program at the Bibb County Adult Education Center.

"You're never too old to learn," he said.

His son, Carl Jr., grew up knowing his father had difficulty fitting words together on paper. As a young man, it never concerned him.

For 45 years, his father was a cobbler on Montpelier Avenue, not far from where he now attends classes at the learning center housed in the old Miller High School. His inability to read never really got in the way at his West End Shoe Shop. He hired clerical work. His wife of 60 years, Marie, kept the books.

"I realized my father had this handicap, but it never was something we discussed that much," said Carl Statham Jr. "Learning to read and write just wasn't a priority with him. And it really wasn't noticeable in

his business, because he knew enough to take care of his daily affairs."

Said his father: "I knew just enough to get by."

But it began to bother him about 15 years ago. He was visiting his granddaughter. She asked him to read something to her, and he couldn't.

"That stuck with him and was a driving force behind his decision to learn to read," said Carl Jr. "And now, 15 years later, he has written his first letter."

Carl Statham Sr. was born in Wellston, the community that later became known as Warner Robins. His father died when he was 4, so he never had the opportunity to attend classes at a schoolhouse nearby.

"I never heard the words: 'Go to school,' " he said. "The only words I heard were: 'Work, or you don't eat.' "

So he labored in the fields for 35 cents a day and a meal. He grew up, got married, joined the service, came home from World War II and was taught a trade. He used vocational training to learn how to repair shoes.

"I did what Moses said to do," he said. "Use what you've got."

The past 10 years have not always been easy. Carl Statham has battled cancer, had two heart surgeries and suffered a brain tumor.

His wife is now in a nursing home.

But reading has opened up new worlds. He can recognize labels and distinguish road signs. He reads his Bible every day.

He even compares his grades and competes with his, grandson Chris, who is in the ninth grade. Chris complains that his grandfather sets the competitive bar too high.

"He has been a man on a mission," said Carl Jr., laughing.

And then there are the letters.

Words, like a new pair of shoes, can take you anywhere.

He sometimes needs 45 minutes to compose a simple 73-word note to his son. But his words come straight from his heart and spill onto the paper.

It took 81 years for Carl Statham to write his first letter.

Better late than never.

"It's pretty special," said the son.

Proud To Claim Annalyn as Kin

May 21, 2004

EASTMAN – I'm proud to claim Annalyn Peele as one of my kinfolk.

OK, I'll admit it's stretching the branches of the family tree. She is

the daughter of my third cousin's sister-in-law, so we're not exactly blood relatives.

Doesn't matter. When she graduates from Dodge County High School tonight, I'll be as proud as if she were my own daughter.

Annalyn is a special young lady. Of course, folks around here already know that. I'm just trying to educate the rest of the world.

On July 30, 1999, Annalyn was a sweet, smart, energetic and friendly girl with a smile that could make you melt like butter on a plate of warm cornbread.

On July 31, 1999, none of that would change — except for one thing.

Annalyn would never walk again.

When you're 13 years old, the prospects of life in a wheelchair can be devastating.

She was a cheerleader in the eighth grade at Dodge County Middle School. Suddenly, those cartwheels were replaced by wheels that would carry her everywhere.

The accident happened on a Saturday morning. Jerry and Karen Peele planned a trip to Macon with their three daughters — Annalyn and twins Kellie and Kristen.

Jerry is the pastor at First Baptist Church, the largest church in Eastman. They were on their way to visit a church member in the hospital.

On U.S. 23 near Gresston, an oil truck topped a hill, skidded into the northbound lane and collided with their van. Everyone was injured, but Annalyn's spinal cord injury was the most serious.

"I spent a lot of days and nights crying," she said. "It was difficult, but I also had the comfort of knowing God had a purpose for me."

You won't find a better attitude. Anywhere.

"I always try to be happy," she said. "If I've got to be in a wheelchair, I might as well have a good time while I'm in it."

She has inspired those around her. A straight-A student, she ranks seventh in a class of 203 seniors. She has been elected president of her class the past four years and voted "Best All Around" senior by her peers.

When she was named prom queen, she was escorted by her 19-year-old cousin, Andrew Sawyer, of Douglas. Andrew is like a brother, a soul-mate miracle. He was born with a heart defect and has had seven major heart operations.

Not much stops Annalyn. Two years ago, at a water park in Orlando, her mother tried to prepare her for the fact that many of the attractions might not be handicap accessible.

Annalyn strapped on leg braces, climbed more than 100 flights of steps that day and splashed in every drop of water in the park.

Tonight, after graduation, she and 11 other seniors in her youth group from First Baptist will leave to set sail for the Bahamas — on a sailboat!

"We're even going through the Bermuda Triangle," she said.

In the fall, she will enroll at Middle Georgia College as a pre-med major. She has always wanted to be a doctor. The accident inspired her even more.

They're going to miss her at Dodge County High.

"The school won't be the same after she graduates," teacher Kathy Brown told Karen Peele. "She just radiates."

From Sea to Shining Sea

December 14, 2003

EUDORA — On his 68th birthday, Frank Harrison dipped his feet in the Atlantic Ocean and turned his toes to the west.

It was Feb. 19, 1999, on the beach at Tybee Island. He told folks he was walking all the way to California.

On Nov. 26, 2003, Harrison waded into the waters of the Pacific Ocean near San Diego and cried.

His journey of 2,380 miles was over. He calculated he had taken 6,127,500 steps along the way.

He had fully intended to make the entire trip in seven or eight months.

It took him more than four years.

That's because he had to start, stop and start back so many times.

Harrison had part of one lung removed before he ever began. Halfway through his walk, he returned home to have part of the other lung taken out because of cancer.

At other times during his trip, he had to recover from open-heart surgery, prostate surgery and was tested to determine if another spot had formed on his lungs.

His dog, a trusted walking companion, died after he made it all the way to Abilene, Texas. Harrison also had to stay close to his home in Jasper County when his oldest son, Mark, developed serious health problems.

Lesser men might have quit. Harrison kept putting one foot in front of the other.

"In the back of my mind, I always knew I would finish," he said. He did not walk to make a statement, raise money, support a cause or call attention to himself. He did not contact every newspaper and television

station along the way to try to get air time on the local 6 o'clock news.

Like a modern-day Forrest Gump, he just started walking for no apparent reason.

"I asked the Cancer Society. They weren't interested. I asked the Lung Association. They weren't interested. I wrote New Balance shoes. They didn't even answer my letter," he said. "So I walked for myself."

In 1991, he retired as a machinist at Robins Air Force Base. Years of smoking cigarettes caught up with him in 1996, when cancer forced him to have a portion of his right lung removed.

In a moment of inspiration and motivation, he decided to attempt to walk across America. It took him 18 months to win the approval of his wife, Liz.

"When he first told me, I thought he was crazy," she said. "I thought he had lost what little sense he had in the first place."

Harrison joined a health club in nearby Covington and trained by walking four or five hours a day. He selected his birthday to start the journey. He scooped some sand off the beach at Tybee (near Savannah), placed it in a Ziploc bag and hit the open road.

Liz would drive the couple's motor home to a designated campground and drop him off every morning and pick him up later in the day.

The only time he felt like quitting was after the first day. He had walked 8 miles. A few days later, near Reidsville, he walked 25 miles. But only because Liz "lost" him.

"I just kept walking, thinking she would be coming around the next curve," he said.

Harrison lost count of the number of people who stopped their cars to offer help.

Some thought he was suffering from Alzheimer's or dementia and had wandered off. One policeman refused to believe his story. He radioed police headquarters to report he had found a "misplaced man" about 5-foot-9 and weighing 180 pounds.

"Who are you talking about?" Harrison protested. "I'm 6-1, 250. And you think I'm confused?"

In case of an emergency, he wore a badge around his neck: "If you see this old man wandering aimlessly, please tell him his name is Frank Harrison and his motor home is located at ..."

He carried an umbrella to use as a walking stick and to fend off the sun, rain and unfriendly animals. He kept a diary and a tape recorder to capture his experience in words and thoughts.

Like the time he found 80 cents on a bridge. Or the time a police officer wrote him a ticket for walking illegally on the interstate highway.

(A judge later dismissed the ticket.)

Or the time the two young women in Decatur, Miss., stopped and asked: "Are you in distress?" They had seen him at the Wal-Mart back in town and had debated whether to stop. But one of them convinced the other to play the role of Samaritan.

"He's an old man with a dog," she told her friend. "He won't hurt us."

He never sought companionship on his walks, except for his dog, Shomere, which means "guard" in Hebrew. Once, though, in the middle of a deserted highway, he thought he heard voices.

"There wasn't another human being for 30 miles, and I heard this voice when I leaned over," he said.

Turns out, he was accidentally putting pressure on the "play" button of the tape recorder in his pocket. "Scared me to death," he said.

Every state line was a sight for sore eyes. He called his friends, Harold and Mavis Odom of Macon, when he left Louisiana and straddled the border with Texas.

"I'm sitting under a bridge in Waskom, Texas," he said on his cell phone.

"You've only got 827 miles to get across Texas," Mavis Odom reminded him.

It took forever and a day to walk the Lone Star state, almost one-third of the trip.

His last return came on Sept. 19, when he arrived in Deming, N.M., to start the final leg of the trip. Liz couldn't be with him because of their son's health situation, so Harrison advertised in a national motor-home magazine for someone to help chauffeur him.

"If you're old, retired and bored out of your mind, come on!" said the ad.

"Five people answered and would you believe I picked the wrong one?" Harrison said, laughing.

The man's name was Lester, but it might as well have been Disaster. He was from Ohio. He drove Harrison crazy for more than 500 miles, then bailed out on him with 52 miles to go.

A young woman named Kelly, who worked at a campground, offered to assist Harrison with the last part of the walk until Liz could fly out and join him for the final miles.

When they got to Ocean Beach, Calif., Liz called XETV, the local Fox affiliate, and asked if they would send a reporter out to cover the event.

Harrison did not have his umbrella that day, so he stopped at a

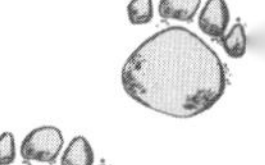

hardware store and spent 77 cents on PVC pipe to use as a walking stick.

"I never got emotional until the end," he said. "I walked out until the water covered my ankles. ... It was the day before Thanksgiving. I was both happy and sad."

Riding home and retracing those millions of steps, Harrison often would point out things he remembered at a certain spot on the road.

Why did he do it? As he sat in his living room on a cold and windy December day, his breathing was labored.

Harrison has to reach deep inside for the answer. Some may call it stubbornness. Others might call it perseverance. Maybe it's because he's a product of the "Greatest Generation."

It's a generation that believes in finishing what it starts.

Fast Friends Take Slow Walk

July 11, 1999

On most days, they never miss their walk.

Seven minutes to the top of the hill. Seven minutes back to the house.

Although it is just the length of a city block, they rarely venture beyond its imaginary boundaries.

They shift their feet into low gear as they ascend the uphill grade of sidewalk along Forsyth Street. They keep their bones and muscles in tow until they can press against the intersection at College Street and turn around.

It is not a breathless climb. They are slow and steady. Besides, they know they can apply the brakes to their stride when they coast back toward St. Paul Apartments.

"It is much easier going downhill," said Jack Morrill, chuckling in the lobby of the high-rise retirement community.

Four years ago, when he moved here, Morrill became fast friends with Paul Brown.

Fast friends bound for a slow walk.

Morrill, 77, is hindered by a bad right leg and an uncooperative left foot. Brown, 72, has been blind since birth.

It is rare, however, that the handicaps of everyday life keep them from their appointed rounds. Morrill lives on the eighth floor. Brown resides on the second. They meet at an arranged time. Some days, it may be in the morning, other times in the late afternoon.

Give us thy daily walk, said the Paul of St. Paul.

It could be the hottest day in July, when the sweat gods attack them

as they leave the door. Or it could be in the chill of a January day that threatens to take their frigid breath away.

Even though the walk is short, it fulfills them. And, when they miss out on it, ... well, the day just doesn't seem quite right.

They are their own support group, leaning on each other as they stroll along. Morrill takes his walking cane. Brown puts trust in his sighted friend. They grab each other by the arm and, occasionally, by the belt loops.

They are faithful in executing the 297 steps from the front door to the corner. They have become familiar with the lay of the land — the curbs along the driveways, the umbrella of shade beneath the distinguished row of Bradford pear trees, and the iron fence beside the Episcopal church.

There is routine in their effort, yet no two steps are exactly the same.

"I tell him what I see," said Morrill. "People walking. Cars passing. Bicycles. Joggers. The trees and birds. The sun as it rises above the tops of the buildings."

Life often laps them at a hurried pace along this inbound artery to downtown.

Soccer moms driving Suburbans. Ambulances rushing toward the Medical Center. Loud trucks idling at the stoplight. Runners testing their torque on one of the city's most famous slopes — dubbed "Heartbreak Hill" by those in the Labor Day Road Race.

Sometimes, if they're feeling a little frisky and a bit hungry, Morrill and Brown will negotiate the busy intersection at College Street to reach the convenience store on the opposite corner.

They have a weakness for ice cream.

Yes, they will cross the road for ice cream.

Brown is enamored by the fresh air and rich sounds of the day. Morrill considers their daily walks both physical and mental therapy. They tell stories, swap jokes, discuss current events and share philosophies.

There is no drudge in their trudge.

The two walkers come from different walks of life.

A Texan, Morrill arrived in Macon four years ago by way of North Carolina to be closer to his son Tom, who lives in Fort Valley. At various times in his life, Morrill has been a teacher, social worker and Methodist minister.

Brown hails from Danville, in Twiggs County, and is a 1951 graduate of the Georgia Academy for the Blind in Macon. He began living at St. Paul in 1994, just a few months before the Great Flood. Of St. Paul's two dozen residents who are legally blind, he is the only one

who is totally blind.

There are times when Morrill wishes he could lead his visually impaired friend into new neighborhoods and different venues in the city. But he is limited by his own bad wheels.

He is afraid of losing his balance. He worries that one of them might take a tumble. Then what would he do?

"I'm more cautious with him, although if anything went wrong, and I had to get him home, I'm sure the Lord would arrange something," Morrill said.

On Fridays, they sometimes walk with a group in the temperature-controlled climes of the Macon Mall.

They prefer their special walk together, though. In the great outdoors, of course.

Seven minutes to the corner.

Seven minutes on the return trip.

It's funny how some folks can travel around the world and never really see a thing.

And then there are others, like Jack Morrill and Paul Brown, who can walk the block and see the whole world.

Walking on Sunshine

December 3, 1999

WARNER ROBINS — It was just a dream. But in that deep sleep, beneath the covers on a cold December night, Clara Gray found her legs again.

She could wiggle her toes. Her feet were gliding across the floor. In her dream, she was getting ready to leave the house. Her friend, Mary, was there. So was her daughter, Michelle.

"Mama, you're walking again!" said Michelle.

Then Clara Gray woke up.

When she talks about the dream, only a few days old, tears roll down her cheeks and tumble onto her lap. Her tear ducts are backwaters of sadness.

But these drops are overpowered by hope.

It has been almost two years since Gray has been able to walk. Diabetes has stalked her for most of her adult life.

First, it nibbled off a couple of toes. Then it robbed her of her right leg (below the knee) in 1996. After nine surgeries, it took away part of her left leg a year later.

In her doses of pain medicine, there was no bitter pill to swallow.

"I've accepted not having my legs," she said. "At least I have my life."

Need some inspiration this Christmas season? Meet Clara Belle Gray. It takes a special lady to tap dance on misfortune with such a positive attitude.

Less than two weeks after her second amputation, she was back for worship service at the Houston Mount Zion Baptist Church in Bonaire.

"Just look at Sister Gray out there with a smile on her face," said the Rev. Nathaniel Jackson Sr. "A lot of us would be hanging our heads."

Life brings its share of swift miracles. This has not been one of them.

Gray has relied on her faith to bring progress in slow, steady increments.

"I promised myself that I wasn't going to let this wheelchair take over my life," she said.

Before Christmas, she is determined to take her first solo flight with artificial legs. She remains confident that grace will triumph over gravity.

"I'm a little scared," she said. "But I know I can do it. I'll be leaning on Jesus."

It would have been easy to quit with no knees to kneel and pray.

Yet Gray never once asked: "Why me?" She accepted her circumstances and refused to become a victim of them.

She grew up in Oaky Woods in rural Houston County. She was the oldest girl in a house with eight children, so she had to start working at age 13 after her mother died.

She later had several jobs in the hotel and restaurant business. She quit work when her daughter was born on a Thanksgiving Day in 1978.

Michelle is 21 years old now. She has a learning disability and still lives in the care of her disabled mother in a tiny trailer on the south side of Warner Robins. Gray plans to move into a larger trailer later this month, closer to her brothers. Her wheelchair is too wide to navigate the small hallway to her bedroom, and she has had to have her bed moved into the living room.

You must walk in her shoes to understand how it feels not to have feet to wear shoes.

"It's something people wouldn't understand unless they had to live that way themselves," she said.

She doesn't complain. She doesn't wallow in self-pity. Of course, Gray holds on to a dream. This one is real.

Her dream is to climb back into the loft to rejoin the gospel choir at church.

"I want to stand up and sing again," she said.

Bet that chorus is going to sound wonderful.

Clara died in January 2001.

Gentle Fellow Had a Big Heart

June 23, 2000

Like most folks, I never knew Edward Whitehead Jr.

So I didn't pay much attention when his 74-word obituary appeared on Sept. 25, 1998. Or that he was buried on an Indian summer day in Rose Hill Cemetery.

He was 69 years old. He had no survivors. A few cousins were listed, but not by name. The obit did not mention that, as a child in the 1930s, he was crowned Little Mr. Macon and was in a parade.

Whitehead lived alone. He never married. He was a radio disc jockey for a few years. After that, he held jobs as a parking lot attendant and elevator operator at the old Grand Theater.

He had a sharp mind. He was passionate about sports and old movies.

Trying to get a movie trivia question past him was like trying to sneak the sun past a rooster. From Cary Grant to Kathryn Hepburn, he knew it all.

He was 6-foot-4 and thin — a long, tall drink of water. A victim of cerebral palsy, he walked with a severe limp, and his right hand was slightly deformed.

Those who noticed might have suspected he was mildly retarded. Sadly, he was one of those lonely hearts that many people choose to keep at a distance.

He lived such a frugal existence, few would have suspected Edward Whitehead died a rich man.

They would be shocked to learn he left almost $500,000 in a trust fund. Or that this gentle fellow, who wore his trademark cowboy hat just about everywhere, would request the establishment of a scholarship program for college students in Macon and surrounding counties.

"He had a heart of gold," said a friend, Dot Anderson.

Whitehead was born with that gold vein on Aug. 2, 1929, just two months shy of the beginning of the Great Depression. He was the only child of Edward Whitehead Sr., a World War I hero, and Sarah Wilson Whitehead.

He graduated from Lanier High but never finished college. His deep baritone voice was the perfect tone for radio. Yet his physical disabilities

and declining health stalked him and limited his options.

"Despite his difficulties, he never complained," said Bill Anderson. "He always kept his sense of humor."

Whitehead met Horace McSwain, a Macon attorney, and McSwain's wife, Gloria, a local middle-school principal, in 1984.

McSwain struck up a conversation with him at Young's Drug Store (now Lawrence Mayer Florist) when Whitehead came in one day to eat lunch.

They even discovered they were distantly related through marriage.

"I told him we weren't exactly kinfolk. But if we couldn't be in-laws, we could at least be out-laws," said McSwain.

Whitehead laughed. He loved that line, and used it often.

He began his friendship with Bill and Dot Anderson when he met them walking their dog near his small apartment on Clisby Place.

A few years ago, Whitehead inherited a large sum of money following the death of a rich aunt, Matthylde Clifton, whose husband, Truman, was a founding father in the accounting firm of Clifton, Lipford, Hardison and Parker.

The Cliftons had no children, and Matthylde's sister was Whitehead's mother. She left him more than $400,000, which has now grown to almost $500,000.

He never spent much on himself. Instead, he insisted his money be used for college scholarships as part of the Clifton Trust Fund. He appointed Bill Anderson, Horace McSwain and Gloria McSwain as trustees.

The Edward S. Whitehead Jr. scholarship program will begin this fall with a dozen college undergraduates each awarded $2,000 scholarships. Three will be selected each year.

Ring the Bell

January 17, 1998

The buzzer bell by the door is a tradition. So are the cook's ears back in the kitchen.

When you reach for the doorknob on your way out of Len Berg's restaurant, you also can grab a toothpick and ring the buzzer. It's a gesture to let the cooks in the back know you enjoyed your meal.

Wilbur Mitcham has heard that sweet sound more times than you can shake a spoon at, and he never has grown tired of it. His reaction has always been one of self-satisfaction. A smile. He forms his fingers to make the "V is for victory" sign.

He used to tell folks he had fed thousands of people in his 51 years at the famous downtown alley restaurant.

Now he has revised his count.

"Millions," he said. "It has to be in the millions now. My goodness. That place down there is known all over the world!"

He has cooked salmon croquettes and fixed turkey and dressing for local royalty. He has baked meatloaf and macaroon pie for ordinary folks. Joe DiMaggio once raised a fork in his honor. Ben Hogan once stopped by to sate his appetite.

It took a heap of turnip greens and Len Berg's trademark H.M.F.P.I.C. (home-made fresh peach ice cream) to put his 10 children through college. It took a lot of long hours at work to feed them at home, too.

"We used to cook black-eyed peas so much one of my daughters said she would pray we would burn them so she wouldn't have to eat them again," Mitcham said, laughing.

The 10 children have blessed him with 24 grandchildren and five great-grand-younguns. At 75, Mitcham still keeps right on working, arriving at the restaurant at 6 a.m. to supervise the day's cooking.

"It wouldn't seem right without him here," said owner Jerry Amerson. "He comes in the morning before anyone else and gets things started. And he makes sure the others follow his recipes."

He now usually leaves by 10, before the lunch traffic begins to pack Len Berg's tiny dining rooms, often spilling into the hallways and along the front counter.

"Working is just part of my life. It's something I've got to do," he said. "If I were to stay at home, Mother (his wife, Annie Mae) would be wanting me to be doing this and that. I might as well be out working. She isn't going to pay me for anything!"

It has been, pardon the pun, a rocky road to this life in the H.M.F.P.I.C. lane. Mitcham never made it past the second grade at Burdell Elementary after his father died of pneumonia in 1935 and his mother suffered a fatal heart attack two years later.

His seven brothers and sisters were split up and went separate ways. At age 9, he found himself on the streets, living in abandoned houses and begging for table scraps.

"I was homeless, basically going from pillar to post," he said. "People would help me, do things for me and give me food. But it was always a hard life. Nothing was easy about growing up."

When he was 12, he began a series of odd jobs, working in what he called a succession of "greasy spoon" restaurants, cafes, fruit stands and

country clubs. He waited on tables, washed dishes and learned how to cook.

He began working at Len Berg's in 1946, when it was located in Wall Street Alley behind what is now the Wachovia Building. At that time, Len Berg's already was one of Macon's oldest eating establishments, opened in 1908 by Leonard Berg.

When fire destroyed the original restaurant on a Friday the 13th in July 1949, owner Art Barry temporarily relocated the restaurant at the Terminal Station. A new restaurant was built in 1950 to replicate the old Len Berg's, right down to the original windows, doors and counter salvaged from the fire. Mitcham continued as the cook under owner Jeff Amerson and has carried on his career under Amerson's son, Jerry.

"I've now been cooking meals in Macon for 65 years," Mitcham said. "I've taught a lot of other people how to cook. You've got to show a lot of love and not think you know it all."

The menu is not as varied as it once was — Len Berg's once served Chinese, Mexican and Italian dishes before ethnic specialty restaurants began appearing on the scene.

Mitcham, a deacon at Memorial Baptist Church, lives the same way he cooks — with lots of love. He has never forgotten his troubled childhood, roaming the streets and wondering from where his next meal would come.

So he helps Macon's homeless, providing them with food and clothing almost daily.

"I help those under the bridge because I've been there," he said. "It's the way I started off — with nothing. I know how it feels not to have food to eat, clothes on your back and shoes on your feet. I can't turn them down. I'm now in a position where I can help them."

Ring the bell.

Our compliments to the old chef.

Wilbur Mitcham died in June 2003.

The Rock of the Valley

February 23, 2001

FORT VALLEY — He was approaching midlife, his hair graying and his children growing.

But Dennis Herbert was still playing rock 'n' roll with a grin as wide as the bridge on the Fender Stratocaster his parents gave him for his 17th birthday.

An old high school classmate advised him to grow up.

"I can't believe you're still doing this," he said. "You just can't seem to get this music out of your system."

Herbert turned up the volume on his smile. You mean you can't play rock 'n' roll forever?

The same man was back a few years later. This time, he was singing a different tune.

"I wish," he said, "I could do what you're doing."

They call Dennis Herbert the "Rock" in his hometown. After all, he operates the family jewelry store. Herbert Jewelers has been cutting diamonds on Main Street since 1945.

But the "Rock" is also a local rock 'n' roll legend. He cut his teeth on everything from Otis to Elvis. And he may need dentures by the time he surrenders his guitar licks. He is a 52-year-old grandfather now, still happily jamming through "Johnny B. Goode" and "Brown-Eyed Girl."

His wife, Peggy, said there is still another reason for his nickname.

"He is as steady as a rock," she said. "All his friends will tell you that."

A surprise will roll for the Rock at breakfast this morning. His wife and two daughters, Jana Anthoine and Lauren Herbert, will no longer be able to keep their little secret from him.

Tonight, they have arranged a reunion of members of all seven bands Herbert was associated with during the past 37 years. Some of the musicians will be reunited for the first time in 25 years.

It all began about the time Herbert heard The Beatles for the first time on WFPM in Fort Valley. Because he knew a few chords, he was asked to play rhythm guitar with a local band, Rockin' Robin and the Velvetones, at the Peach Theater.

Since then, his life has usually consisted of another "garage" band, another gig and another memory for the scrapbook. Herbert once toured with Billy Joe Royal and B.J. Thomas. (Yes, he has played "Down in the Boondocks" more than he cares to admit.)

Peggy usually marks their first date in high school as the week before her hubby joined the Malibus. That group later became Sixpence, having picked up a horn player and a British influence. By the time the group split up and reunited to play for Peggy's 10-year reunion at Fort Valley High, their music was considered "oldies."

Along with original band members Eddie Byrd and David Luckie, the band changed to Nightlife during the disco years. It then became Boardwalk and Sensations before evolving into the current band, Celebration.

Two weeks ago, Celebration played at a party for Gov. Roy Barnes and state legislators.

Tonight will truly be a celebration — a chance to relive those good times of cutting scratchy 45-rpm singles on homemade labels, of playing everywhere from high school proms to senior citizens' parties.

There are no regrets. Well, maybe one.

There was a chance to sign a record contract and go on tour. But life got in the way. Band members were finishing college, getting married and starting careers.

So, they turned it down. The opportunity never came again. Herbert sometimes wonders if there might have been a bigger stage.

A few years ago, he attended a Rolling Stones concert in Atlanta. As Herbert watched the aging Mick Jagger sing and strut, he turned to Peggy.

"We could be doing that," said the Rock.

MAKING A DIFFERENCE

Good Deed Along Life's Highway
September 21, 2003

To become a member of the Beverly Deese Fan Club, I know I must take a number and get in line.

We live in a society where we rush to crown our heroes. We don't hesitate to loosely label good Samaritans as those who come to the aid of their fellow man.

But rather than getting caught up in semantics, let me simply tell you what Beverly did.

A few weeks ago, she was driving on Northside Drive to pick up a bowl of won-ton soup from a Chinese restaurant. She witnessed a jogger who had been struck by a hit-and-run driver.

She pulled to the curb and stayed with the man until police and an ambulance arrived.

No big deal, huh? Happens all the time.

Beverly Deese has no legs.

Seven years ago, the 44-year-old Macon woman was stricken with reflex sympathetic dystrophy, a neurological disorder so rare it is found in only one of every 250,000 people.

Her left leg was amputated above the knee in July 2001. Her right leg was cut off six months later.

After she learned to walk with two artificial legs, doctors discovered a tumor in her right leg earlier this year. Recently, she has been unable to use a prosthesis.

She continues to be an inspiration to others, though, doing volunteer work at HealthSouth Central Georgia Rehabilitation Hospital. She visits with patients and offers them encouragement. One thing is for sure. She doesn't host any pity parties.

"People ask me how I can smile all the time," she said. "And I tell them I woke up this morning."

When Beverly woke up the morning of Aug. 20, two days after receiving chemotherapy, she started craving a bowl of won-ton soup. She uses special hand controls to drive. She didn't think she would need her wheelchair in the back. She usually calls ahead to the Golden Palace restaurant, and they are gracious enough to bring her order to her car.

A block from the restaurant, she noticed the injured pedestrian. "Beverly, you can't just keep going," she told herself.

So she U-turned to the rescue. She grabbed several towels and lowered herself onto the hot pavement.

The man was bleeding and incoherent. She stabilized his head and

controlled the bleeding with napkins.

Others offered help before the police and ambulance arrived. One man looked down at Beverly and couldn't believe it.

"You don't have any legs! How you do that? Why do you do that?" he asked.

Said Beverly: "I just hope if it happened to me, somebody would stop to help. I believe we were put here on this earth to help one another."

Later, a police officer told her he admired her. Two men helped her wash the blood from her hands and lifted her back into her car.

After the adrenaline stopped flowing and she picked up her soup order, she pulled into a space in the Kroger parking lot and cried tears of joy and gratitude over her good deed.

"It was a reassurance," she said. "God still has plans for me."

Where the 'Golden Rule' Works Miracles

March 14, 2004

MAUK — They joined hands and said the blessing. After they had nibbled the last bites of turkey at the end of their forks, they began to rise slowly from their chairs.

One by one, they stood and summoned the courage to tell their stories in front of everyone in the crowded dining room on a Sunday afternoon.

There was Sandy from Macon and Jennifer from Cochran. There was Kristen from Cairo and Melanie from Milledgeville.

They emptied their hearts and spoke honestly about the demons that still stalk them. They recalled the times in their lives when they couldn't bear to look in the mirror because they hated the person they saw there.

Still, there was hope in their voices.

There were soft sobs around them, as they reached for napkins to dry their own tears.

The Golden Rule is a home for women who are victims of drug and alcohol abuse. They come from small towns and big cities, from wide avenues and dirt roads.

Some are married and have children. Others are single or divorced.

They answer to names like Libby, Michelle, Kerri and Trinity. They could be your mother. Your daughter. Your sister. Your neighbor.

They arrive with suitcases and plenty of physical and emotional baggage. They've abused their lives. And they've had their lives abused by others. Many have limited financial resources, and most have legal

problems as a result of their addiction.

Background is their common ground on this western edge of Taylor County, about 10 miles from Butler.

They've come here to pick up the broken pieces.

They find God. They learn to pray. They help others as they help themselves.

"We learn to live all over again," said Susan, a wife and mother from Hillsboro.

Charles Weston, a former Bibb County district attorney, is a member of the board of directors at The Golden Rule. He attends these Sunday dinners every three months.

He has learned how to eat with a lump in his throat as he listens to their stories. He rejoices in their personal triumphs.

"This is holy ground," he tells the women.

Weston has been lifelong friends with Norman Carter, who started The Golden Rule in a single-wide trailer in 1998 and has built it into a model program.

Carter, 65, is one of the most revered high school basketball coaches in state history. A former star athlete at Mercer, he married Jane, a Mercer cheerleader, and moved to Taylor County in 1960 to teach and coach.

From 1967-72, his Taylor County girls basketball teams won 132 straight games, which remains a state record. His career record was 350-32 with six state championships. He also served as the county's school superintendent for 21 years.

Despite those successes, he experienced heartache within his own family. His two children became victims of substance abuse. It's one of the reasons why he and Jane put their time, talent and resources into founding The Golden Rule.

(Their son, Trey, a former University of Georgia tennis star, has since turned his life around. In 2003, he became CEO of the same Atlanta rehabilitation hospital where he had been admitted 10 years earlier with a substance abuse problem.)

Carter originally had hoped to operate The Golden Rule in one of the county's larger towns, either Butler or Reynolds. But his plans came just six months after a 16-year-old youth at the Georgia Center for Youth in Reynolds stabbed a local man to death on Oct. 18, 1995, after running away from the group home for emotionally disturbed teens.

There was opposition in the community to Carter's idea, so he bought property in a remote part of the county.

In a way, it was a blessing. Seemingly miles from anywhere, there were fewer distractions and temptations in the deep woods along a sandy

ridge. There are now nine mobile homes, including a halfway house for those who elect to stay longer than the required nine months. The Golden Rule operates on donations by private individuals, businesses and churches, some state money and a grant from the Peyton Anderson Foundation.

Most of the women at The Golden Rule have been sent there by the court system. The program doesn't accept violent or emotionally disturbed women.

The residents are expected to follow strict rules. If they don't, there's always somebody waiting to take their place. As of last week, there were 30 in the program and 42 on a waiting list.

Their daily routines include developing work skills, attending devotionals, keeping journals and taking part in educational training. Carter is most proud that 35 of 37 residents who have taken the GED since 1999 have passed it.

Whenever a new resident arrives through the Golden gates, the women all show up to greet them.

"They're scared," said Harriet Felts, an addiction counselor and case manager at The Golden Rule. "I know how they feel. I was scared, too."

Felts was among the first women to see the sun come up again in her life beneath these tall pines. She was working as a nurse in Ocilla and was forging prescriptions for the 80 pain pills she was taking just to get through the day.

She got caught and went to jail.

She also realizes she could be dead.

"I came here wanting help," she said. "The thought of staying and working here never crossed my mind. But God had other plans."

She leads by example. This is where you've been. This is where you need to be. This is how you get there.

"There's nothing I ask them to do that I haven't been through myself," she said. "There's not a lie I haven't heard. There's not a story they can tell that I haven't experienced."

Although The Golden Rule has been successful with almost two-thirds of the 170 women who have come through the program, there are no guarantees.

Some have had to return. Others left only to become trapped again in the same lifestyle that brought them here.

Susan, from Hillsboro, has two children and a husband waiting for her at home when she leaves in late July. She was barely a teenager when she got hooked on drugs and alcohol. Now, 23 years later, she is trying to

"get out all the trash."

"Coming through those gates," she said, "was the first day of the rest of my life."

Sandy, of Macon, has been here for three years and three months, longer than any other resident. Addiction nearly ruined her life. She found herself homeless on the streets.

"I'm so grateful I don't have to live that way again," she said.

Sharing their stories is part of the healing process. Dee, from Milledgeville, talks about stealing two guns and selling them to buy crack cocaine.

In jail, she said, "You could swim home on the river of tears I cried."

Others weep about not being home for a child's birthday. Or how they had to spend Christmas in prison. They talk openly about how they must remain vigilant — to be on guard for that unguarded moment.

When they first arrive, their photographs are taken and placed on a bulletin board near the chapel.

Of course, most look different when they leave. You can see it in their eyes, their smiles.

Most of all, they have changed on the inside, too.

Working for Those Cherished Children

May 28, 2000

WARNER ROBINS — When they asked how much she needed, she told them. It would take a million dollars to build a new day-care facility.

Jean Coleman stood before a local church group two years ago and asked for blessings and financial support.

They wrote her a check for $50, and she thanked them. After all, you've got to start somewhere.

She wondered if she took the $50 home and watered it, would it sprout a few more pictures of Ulysses S. Grant? Maybe it would have some Ben Franklins as offspring. Who wants to grow a millionaire?

It was exasperating to realize that it would take another 19,999 chicken-dinner speeches to reach her fund-raising goal.

A year passed, and the nickels trickled in like drizzle in a drought.

Coleman kept barnstorming and begging. When she wasn't twisting arms, she was clasping those same hands in prayer.

Last summer, on her 50th wedding anniversary trip to Europe with her husband, Bob, she sat in great cathedrals. She thought about the

hundreds of years it took to build those cathedrals. She imagined the thousands of laborers who never lived to see the finished product.

Would it be that way for her?

She has fought on this socioeconomic battlefield before, ever since she was the co-founding mother of this non-profit day-care center for low-income, working families.

"It was a struggle 35 years ago," she said. "It's still a struggle today."

She has remained a constant, the perfect spearhead. She has lived in Warner Robins for almost 40 years and is one of its leading citizens. In a town neither blessed with "old" money nor a major philanthropist, she has personal and professional contacts and the power of persuasion.

Coleman is 71 years old and has been slowed by Parkinson's Disease. Still, there is plenty of bounce in her step. She remains committed to the cause. She is anxious to help facilitate the move out of the aging buildings that were deemed barely adequate when Warner Robins Daycare opened in 1965.

Now the center is called "Cherished Children: The Education Station." A new facility has been proposed on 3.5 acres along Myrtle Street behind City Hall. It is planned to handle the needs of 100 children from 6 weeks to 12 years old.

Such a facility would be a marked improvement from the two locations that now serve as the daytime homes for 65 children.

Conditions are so antiquated that meals are cooked and prepared in one building, then pulled in children's wagons across the street. About 85 percent of funding comes from the community and non-government sources.

The capital campaign will soon be entering its third year, still looking for enough shovels to break ground. Coleman remains optimistic.

She is well-conditioned for such challenges. In 1979, she co-founded Golden Key Realty, now one of the city's largest real estate firms. She was a member of the county's planning and zoning board for eight years. She wrote the application for Houston County's first Head Start and secured its first pre-K program.

Of course, this was not a pre-ordained resume' when she met Bob at a Methodist church in Memphis, Tenn. They married in 1949. Her father had been a mill superintendent, and her family moved many times.

"My goal was to marry a man and live in a cottage with a white picket fence and ivy in the yard," she said. "I wanted stability."

Instead, she fell in love with an Air Force pilot. They had five children in eight years and endured the nomadic lifestyle of the military.

"Mama, where is our home?" her children asked her during one of the moves.

At that moment, home was a station wagon.

"I said it was wherever we were," said Coleman. "What was important is that we were together."

The family was stationed in Warner Robins in 1960. They moved into base housing and finally were able to put down stakes. Coleman, however, eventually was faced with the decision of having to work to cover some of the bills. With five children, three of them preschoolers, it was not an easy choice when she began looking at day-care options.

In the process, she discovered an even greater need than her own. She met a young, black woman who was working as a housekeeper. The woman was living in a room behind a bar. She had to leave her two children with a relative during the day.

Day care was available in Warner Robins in the early 1960s, back when the town's main thoroughfare, Watson Boulevard, was a two-lane street with storefront parking.

But child care was expensive and even exclusionary. And, in the segregated South, it was not readily available to people of all skin colors.

Coleman could somewhat identify with discrimination. Though raised in the Methodist church, her maiden name was Kressenberg.

"Growing up, people always assumed I was Jewish, even though I wasn't," she said.

She enlisted the help of another woman, Anita Brown, who shared the same passion for starting the day-care operation for needy families. Coleman and Brown convinced city officials to permit the use of an older building on Oak Grove Road in south Warner Robins. (The original center is still in operation.)

"I've always had a heart for the underdog," said Coleman. "We saw a real need, and we met that need."

It was a massive undertaking. Coleman kept supplies in her carport and storage room. She spent long hours at the center. She did everything within her power to make it work. The first employees worked 12-hour shifts and earned $25 per week.

"Some weeks, we didn't have enough money to pay them," she said. "I would have to borrow from my friends. We had a lot of volunteers. It was all hand-to-mouth during those early years."

It's not nearly as much hand-to-mouth now, although there are times when she admits the capital campaign would benefit from a little mouth-to-mouth.

There have been no blank checks.

A million dollars. Coleman is determined to get there, even if it has to be with one $50 pledge at a time.

Helping Others Help Themselves

January 21, 2001

The idea was born between sips of coffee and the slow puffs of cigarette smoke.

Frank Abbott cannot remember what the weather was outside. He just knows he was having a brainstorm inside the Waffle House on Hartley Bridge Road.

Abbott had helped needy folks plenty of times before. So had the other Good Samaritans at his table. He had given rides to stranded motorists. He had delivered hot meals to the hungry and warm coats to the cold.

Three years ago, he donated a kidney to a man he did not know. But in October 1998, Abbott decided there was strength in numbers. So he pulled together an organization he called "People Helping People."

He enlisted the help of his coffee-drinking buddies at the Waffle House and Janet's Home-Cooked Meals on Pio Nono Avenue.

Something special has been happening ever since. By bringing together a hard-core collection of soft hearts, Abbott created a tour de force. About 15 low-profile volunteers do everything from distributing diapers to assisting folks with their utility bills.

People Helping People could best be described as helping people help themselves. Through the organization's "Angel Food" program, for example, needy families can purchase $80 worth of groceries for $27.

"It's a hand up, not a hand out," said Abbott. "Most of these people have pride and dignity. They are not looking for charity. Once we get them back on their feet, we expect them to help someone else."

Usually, the needy are screened and referred by churches and social agencies. Many times, they have fallen through society's cracks. Help is given unconditionally.

"I don't always believe people's stories," said Abbott. "But I always try to help them."

Sometimes, all that is required is a simple act of kindness. Other times, Abbott refers to it as "life-saving." It could mean collecting school clothes for children or medicine for senior citizens. It could mean gathering eyeglasses for the local Lions Club or wheelchairs for the international Wheels for the World.

The organization accepts donations and contributions but does not

solicit money. (When the cash runs low, there are always raffles and yard sales.) Donations are taken for items such as clothing, food and household goods. A distribution warehouse has been opened on Guy Paine Road.

Abbott has allowed himself to be amazed. Someone once donated a baby walker. "Now what am I going to do with that?" he asked himself.

The following day, a woman approached him at the Waffle House. Her baby desperately needed a walker. Abbott smiled at the small miracle. He just happened to have one in his trunk.

Another time, he ended up with an electric can opener. Within 24 hours, he received a call from Loaves and Fishes Ministry downtown.

"We have a one-armed man down here who needs an electric can opener. Do you have one?"

When Abbott went to help victims of the 1999 tornado in Vienna, a minister at a black church was so grateful he made him an honorary deacon.

Abbott is a retired bookkeeper, a lifelong bachelor and is financially secure. But, until recently, he had gone 592 straight days "helping people" without a day off.

"From May 12, 1999, until Christmas last year," he said. "Somebody needed assistance every single day. I can remember it was May 12 because that was the last time I went fishing."

No, he hasn't been fishing much. But the brainstorm has brought showers of blessings.

Parents Gave Him Gift of Hope

August 24, 2003

This is a column about Larry Lawrence. But it is really about his parents, Malachi and Julia Lawrence.

You won't find any streets in Macon named in their honor, no monuments placed in any civic square. They had neither money nor political influence.

They just rolled out of bed each morning and raised 12 of the finest children you could ever hope to meet. If there was a hall of fame for parents, the ballot would be unanimous.

Malachi never made it past the third grade. Julia was a dropout in the fourth grade.

Didn't matter.

"They were the smartest people I've ever known," Larry said. "They understood what it took to be successful. Hard work. Honesty.

Loyalty. They changed the lives of an entire generation. Thanks to them, my own children will know a different way of life."

It's a long way from Bell Avenue in Macon to Wall Street in New York. Larry has felt the presence of his parents every step of the way. Malachi died in 1980. Julia passed away nine years later.

Their spirits linger.

Now Larry puts on a coat and tie every morning in Westchester County, N.Y., hugs his wife and two kids and counts his blessings.

His mother and father made endless sacrifices. And they have never stopped teaching, even though they're gone.

Among the seven boys and five girls in the Lawrence family, eight graduated from college. The honor rolls have produced an aerospace engineer, an attorney, an Air Force officer at the Pentagon and an executive with the Southern Company.

Larry went on to become a star basketball player at Dartmouth, where he was the Ivy League Player of the Year in 1981. He played professionally in France, and once a French newspaper referred to him as another Larry — the "Larry Bird of France," likening him to the former Boston Celtics great.

An economics major, he now works in institutional sales at Salomon Smith Barney in New York City.

"It's a family of achievers," said Joe McDaniel. "Larry will tell you everything he has accomplished is the direct result of good and godly parents."

McDaniel was Lawrence's basketball coach at Mount de Sales in the mid-1970s, and often he would give him rides home after practice. Larry lived in a concrete block house on an unpaved road in Hillcrest Heights.

It was a home with boundaries.

"Growing up, we weren't allowed to play anywhere except our own yard," he said. "The only time we could leave the yard was to walk to Lizzie Chapel Baptist Church, which was a couple of miles away."

A deacon at Lizzie Chapel, Malachi was a concrete mason by trade. He built his house on a solid foundation in more ways than one. His family's life revolved around the church.

Malachi left for work each morning before his children woke up. He returned home after Julia had already tucked them into bed, his supper still warming on the wood stove.

Julia never worked outside the home until Larry started attending Mount de Sales. All her children received scholarships to St. Peter Claver for elementary school, then went to public high schools. Larry, an excellent student with an incredible work ethic, had an opportunity to

go to Mount de Sales. Julia took a job at the S & S Cafeteria in Bloomfield to help pay his tuition.

McDaniel was devoted to helping the tall, skinny kid get a college basketball scholarship. When the local schools weren't interested, he turned to the Ivy League.

Larry had never flown on an airplane until he traveled to Dartmouth for the first time.

Julia knew the college was located in New Hampshire, which was a thousand miles north.

So she sent him to college wearing a heavy sweater.

In August.

Larry was drafted by the NBA's Atlanta Hawks after his junior season. He turned down the offer, and draft rules for underclassmen at the time allowed him to retain his college eligibility his senior year. He played in a summer basketball league with Dominique Wilkins and Spud Webb, and spent several seasons in the Continental Basketball Association before going to France.

When he retired three years ago at age 41, he had spent 15 years in France. He was such a celebrity athlete he had his own TV show.

Frenchmen would knock on his door on Saturday mornings and ask if there was anything they could get for him.

McDaniel left coaching and became an associate pastor at Mabel White Baptist Church. On many occasions, he evoked the name of Larry Lawrence in his talks and sermons.

It was a lesson about respect. About excellence. About the need for strong parents and good role models. About love.

When Larry shares his life story with others he always gives credit to the two "smartest people I've ever known."

They gave him a gift he has opened every day of his life.

The Stars in the Galaxy

Macon's Most Famous Caveman

January 19, 2003

He lost his leg in the war. An artillery shell hit his bunker. The two men who were in the bunker with him were killed.

He spent more than two years recovering in the hospital. Doctors amputated his right leg and took 4 inches of bone from his leg to save his mangled arm.

But the tragedy of war could never crush his spirit. He returned home, built a life and raised a family.

He reads the newspaper every day.

Some mornings, he even sees himself in the funny pages.

Wiley Baxter is Macon's most famous caveman.

You may recognize his likeness as the peg-legged character in the comic strip "B.C."

The strip appears in more than 1,300 papers worldwide, including *The Telegraph,* and reaches more than 100 million readers.

Yes, he is Wiley, the grubby baseball coach. He is Wiley, the poet resting beneath a tree with pen and tablet in hand.

Sometimes the other characters look up definitions of words in "Wiley's Dictionary" or sip a few suds at "Wiley's Bar."

"We've never really gone around telling people Wiley is in the funny pages," said his wife, Fran Baxter. "Oh, I told a few of the neighbors last year. But I don't think there's even a dozen people in Macon who know about it."

They do now.

"I'm a shy, private person," Wiley said. "I'm not one to toot my own horn. But I was thrilled when Johnny started doing this 45 years ago. And I'm still thrilled."

Fran Baxter's younger sister, Bobby, is married to Johnny Hart, the creator of the famous comic strip. The Harts celebrated their 50th wedding anniversary last year.

They met in 1951, while Bobby was a lab technician at Macon Hospital. Johnny was stationed at Robins Air Force Base, where he worked for the base newspaper and trained as a photographer.

The Harts were married at the RAFB chapel. As newlyweds, they lived in an apartment in Macon on Georgia Avenue, where Johnny penned his early aspirations to draw cartoons for a living. They now reside in Ninevah, N.Y.

Wiley, the 80-year-old World War II veteran, is the inspiration behind his Neanderthal namesake.

But the comic strip character is not exactly a Wiley clone. "When Johnny was coming up with the characters, he completely reversed Wiley's personality," Bobby said.

"Wiley is so neat and clean and a sharp dresser," said Johnny Hart. "In the strip, he's a slob who doesn't like to bathe. In the early days, I would even have Wiley run at the mention of water."

Wiley Baxter also isn't much of a poet, as he often is portrayed in the comic strip. He's no wordsmith. In fact, he's a man of few words. "Wiley's Dictionary" is a reflection of Wiley's somewhat unique way of defining the world around him.

Still, there are similarities besides the name. Hart describes Wiley the caveman as having "an adherence to sports in any shape." So he made him the "B.C." baseball and football coach.

Art does, indeed, imitate life. The real Wiley has been a fan of the New York Yankees' pinstripes since the days of Joe DiMaggio. He also is a devoted football fan of the Auburn Tigers.

Wiley is one of the many characters Hart chose to fashion after friends and family members who make up the world around him. Among them are B.C., who most closely represents himself, and the "Cute Chick" — his wife, Bobby.

Peter, Thor, Grog and Clumsy Carp are all composites of others Hart has chosen to immortalize in the strip.

Fran's mother, the late Janie Hatcher, was a small, thin woman. But Fran is convinced she was the inspiration behind the "Fat Broad." After all, Johnny once watched her kill a snake with a hoe in the hen house.

"That woman," Fran said, "could pulverize a snake."

Wiley grew up in Clio, Ala., and met his future wife at a party while he was in the service. Fran is a native of Boston, but not the Massachusetts variety — Boston is a small community in Thomas County in south Georgia. The Baxters were married on June 28, 1942.

Wiley went to Europe with the 3rd Infantry during World War II. He was engaged in heavy fighting in France, near Strasbourg, when he was injured.

Back home, Fran received a telegram notifying her that Wiley had been critically injured. Before she could hear from him, the Army sent word that his right leg had been amputated above the knee. He also had sustained severe injuries to his right arm and jaw.

After spending more than two years in military hospitals, Wiley was discharged in 1947. The Baxters moved to Macon in 1951, where he began working with munitions at the Naval Ordnance Plant on Guy Paine

Road. Johnny used to tease him about that.

"If anything happens out there, working around all those explosives, you're going to get blown up in Macon, too," he said, laughing.

Wiley remembers he wasn't too impressed with his future brother-in-law when they first met. He barely looked up from his newspaper when Johnny arrived at the door to court Fran's baby sister.

While working at RAFB, Johnny was always drawing silly caricatures and giving them to friends. Not long after he graduated from high school in New York, he had met Brant Parker, a young cartoonist who later became a partner in the creation of the Wizard of Id. Parker was a major influence in shaping Johnny's career as a comic strip artist.

After he got out of the service, his career didn't exactly take off like the invention of the wheel. In fact, Johnny remembers drawing at a card table one night in their two-room apartment in Macon, near the old Wesleyan Conservatory.

Frustrated, he slammed his fist on the table, sending the ink well flying. He then looked over at Bobby and swore he was going to have a syndicated comic strip by the time he was 27 years old.

"At the time, I'm not sure I even understood what being syndicated was," he said.

They moved to her family's farm in south Georgia, where he later sold his first free-lance cartoon to *The Saturday Evening Post.* He began admiring the work of "Peanuts" creator Charles Schulz. Since he loved to draw cavemen, a friend jokingly suggested that he start a strip that took place in prehistoric times.

In 1958, the day before he turned 27, "B.C." made its debut in the *New York Herald Tribune* and 30 other newspapers. Bobby reminded him of the pledge he had made before his 27th birthday.

"I now laugh and say that's the last deadline I ever made," Johnny said.

Two years later, he began work on "The Wizard of Id." His combined work on both strips inspired *Time* magazine to call him the world's "most syndicated comic author." *The Washington Post* went a step further. In 1999, the newspaper hailed Hart as "the most widely read writer on earth."

Through the decades, Johnny and Wiley have been best buddies, even though they only get to see each other a few times each year. They love to fish together and once went to see the Yankees in spring training every year. They still sit around and try to solve the problems of the world while wetting their whistles.

Hart's admiration for Wiley comes through in the cartoon strip in

its own special way.

Once, a lady wrote who thought he was making fun of handicapped people.

Hart responded by explaining that he was trying to find a way to honor him.

Another time, when he made the mistake of flipping the transparency so that Wiley's "peg leg" appeared on his left, several observant readers pointed it out.

He soon hopes to compile a "Wiley's Dictionary" book and perhaps come to Macon for a book signing with the real Wiley.

In the 45 years Johnny Hart has brought a smile to the faces of "B.C." fans, Wiley has managed to contribute only one "gag."

He got the idea watching former Atlanta Braves third base coach Ned Yost, now manager of the Milwaukee Brewers, go through several animated hand gestures. Wiley told Hart about it, who drew several frames of Wiley going through assorted gyrations.

"What does all that mean?" the batter asks.

"Nothing. I'm trying to make the other team think we're up to something," Wiley says.

Fran said she and her husband have always kept a low profile about their association with the cartoon strip, even though the walls of their home are filled with "B.C."

"Neither one of us can draw," she said.

Then she laughed. "About the only thing I can draw is water from a well."

Time Flies for Miss America
September 6, 2002

On the night that changed her life forever, Neva Langley Fickling took a deep breath and prayed.

They placed a crown on her head and draped a red velvet robe across her shoulders. It was nearly midnight. Flashbulbs along the runway twinkled like the stars above the boardwalk in Atlantic City, N.J.

Back in Macon, where she was a college student at the Wesleyan Conservatory, a crowd gathered at the Pinebrook Inn to cheer the radio broadcast.

Being named Miss America was once the dream of every young girl. For Neva Langley, it soon was as permanently affixed as her married name — Fickling.

Both her landscape and legacy were ordained the night of

Sept. 6, 1952, when she began her year-long reign as Miss America 1953.

She returned to Macon for a parade on Cherry Street. A path of rose petals was spread along the steps of City Hall. (The parade route passed Goldman's, the store where she bought the swimsuit she used to win the national competition.)

On tour, she brushed elbows with Marilyn Monroe and President Eisenhower. She was in the Rose Bowl parade and on "The Ed Sullivan Show." She graced the cover of *Ladies Home Journal.*

Fifty years later, people still brag that they saw her win on TV. She smiles, even though they are mistaken. The pageant was not televised until 1954. Her crowning also came three years before the debut of master of ceremonies Bert Parks and his coronation song, "There She Is, Miss America."

Fickling still looks back with wonder at that time of her life. At 19, she was one of the youngest winners in pageant history and the first to have a full-time chaperone. She is the only Miss Georgia to win the coveted crown.

She has aged gracefully, with hardly a dent in the 10-car-pileup beauty of a half-century ago.

She has been married to Bill Fickling for 47 years and has five grandchildren. She is a renowned classical pianist. Three years ago, she underwent heart bypass surgery.

"I chose not to be on stage the rest of my life, to live in a fishbowl," she said, explaining her retreat from the spotlight.

But, in many ways, Miss America has been a career from which she can never formally retire.

"Of course, there has been the pressure to lead an exemplary life, and that is good," she said.

Other pressures, though, are relentless. The private person is still a very public figure.

"I can never go to the grocery store and wear an old pair of jeans," she said, laughing.

She admits she was nervous the night of the pageant, but not terrified.

After all, she had been playing the piano in church since she was 13.

During the Miss Macon pageant at the City Auditorium, she impressed the judges by continuing to play the piano after a storm knocked out all the lights.

She has never lost that composure.

Fifty years?

Time sure flies, even when you're Miss America.

The Shake 'N Bake Twins

February 3, 2002

REYNOLDS — Remember those old SHAKE 'N BAKE commercials?

Remember the one where the father walks into the kitchen, and the mother proudly displays a platter of fried chicken?

"Honey, did you make this?"

Sure did, she says. Then those cute-as-a-button twin girls answer in a deep-fried Southern drawl.

"And we helped!"

Jennifer Wilder and Natalie Bell Dent remember that commercial. After all, they really did "help."

Twenty-seven years ago, they stood beneath the hot glare of television lights in a small kitchen in Atlanta and recited that famous line.

"And we helped!"

They introduced a nation to Georgia drawls one year before a peanut farmer from Plains made "Southern" the official national language.

Today is Super Bowl Sunday, when considerable attention is placed on TV ads. (Sometimes they are more entertaining than the game itself.)

I'm not sure if the SHAKE 'N BAKE twins ever made the Super Bowl lineup, but they certainly uttered a classic line in advertising history.

No, Jennifer and Natalie Bell didn't shake and bake their way to fame and fortune.

They settled into life as small-town girls from Reynolds. They cleaned their rooms, said their prayers and did their homework. Their parents, Bobby and Frances Bell, still run a drug store in Roberta.

Now the twins are wives and mothers. Jennifer is a kindergarten teacher at Taylor County Elementary in Butler. Natalie lives in Fitzgerald and teaches fourth grade at Irwin County Elementary in Ocilla.

"We never bragged about it," said Jennifer. "We never even bring it up unless someone mentions it. All my life, people have tried to get me to say that line: 'And we helped!' "

Natalie said she gets as much reaction from the fact that she is part of two sets of twins from the same family. Her sisters — twins Christy (Bullard), who lives in Macon, and Michelle (Evans), who lives in Watkinsville — were born five years after Jennifer and Natalie.

Frances and Bobby Bell met as teenagers while water skiing on

a pond in Potterville. Bobby was from Reynolds. Frances grew up in Marshallville.

They married in 1966. Jennifer and Natalie arrived the following year, while Bobby was in pharmacy school.

They moved to Reynolds in 1969. This past Friday marked Bobby's 31st anniversary as the owner and pharmacist at Roberta Drugs.

Reynolds native Sara Ann Fountain was living in Atlanta in March 1975. Her roommate worked for a talent agency and was searching for twin girls for a speaking part in a commercial.

"I've got just the twins for you," Fountain told her. Natalie and Jennifer were first-graders at Beechwood Academy (now closed) in Marshallville. They had no previous acting experience. Their aspiration was to become gymnasts.

On their way to Atlanta for the audition, they stopped in Griffin, where their mother bought them matching pairs of peach-colored overalls.

At the audition, Frances filled in and read the script, playing the part of the mother.

Jennifer and Natalie were chosen for the parts and returned to Atlanta a few weeks later.

It took eight hours to film the one-minute commercial in the kitchen of a private home near the Governor's Mansion on West Paces Ferry Road.

They remember their TV mom's instructions.

"Here, Susie, you shake! Here, Sally, you bake!"

They fought over who was going to get to play the part of Susie. (It seemed that neither liked the name Sally.)

Jennifer recalls the hot lights melting the butter on the table. Her part also called for her to drink some milk. It, too, was hot from the lights.

She also remembers the "father" repeatedly taking bites into the juicy chicken.

"I shook the bag, and Natalie pushed it in the oven," she said. Months later, when the commercial began airing, the Bell family would rush into the living room every time it appeared.

"We never knew when it was going to come on," said Frances. "We would just have to run in there and catch it."

At first, Frances thought the commercial was only going to be test-marketed in the South. Then, a friend from Roberta told her he had seen it on a trip to Bangor, Maine.

Otha Dent was a pilot for Delta and had watched it during a

layover. “He said if it was playing in Bangor then it had to be playing everywhere!” said Frances, laughing.

There were times when other children teased Jennifer and Natalie about being in the commercial.

“But we were laughing all the way to the bank,” said Natalie.

Royalty checks over the next several years earned them about $17,000. They used it to buy new bedroom furniture. The rest was put away for their college education and other expenses.

They’re not sure what happened to the other actors in the commercial. They later heard rumors that their TV “mom” ended up in *Playboy* magazine and was a body double for Angie Dickinson in a movie. They are convinced they once spotted their TV “dad” modeling underwear in the Sears catalog.

Friends still remind them about their famous commercial stint. Others don’t even know.

Natalie said she has been talking with people unfamiliar with her childhood when the SHAKE ‘N BAKE commercial sometimes comes up in the conversation.

“Most people hated it,” she said. “It was annoying. It got on their nerves. When they mention the part about the twin girls, I always say: ‘That was me!’ ”

Just this past week, in Jennifer’s kindergarten class, she told her students she had a twin sister.

“You’re one of the SHAKE ‘N BAKE twins!” said a little girl, whose mother apparently had told her the story.

Penny Windham used her longtime friendship with Jennifer and Natalie as part of a personal trivia question.

Windham, the director of Diabetes Health Ways at The Medical Center of Central Georgia in Macon, was attending a seminar in Orlando, Fla., two years ago.

At one of the meetings, everyone was asked to write down an obscure fact about themselves. The group was supposed to guess the person when the fact was read aloud.

“My two best friends are the SHAKE ‘N BAKE twins,” Windham wrote.

Her accent, of course, gave her away. Later, Windham was invited to get up in front of more than 100 people and do her best “And we helped!” impression.

“It was hysterical,” said Windham. “Everyone there remembered that commercial.”

Frances Bell said her only regret is that the family does not own

a copy of the commercial. It was filmed in the days before videotapes and VCRs.

For years, the Bells have been trying to locate a tape. Maybe they'll get lucky and find it on one of those "retromercials" on the TV Land cable network.

Of course, plenty of folks probably thought SHAKE 'N BAKE was a staple on the Bells' supper table.

"No way," Jennifer has always told them. "My mother fries chicken the way you're supposed to fry chicken!"

In Pursuit of the Perfect Word

October 3, 2004

HAMILTON — Allen Levi's fingers moved up and down the guitar strings. His songs swept across the front porch like the dew tickling the grass.

When I asked him a question, Allen usually had the answer tucked away in the lyrics of one of his songs.

"I live," he said, "in pursuit of the perfect word."

Maybe that's why I'm so drawn to Allen Levi. We both try to find stories in the fingerprints of everyday life.

There are times when I can listen to one of his songs, watch the goose bumps rise and walk away convinced we are kindred spirits.

I first met him three years ago at a concert at Mabel White Memorial Baptist Church in Macon. Last year, Joe McDaniel and I attended one of Allen's sold-out shows at the River Center in his hometown of Columbus.

Monday night, Allen will perform at a banquet for Young Life, a Christian youth ministry. It will be held at the Methodist Home for Children and Youth in Macon.

Allen sings about everything from loyal dogs to old bridges to Sunday drivers to refrigerator art to changing the strings on his guitar.

"I'm one of those people who writes from the heart about things important to me," he said.

At the top of his treble clef is his faith. No, it doesn't choke the neck of his guitar like a stiff collar. He simply sings about goodness and grace, then allows the gift of music to do the spiritual labor.

He lives on 1,200 acres in Harris County, where he can stretch his eyes across the pasture and see the chapel his daddy moved from Suggsville, Ala., then rebuilt piece by piece and pew by pew.

They hold services a couple of times each year. It's nondenomi-

national and, as Allen puts it, “open to any old dog who wants to come.”

It would be easy to be envious of Allen. Eight years ago, at age 40, he traded a rewarding law career for a pair of jeans, a porch full of rocking chairs and guitars within arm’s reach of any room in his house.

His firm kept his name on the letterhead, hoping he would come back. But he never did.

He calls his decision the “choreography of ‘coinci-dance.’ ”

“God has directed the steps of my life,” he explained.

He discussed his life-changing decision with his father. After all, A.C. Levi had paid for his son’s education, often attended his trials and took great pride in Allen being an attorney.

He gave his son his blessings.

“He had a chance to play professional baseball, and he didn’t,” Allen said. “He said I wouldn’t want to go through life wondering ‘what if?’ ”

Allen has now recorded 13 albums. He plays in living rooms, fellowship halls and packed concert venues across the country. Last week, he performed in Dallas, Chicago and schools in nearby Columbus and Hamilton.

“It’s not that much different from being a lawyer,” he said. “My tool is words, my job is to tell stories and my goal is to persuade.”

He picked up his guitar.

Sometimes you’ve got to give up something good to get something better.

The answer can be found in his songs.

Songs still in pursuit of the perfect word.

Ace Is the Place

February 9, 1998

MOUNT VERNON — If he wants to see a former version of himself, Ace Azar can always aim the satellite dish at the corner of the house toward the sky and find an image.

On any given day, at any given hour, some superstation or cable network will be showing reruns of “Andy Griffith,” “Make Room for Daddy” or “The Munsters.”

Years ago on “I Dream of Jeanie,” Barbara Eden rubbed a genie’s lamp and poof! Azar appeared on the television screen. He once played the character of a tougher sergeant than the buffoon Sgt. Carter on “Gomer Pyle.”

He was a pots-and-pans salesman on “Make Room for Daddy.”

He had some connections on the set. The star of the show, Danny Thomas, was his real-life second cousin.

He developed a reputation for playing bad guys on shows such as "I Spy" and "The F.B.I." He was a classic con man on "The Andy Griffith Show."

"I played crooks so well the Hollywood police department made me an honorary suspect," he said, laughing.

He touched elbows and traded punch lines with a parade of stars from Bob Hope to Jimmy Durante to Lucille Ball to Jerry Lewis to Shirley Jones. His own fame and fortune arrived in gentle doses. It came during a span of 30 years of nightclub routines, TV shows, theater performances and as a backstage singer for burlesque acts.

"I was once sitting next to a guy in a bar in Chicago. I don't remember what was on, but he looked up at the TV and said: 'Hey, that's you!'" Azar said. "And I said: 'Yeah, that's me.'"

Now 76, he called Macon home for almost half his life. He owned a nightclub on Cotton Avenue in the 1940s, took off for Hollywood in the 1950s, then returned in the 1970s to own and operate a string of restaurants and clubs.

About a year ago, he moved to an 80-acre farm in Montgomery County where his wife, Flo, grew up.

Now, the only fast lane is a downhill stretch of U.S. 221 between Soperton and Mount Vernon.

"I've entertained in Las Vegas and New York, so a lot of people have asked me what I am doing here," Azar said. "I tell them that my wife is happy, which is a good reason for me to be happy. I don't miss life in the fast lane. I've met a lot of wonderful people here.

"I joined the country club over in Vidalia. At one time in my life, I belonged to Riviera (Riviera Country Club in Los Angeles). Well, I wouldn't trade this place for the Riviera. When people tell you something here, you can put it in the bank."

He grew up in a large family of aspiring entertainers in Detroit. When he was a teenager, a cousin from Toledo named Amos Jacobs came to Detroit to live with them. Jacobs was looking to crack into show business. He began working at local nightspots and even performed "The Lone Ranger" series on a Detroit radio station.

"He got me on one time doing the voice of a kid," Azar said. "I still remember my line: 'Who was that masked man, Ma?'"

Jacobs got his first big break when a well-respected talent agent from Chicago discovered him. He offered to sign him for $50 a week with a week's option at a club in Chicago. There was one condition — he

change his stage name.

Jacobs borrowed his younger brother's name, Danny, and mixed in his older brother's name, Thomas. Danny Thomas was on his way to becoming one of the most beloved entertainers of his generation.

"Danny got his break, and that's just what you have to call it in show business — a break," Azar said. "There is no formula for success. I knew guys who could sing better than Bing Crosby and dance better than Fred Astaire who ended up pumping gas somewhere waiting for their breaks."

Thomas built a national act while Azar was overseas during World War II. When Azar returned to Detroit at the end of the war, he chose not to stick around.

"It was below zero and snowing," he said. "I stayed a couple of days, said hello to everybody and headed south."

He stopped to visit relatives in South Carolina and dropped by Macon to see some friends on his way to Florida. "It was January. Everybody was wearing short sleeves. I decided to stay," he said.

He opened a club on Cotton Avenue and called it the Tropics. He served lunch and dinner, and entertained in the cocktail lounge. He soon was joined in Macon by his younger brother, Johnny, also an entertainer.

In 1952, he sold the club after a six-year run and packed his bags for Hollywood, where he continued working in nightclubs and making appearances in situation comedies. He also did some theater work in several other cities.

"Television was in its infancy, but it was necessary to do something on national TV to promote your nightclub act," Azar said. "It was important to be introduced as someone who had appeared on television." By the 1970s, Azar was weary of California. His first marriage had failed. The residuals soon ran out. He returned to Macon in 1975 for "just a few weeks." He ended up settling down. He operated several restaurants, including the Rib-N-Chick Inn on Emery Highway and the Grey Goose on Gray Highway. He ran the Fraternal Order of Eagles when it was located downtown on Third Street.

Since he remarried, he and his wife have been active in various telethons, benefits and golf tournaments to help raise money for St. Jude's Research Hospital in Memphis. It was founded by Thomas in 1962 and is one of the world's largest research and treatment centers for children with cancer. Thomas died in 1991.

Azar adjusted to life in Macon after living in Detroit and Hollywood. Now he is adjusting to life in a small, south Georgia town after living in Macon.

Show biz still flows in his bloodstream, although the pumps have been slowed by age. Last year, he appeared in a community theater production of "Guys and Dolls" in Vidalia.

"I can't sing anymore, but I had a great time," he said.

They don't call him Ace for nothing.

Where Every Day Is Windy

April 29, 2001

BARNESVILLE — When guests ring the doorbell and step across the threshold, they can hardly believe the sound of their own feet as they move across the wooden floors.

The staircase looks like a scene right out of Tara. There is a swatch of Scarlett's dress in a frame on the wall.

Then the man in the parlor reaches to shake their hands and welcome them to historic Tarleton Oaks, a bed-and-breakfast inn that once served as a Confederate headquarters and hospital during the Civil War.

That is when many of them become so emotional they begin to cry.

"I can't believe I'm in the same room with Brent Tarleton!" they say.

Fred Crane nods and smiles. Above all, he understands.

Many who come to Tarleton Oaks are known as "Windys." Everything about the most-revered movie of all time — "Gone With the Wind" — leaves them breathless.

Clark Gable and Vivien Leigh have been dead for more than a generation. Tara exists only in the pages of a masterpiece that was written on a second-hand typewriter. A taxi ran over Margaret Mitchell. Butterfly McQueen tragically died in a house fire. A lawsuit to block the publication of a controversial sequel, *The Wind Done Gone,* is now making its rounds in federal court.

So this is among their final chances to press the flesh of a man whose lines have been echoed throughout history.

Fred Crane played one of the handsome Tarleton twins. Both were listed as casualties in the Battle of Gettysburg.

He may have been killed off in celluloid, but the real-life Tarleton is a survivor who lives and loves to tell the story.

He is 83 years old and never tires of answering questions about the motion picture that defined his life.

After renovating the inn, Crane and his wife, Terry, opened this four-bedroom, bed-and-breakfast (the former Rose Hill Inn) on June

30 — to coincide with the 64th anniversary of the release of Margaret Mitchell's book.

Three weeks later, Crane was in a Macon hospital undergoing heart bypass surgery.

His body dropped 40 pounds, but he never lost an ounce of his spunk.

"I went from looking like Fred Crane to looking like Ichabod Crane," he said.

The flaming red hair of Brent Tarleton, which was dyed for his scenes as one of Scarlett O'Hara's suitors, now has taken on the look of the distinguished white hair and beard of Crane's ancestor, Robert E. Lee.

He claims he has returned to Georgia after "60 years as a Yankee POW."

Each evening, he gives the inn's guests a real treat — a slide show with rare photographs from the movie. He fields the visitors' questions and keeps them captivated.

"For two-and-a-half hours," he said, "nobody yawns."

Crane grew up in New Orleans during the Great Depression. His mother bought him a one-way ticket to Hollywood. While there, he contacted his cousin, a silent-film actress named Leatrice Joy, who took him with her when she went to audition for the role of Scarlett O'Hara's sister, Suellen.

Crane was 20 years old. He had never read the book and was unfamiliar with director David O. Selznick. But casting director Charles Richards overheard Crane's Louisiana-laced Southern accent and was convinced he could fill the role of one of the Tarleton brothers.

Crane read the script with Leigh and signed a contract for $50 a week for 13 weeks. (His cousin did not get the part of Suellen, which went to Evelyn Keyes.)

Of course, both Windys and non-Windys are more familiar with Brent Tarleton's twin brother, Stuart. After all, he was portrayed by the late George Reeves, who was faster than a speeding bullet in the Superman television series of the 1950s.

Crane still remembers his own opening lines:

"What do we care if we were expelled from college, Scarlett? The war is gonna start any day now, so we would have left school anyhow."

To which Scarlett replies:

"Fiddle-dee-dee. War, war, war. This war talk's spoiling all the fun at every party this spring. I get so bored I could scream."

The scene was remade three times. In the first take, the twins' dyed red hair was too curly.

"We looked like Groucho Marx," said Crane.

Then, before the movie premiered in Atlanta in 1939, film advisor Susan Myrick, a well-known columnist for *The Macon Telegraph,* suggested Selznick rework it.

Scarlett was in a low-cut dress, and Myrick said the movie's producers would have a difficult time convincing the United Daughters of the Confederacy that Scarlett would "be showing that much bosom in the morning."

Crane spent the next 40 years as a radio and television announcer in Hollywood. He broadcast classical music and had acting roles in everything from "The Twilight Zone" to "Peyton Place."

After his wife died in 1998, Crane was in Memphis for an appearance at the Hunt-Phelan House, which once served as Ulysses S. Grant's headquarters.

Terry was there searching for Civil War items to use in a theme for a Shirley Temple collectors convention. She paid $30 for two autographed photos of Crane and struck up a conversation.

When she learned he was widowed, she switched to her match-making mode to see if he might be interested in a date with her former mother-in-law.

Although Terry was 40 years younger, she was the one who was charmed by his wit and touched by his kindness.

"He didn't shake my hand goodbye," she said. "He kissed it." They exchanged some 1,600 e-mails and were married in October 1999.

"I found my Scarlett," said Crane.

Terry had always been a huge GWTW fan. She wrote term papers on the book and once did a Scarlett soliloquy in a school play.

"I saw the movie for the first time when I was 10 years old," she said. "I can't explain it, but I had the strangest feeling when I saw the Tarleton twins."

They moved from Terry's home in Hiram to Barnesville last year. They had never been to Barnesville — they had never even heard of the town — until they found the inn listed for sale on the Internet.

They walked in the door and, even though the old place needed some work, their instincts told them they were "home." They filled it with antiques, family heirlooms and their 7-year-old son, Trey.

The house, which was built in the 1850s, is a southern Greek Revival mansion listed on the National Register of Historic Places. Historic Greenwood Cemetery is located behind the property. More than

350 soldiers are buried there, including some 150 killed in a head-on train collision.

"We have two secret passages in the house," said Terry, "and a ghost."

The inn has been written up in *TV Guide* and shown as part of a documentary on The Travel Channel. Visitors have come from as far away as England and Japan.

The Cranes have developed an appropriate slogan: "... where true Southern hospitality is not gone with the wind."

They are working on several book projects about their adventures, as well as a cookbook. They truly love what they're doing. They can't remember when they've had so much fun.

Crane still gets requests for autographs almost every day. And he never seems to grow weary of reminiscing about the movie he became a part of by "accident and good fortune."

"All this has been a great joy to me, because it has been such a great joy to others," he said.

Courtroom Becomes Her Saving Grace

June 1, 2003

When she comes home to Macon, Nancy Grace runs through the nearby soybean fields and eats barbecue at Fincher's on Houston Avenue.

She argues politics with her brother and listens to her mama playing the organ on Sunday mornings at Liberty United Methodist Church.

She relishes the warm sunshine, the tall pines and the smell of flowers.

"It's great to see the sky," she said, "without having to look straight up."

You can take the girl out of Georgia, but you can't take Georgia out of the girl.

She now lives in Manhattan, surrounded by skyscrapers along the East River. Her apartment is 21 floors above the ground. She walks 16 blocks to work. People often stop her on the streets of New York and ask for her autograph.

Grace never went looking for celebrity. It found her.

She only went searching for justice. And she won't stop until all the evil in the world is behind bars.

Grace is an anchor for Court TV cable network and one of the country's high-profile legal minds. She has been featured on CNN and is

a regular guest on "Larry King Live."

She has been interviewed on "The Today Show" and "Good Morning America."

She also contributed an essay to the recent best-seller book, *I Love You, Mom.*

There may be a star on her dressing room door in the Big Apple, but she never has forgotten her roots in south Bibb County. Her parents, Mac and Elizabeth Grace, still live in the house where she grew up.

On a recent Saturday afternoon, she sat on the front porch and waved to neighbors as they rode by.

Look! Nancy's home! And, to think, we just saw her on TV the other night interviewing Laci Peterson's mother!

It didn't start out this glamorous. Grace had planned to be an English teacher. She wanted to marry and start a family. Drive a mini-van. Be a soccer mom. Carry a PTA membership card.

"I didn't get my dream," she said. "God gave me a different life and purpose, and I'm not going to second-guess that. When he shuts a door, he opens a window."

As a child, she attended Heard Elementary School and graduated from Windsor Academy. An avid reader, she went to Valdosta State to major in English.

She loved Shakespeare, but she fell in love with Keith Griffin, a handsome young baseball player from Athens. They planned to get married.

Then, in the summer of 1980, Griffin was murdered. He was working at a construction job in Madison and had gone to get soft drinks for everyone at lunch. He was mugged for $30 in his wallet. He was shot five times.

Grace was devastated. She testified at the trial. To this day, 23 years later, she has not married. She refuses to enter the front bedroom in her parents' house. It is where Griffin stayed after returning with her family from a beach vacation.

"I couldn't eat. I couldn't sleep. I couldn't even think," said Grace. "So I dropped out of school."

She went to visit her older sister, Jenny, who lived in Philadelphia. She hoped getting away would help her start piecing life back together.

Nothing seemed to fit.

"My whole world had exploded," she said. "I didn't know where I was going to go or what I was going to do. I didn't have any hope or direction for the next hour, much less for the rest of my life."

Then, while sitting on a bench on the campus of the University of Pennsylvania, it suddenly became clear. She remembered a book that had influenced her life almost as much as the Bible.

It was *To Kill a Mockingbird,* by Harper Lee. She admired the character Atticus Finch — a widowed attorney in a small, Southern town who defended a black man accused of raping a white woman.

That day, she decided to go to law school to become a prosecutor and victims-rights advocate.

The next day, she returned to Macon, enrolled at Mercer and was later accepted at Mercer's Walter F. George School of Law.

She rented an apartment near the law school and immersed herself in academics. She had no interest in a social life. She worked as a law clerk and at a downtown sandwich shop.

Eventually, it all led to a job with Atlanta's Fulton County District Attorney's Office, where she became a daring inner-city lawyer in the heart of the nation's murder capital.

Grace didn't want to fool with misdemeanors or petty crime. Her intent was to put away hard-core criminals. She became the first female special prosecutor in the office of longtime district attorney Lewis Slaton. She worked on major felony cases involving serial murder, serial rape, serial child molestation and arson.

"The first time I tried a case, I felt like a bird let out of a cage," she said.

It was an affirmation. One person could make a difference. She considered it an honor — and a duty — to speak out for victims who could not speak out for themselves.

A decade's work produced more than 10,000 guilty pleas. She compiled a perfect record of nearly 100 felony convictions. She never lost a trial.

She also developed a loyal following for her theatrical style in the courtroom. She earned respect for her relentless pursuit of criminal evidence.

It wasn't long before she became a darling of the media. The Atlanta newspapers referred to her as "Amazing Grace." During lunch, she would race over to the CNN studios, still wearing heels, and provide legal commentary.

So it shouldn't have been a surprise when a noted writer, magazine editor and former attorney named Stephen Brill, the founder of Court TV, took her to dinner in 1996 and offered her a job.

In the post-O.J. Simpson trial days, he "courted" her as a sparring partner with Simpson's lawyer, Johnnie Cochran, on a legal af-

fairs show called "Cochran & Grace."

"I never imagined doing anything like TV," she said. "It just evolved."

She left for New York on Jan. 6, 1997. She packed her clothes, a curling iron and $200 in savings.

And now here she is — a famous name, a famous face. Here she is, trying to convince millions of TV viewers in a jury box that knows no boundaries.

There are days when she casts her big eyes toward the camera and unleashes the bite of a pit bull.

There is a soft side, too.

"Sometimes I will cry during a commercial break when something comes up that reminds me of Keith," she said.

When she comes home to Macon, she heads over to the S & S Cafeteria for fresh vegetables. She calls old high school friends and listens to her father's fascinating stories about working for the railroad.

You can't take Georgia out of the girl.

That much will never change.

Cutting Edge of Southern Food

June 9, 2002

When he was a kid growing up in the former home of a Confederate general, John T. Edge would ride his five-speed Schwinn bicycle to Old Clinton Barbecue, just a few miles south of Gray.

He would wash down a pork sandwich and Brunswick stew with an Orange Crush.

He ate there so often, his family had a charge account. It was the beginning of what would become a passion — and later a career — dedicated to the finger-lickin' bounty of kitchen tables in the deep South.

His appetite for life was whetted by recipes passed down through generations of Southern cookbooks.

And the fire in his belly was stoked by the menus in restaurants where people gathered for second helpings of catfish and fried green tomatoes.

They shared a sense of community as they wiped the red-eye gravy from their collective chin.

His father, John T. Edge Sr., remains an avid reader and adventurous cook. His mother, the late Mary Beverly Evans Edge, loved antiques and history.

Those qualities were passed down to provide Edge with the edge he needed. He became a writer, lecturer and, according to *USA Today* newspaper, a "studious chowhound ... the country's brightest young proponent of Southern food."

The pot didn't stir all at once for Edge, who now holds a fancy title. He is director of the Southern Foodways Alliance at the Ole Miss Center for the Study of Southern Culture.

When he graduated from Macon's Tattnall Square Academy and headed for the University of Georgia, he had no idea what he wanted to do in life.

After getting his diploma from UGA and taking a job in the Atlanta corporate world, he still had no clue.

Working nine years as a salesman for a financial news service left him with a revelation: He was bored.

So he shucked his yuppie lifestyle and showed up on the doorstep at Ole Miss to pursue a master's degree in Southern Studies.

"I didn't know what was going to happen on the back end," he said. "I just knew the front end was going to be exciting."

Soon, he was eating and writing his way through the South. His byline appeared in national and regional magazines. His books showed off their dust jackets in bookstores and libraries.

Edge brushed elbows in the Oxford, Miss., literary community with folks like John Grisham.

A Gracious Plenty isn't simply a collection of Southern-fried recipes. It's more of a storybook than a cookbook. Edge was keenly interested in telling stories rather than just listing ingredients.

His *Southern Belly* is a fun-filled grub tour of the South. Once again, the people are more important than the palate.

There is always a great story out there waiting to be told.

"And food is a great way to tell it," he said.

Bon appetit.

New Delivery at General Hospital

April 13, 2003

There are stars in Hollywood we will never see.

They are hidden behind cosmetic counters and cash registers. They pump gas, wait tables and line up for auditions, hoping for their big break.

Natalia Livingston once worked at a Home Depot in Los Angeles. She tended plants in the garden department while nurturing her

dream of an acting career.

She had faith that one day her script would come in.

"Working at Home Depot was a good experience," she said. "If I ever build a house, I'll know what I'm doing."

For the past month, she has been building a "hospital."

Her family and friends back home in Macon, who know her as "Naty," can now turn on their TVs every afternoon at 3 p.m. and watch her in living color.

In March, she was cast as Emily Quartermaine in ABC's "General Hospital," which has won more Emmys than any daytime soap opera in television history. She made her debut the first week of April.

"I still can't believe it," she said.

Her proud parents, James and Martha Livingston, are pinching themselves, too.

It seems like only yesterday Natalia was dancing on stage as a tiny snowflake in "The Nutcracker." Or was being crowned homecoming queen at Mount de Sales, where she graduated in 1994.

James Livingston is a physician who has his practice in Byron. After graduating from Emory University five years ago, Natalia was a social worker at The Medical Center of Central Georgia.

So the family is somewhat amused that all this medical background has nothing to do with "General Hospital."

James met his Mexican-born wife, Martha, while studying in Guadalajara. Natalia, 27, has a younger brother, Jimmy, 24.

When James took Natalia to Emory for her freshman year, he pointed to a sign in her dormitory that said: "You cannot take the elevator to success. You have to take the stairs."

He still reminds her of it almost every time they talk. She returned to Macon after graduation and gained some TV experience working for "Unique Discoveries," a local cable show.

Only she wanted to be "discovered," too. Three years ago, she decided to move to L.A.

"Leaving was the hardest thing I've ever had to do," she said. "I felt I had to give it a shot, though."

She landed acting parts in local theaters. She spoke Spanish fluently and got a part in a McDonald's commercial for Hispanic audiences.

While in Macon for Christmas, her agent called and asked her to make an audition tape for "General Hospital." That led to a screen test, and she was offered the part.

Goodbye, Home Depot.

"It's so much fun we can work on a show for nine hours and it

feels like nine minutes to me," she said.

Twenty years ago, "General Hospital" launched the career of actress Demi Moore.

Now that Natalia has gotten her big break, she is anxious to see what she can do.

We'll be pulling for you, Naty.

Bold, Beautiful Bobbie

April 20, 2001

I'm sure Bobbie Eakes would have made a great dentist.

I'm sure she could have nailed fancy diplomas on the wall, chatted away about tooth decay and reminded us to floss every day.

Gosh. With her heart-stopping beauty, she could have had people lining up — for root canals.

But she had enough sense to follow her heart. And something told her heart to escape the misery of chemistry class at the University of Georgia.

So she switched to journalism and plotted a career in broadcasting.

What she really wanted, though, was to be a singer. Whenever Bobbie Eakes sang, heads would turn and goose bumps would gather.

"I wanted to find out what I could do as a singer. I decided to give it a shot while I was still young," she said.

So she chased that dream across eight states. She didn't stop until she stuck her big toe in the Pacific Ocean.

She discovered Hollywood, all right. But Hollywood discovered her first. She became an actress.

Of course, she carried some lofty credentials with her. Seven months after graduating from Warner Robins High School in 1979, she was the first runner-up in the Miss Teen USA pageant.

In 1982, she was crowned Miss Georgia and was a finalist in the Miss America pageant. Two TV producers were impressed with her performance in Atlantic City, N.J. Before she knew it, there was a star on her dressing room door.

Anyone who knew her family was not surprised when Bobbie — the youngest of five talented Eakes sisters — eventually assumed the role of the popular Macy Alexander Forrester on the CBS soap opera, "The Bold and the Beautiful."

Her older sister, Sandra, also was Miss Georgia in 1979. Together with sisters Susan, Sharon and Shelly, the Eakes assembled a family

record for winning pageants that may never be broken.

They are the pride of Warner Robins, a city that popped so many proverbial buttons over the success of the Eakes sisters it needed to hire a municipal seamstress.

Although Bobbie Eakes has been a California girl for almost half of her life, she remains true to her Georgia roots. Her parents, Bob and Audrey, still live in Warner Robins, where Bob is retired from the Air Force.

Bobbie may have met her husband, David Steen, and her best friend, Caia Coley Feifer, in Los Angeles, but they both are native Southerners. David is from Memphis. Caia, who recently was married in Eakes' home, is from Atlanta.

Bobbie will return to home turf today as one of the celebrities participating in the ninth annual Children's Hospital Celebrity Golf and Tennis Pro-Am Classic at Macon's Idle Hour Club.

She'll be coming home under somewhat different career conditions. Macy's character on "The Bold and the Beautiful" was "killed off" the show last year in a fiery car crash. It was a shock for Eakes to be given such an unceremonious boot from the show after 11 years.

Although acting is still in her blood — she has made guest appearances on "Falcon Crest," "Cheers," "The Wonder Years" and "Full House" — she has been re-focusing her career on her first love, which is music.

She has recorded several albums in Europe (one with former soap co-star Jeff Trachta) and performed a duet with country star Collin Raye on the single "Tired of Loving This Way." Her yet-unnamed new CD is due out this summer.

"I'm sure a lot of people know me from my soap opera days, but I want my music to speak for itself," she said. "I want to win people over that way."

That's bold. That's beautiful. That's Bobbie.

Bobbie is back on the afternoon soaps in the role of Krystal on "All My Children."

ABSENT FRIENDS

In the Company of a King
December 26, 2002

I've always believed you could travel to the far corners of the earth and someone there would know Harley Bowers.

His influence stretched beyond the circulation boundaries of *The Macon Telegraph*. It didn't matter if you were at the airport in Atlanta or in a country store outside of Thomasville.

With Harley, you were in the company of a king.

For years, he wrote a prolific six columns every week. In Middle Georgia, he had the most recognizable mug this side of Col. Sanders.

Generations of sports fans grew up reading the more than 11,000 columns he typed for the *Telegraph* sports pages between 1959 and 1996.

Harley knew the formula for a good sports story. People watch games to have fun. They read about those games the next day to have fun again.

Coaches, players and officials all respected him. Although he was tough, you rarely saw poison drip from his pen.

He understood a journalist's fingers must not be disconnected from his heart, and he had a good one. I once heard him described as the "consummate Southern gentleman."

Whether he was writing about his beloved Georgia Bulldogs, the green jacket at Augusta, native son Dan Reeves of Americus or the rabbits he chased from his backyard garden, Harley always let you know where he stood.

He may have built a few fences growing up on a farm near Moreland. But, in a career that spanned 54 years at five newspapers, he never straddled them.

Over the past century, no figure in Macon sports history has wielded as much influence or been a more worthy ambassador for our city. He helped bring the Georgia Sports Hall of Fame and minor-league baseball to town.

Harley was one of the saints in my life. In my sportswriting career at *The Telegraph,* he was a father figure. He coached me. He encouraged me. He opened doors and took me into new territory.

My only mistake about Harley was thinking he was invincible. Even after the cancer in 1991, when doctors amputated his right arm, he typed his columns with one hand.

On Christmas Eve, I returned from a church service and sat down to watch "It's a Wonderful Life." At 8:05 p.m., the phone rang. It was Martha Clare Bowers.

"Daddy died tonight," she said. An hour earlier, she and her mother, Joyce, had tried to wake him from his easy chair to come to the supper table. He had gone to sleep in front of the TV and closed his eyes forever.

"One of the last things he read before he died," said Martha Clare, "was the Christmas card you sent him."

It has been a tough year for the *Telegraph* family. In March, we buried a true matriarch — retired food editor Clara Eschmann. In September, editorial page editor Ron Woodgeard died after a long and courageous battle with cancer.

And now, as this sad year draws to a close, we must mourn Harley's death while celebrating his life.

"He always loved you, Ed," Martha Clare told me.

"And I loved him," I said.

Dog Crossing's Best Friend

December 14, 2001

DOG CROSSING — It wasn't easy to remember the first time you met Ed McHargue because he made you feel as if you had always known him.

He was the kind of neighbor who came running when you needed help and dropped by to check on you even when you didn't. He wasn't being nosey, just neighborly.

Folks claimed he had a dry sense of humor, even on the wettest days. He loved to compare rain gauges. If you had more drops than he did, he would scratch his head and wonder how the rain could have missed his house.

"He was everybody's friend," said a neighbor, Cindy McInvale. "He had a heart as big as the world."

When folks die in the big city, the population figures barely move.

But, when somebody dies in Dog Crossing, the whole place seems to lose its collective breath. That's because only about two dozen folks, and a couple of dozen dogs, live at this Upson County crossroads.

Mr. Ed didn't just live in Dog Crossing.

In many ways, he was Dog Crossing.

He was the town historian, caretaker and ambassador. If the place had a mayor, he would have been elected in a landslide along Rocky Bottom Road.

At age 80, he still worked with his son, Roy, in the cabinet shop

across the road from his house. In the evenings, he would retire to his front porch swing at the home where he grew up. He knew just about every car and truck that would come around the curve from Mud Bridge.

They would honk, and he would wave. That's the way his world worked.

They laid Mr. Ed to rest Thursday afternoon in the drizzle at Mount Zion Baptist cemetery. A line of cars followed the black hearse down Rocky Bottom, carrying him past his front porch one last time.

On Monday, he had taken his daughter, Earlene, to the doctor in Thomaston, and his own heart gave out right there at the hospital.

Above his casket in the chapel at Coggins Funeral Home, they placed his hammer, his saw and his measuring tape.

"With Mr. Ed, it was always: Measure twice, cut once," said Kenny Coggins.

A year ago, I wrote a column about Dog Crossing and other tiny Georgia communities with interesting names.

I had never been to Dog Crossing, and I admitted I wasn't sure I would even know it when I got there.

That same morning, I got a call from Ed McHargue. He had been at the post office over at The Rock and heard folks talking about the story.

He invited me over for a wonderful history lesson. According to his daddy, John Henry McHargue, a mule wagon once ran over a dog crossing the road, hence the name.

In response to my column, residents Tommy and Cindy McInvale put up a sign: "DOG CROSSING."

A few months later, I went for a visit. I had my picture taken kneeling at the sign with Mr. Ed and a basset hound named Buster.

Mr. Ed would have been 81 years old on Jan. 4. After his funeral Thursday, the McInvales said they now plan to place another sign beneath the big letters: Dog Crossing.

It will say: In Memory of Ed McHargue. 1921-2001.

As Good as It Gets

May 31, 2002

TIFTON — Tuesday morning, I rode in a pickup truck with Gene Brodie.

We cruised the streets beneath the tall pines where the coach put down roots 26 years ago. We passed the stadium that now bears his name, the stadium where his funeral is expected to be held in a few days,

although we had no way of knowing that at the time.

I asked him what it was like to be king — the head coach in a small south Georgia town, where Friday nights revolve around football the same way the planets orbit the sun.

"It's as good as it gets," he said.

Later that same day, Gene Brodie was scrambling for his life, like a quarterback trying to avoid a heavy rush.

He has always been a fighter. This time, however, the 60-year-old coach was clearly overmatched.

By Thursday morning, a Catholic priest was summoned to the hospital in Thomasville to administer last rites to Brodie. Family and friends waited into the night for the end. A few coaches and former players returned to Tifton and began building the cedar casket Brodie asked to be buried in.

By all counts, Brodie was a coaching legend. He won a pair of state championships at Central High School (1975) and Tift County (1983).

Last month, he was inducted into the Macon Sports Hall of Fame. He was the consummate hard-nosed, throw-back coach. He turned boys into men in the sweat of weight rooms and on the dirt and grass of practice fields.

His players believed he was tougher than a pit bull and meaner than a timber rattlesnake.

But there were soft pads beneath the hard shell. There was a deep devotion to making the world around him a better place.

In the summer of 1993, he and his son, Brooks, hopped on a pair of motorcycles and took a 4,150-mile trip to Death Valley and back.

It was the summer before Brooks' senior year at Tift County. (He is now a graduate assistant coach at Valdosta State.) Brodie had never been west of the Mississippi River. That summer, a couple of Blue Devils became Hell's Angels.

Brodie retired in 1994, and he was diagnosed with cancer that same year.

The doctors gave him just two years to live. The prostate cancer later developed into bone cancer.

Brodie needed a reason to get out of bed every morning. So he bought 10 acres on a lake a few miles outside town.

He drew plans for a log home on the back of a paper sack the same way he might diagram a football play with X's and O's.

Then he went to work.

"It helped get me through some tough times," he said. "There are

plenty of folks who worry themselves to death. But I've never heard of anyone working themselves to death."

The son of a carpenter, he purchased a sawmill and spent an entire year cutting 16-foot sections of cypress logs. He drove to Michigan and brought back three black walnut trees. He traveled to Indiana to fetch igneous rock for the fireplace.

Brodie worked on his log home almost every day for four years, stopping only for his chemotherapy and radiation treatments. The family moved into the home in 1998.

"This will be here long after I'm gone," he said. "I'm leaving my mark."

There are other ways Brodie will be leaving his mark.

He was a father figure to hundreds of young men. One of them, Michael Jolly, was the star quarterback on Central's state championship team. Jolly stopped by to visit with Brodie earlier this week.

Brodie influenced countless others. The story of Andy Summers is an example of the circle of life.

Summers' father died when he was 2 years old. His mother battled alcoholism, and he went to live with relatives in Macon. In the late 1960s at Lanier High School (now Central), Summers started in the same backfield with running back Isaac Jackson (of "See Isaac Run" fame.)

Summers was white. Jackson was one of Lanier's first black players.

Fans called them "Salt and Pepper."

Andy signed with the University of Florida, and he was working on a construction job in Tallahassee when Brodie contacted him in 1976. Brodie had been hired at Tift County. He asked Andy to join his staff to coach the defensive backs.

In March 1983, the spring before the Blue Devils won the state championship, Andy was killed in a car accident on U.S. 41 north of Tifton.

His young son, Tyson, was 10 days shy of his third birthday.

Brodie immediately established a trust fund for Tyson. He was a father figure to him, just as he had been to Tyson's father.

"I still call him Andy half the time," said Brodie. "He looks just like his dad."

Three weeks ago, Tyson graduated from Presbyterian College, where he played football. Brodie advised him to return to Tifton and buy a small house rather than pay rent.

That's because Tyson Summers has been hired to coach the

defensive backs at Tift County, just like his dad once did.

Everyone was praying the old coach would be there to see it.

We're Richer for Having Known Him

February 21, 2003

They laid Bob Bonifay to rest Thursday morning on a warm February day that fit like a baseball glove.

At Riverside United Methodist Church, friends and family wept softly and said their goodbyes. The 23rd Psalm was read. The organist played "Amazing Grace."

Bob Bonifay was one of those folks who made your life richer just by knowing him. He was passionate about living. He made every one of his 86 years count.

In his native Montgomery, Ala., he was a high school classmate of legendary country singer Hank Williams Sr. During World War II, at an Army office in San Bernadino, Calif., he discharged a fellow by the name of Ronald Reagan.

His name was synonymous with Macon sports. Of course, his main claim to fame came as general manager of the Macon Peaches baseball team when Pete Rose played here in 1962. He also was executive director of the Georgia Professional Golfers Association for 17 years.

But his footprints were everywhere else, too. He once managed the City Auditorium and a local cable company. He chaired a local recreation commission and several political campaigns. He even ran for City Council himself one year, losing his race by about 100 votes.

"I've been nearly a little of everything," he once told me.

I will always remember his throat-clearing grunt. He used it to emphasize every point, his eyebrows rising and falling across his forehead.

In the days before videotape, he operated a film-processing business for high school football coaches on Friday nights out of a small house on Walnut Street.

His most interesting job, however, may have been doing play-by-play for a St. Petersburg, Fla., radio station. When the local minor-league team played on the road, reports were phoned in after every inning.

Bonifay gathered the details and "simulated" the game in front of a live studio audience, right down to the crack of the bat. Just call it "reality" radio. The station even sold popcorn.

But, for all his accomplishments and public recognition, his

proudest moment was when he was named "Father of the Year" by the Macon Junior Chamber of Commerce in 1967.

Every time I visited him in that pack rat of a "baseball room" at his Shirley Hills home, he mentioned receiving the fatherhood honor.

He and Catherine, his childhood sweetheart, were married for 62 years. Their three sons — Ken, Cam and Brannon — all were outstanding high school athletes in Macon and at Georgia Tech.

What was the measure of the man? Several years ago, he read a column I wrote about injustice being done to a 10-year-old boy in south Macon.

The youngster, who had been diagnosed with leukemia, was dropped from his league's all-star baseball roster.

Bonifay asked me to take him to the young man's home, where he presented the boy with a major-league all-star shirt, cap and autographed baseball.

I never forgot that gesture, just like I'll never forget the man who made it.

If They Played, He Was There

June 26, 2002

Bobby Fay could tell you how many stolen bases Ty Cobb had in 1912 and the name of the Atlanta Braves pitcher who once hit two grand slams in a game.

Trying to slip a trivia question past Bobby was like trying to sneak a hanging curve past Barry Bonds.

He would never fail to call me on the telephone, always full of facts and figures.

I'm really going to miss those conversations.

When they buried Bobby on Tuesday, we lost one of Macon's most loyal sports fans. It was practically impossible to attend a local sporting event without seeing him there.

"He was everywhere," a friend whispered during the funeral Mass at Holy Spirit Catholic Church.

Bobby kept his own statistics in his own score book and often brought his own PA system. He wore a grin so wide you could park the team bus inside.

"He was a legend," said Bobby Pope, Mercer's athletic director.

Bobby died Sunday at age 45. He had endured a variety of health problems since birth. This time, the cancer struck so quickly he never realized the seriousness of his illness.

To know Bobby was to love Bobby, and there was a lot of Bobby to love. His appetite for food rivaled his passion for sports.

He was born with a slight birth defect. Some might have called him simple-minded.

"It always hurt me when people said he was retarded," said his mother, Catherine. "He was just a slow learner."

While part of Bobby's personality bordered on innocence, the other side of his brain functioned like a computer.

He could recite statistics. He rarely forgot a name or face. He could remember entire casts of TV shows.

I first met Bobby at a high school football game. He was in the press box, pretending to be broadcasting the game. He dreamed of becoming the next Keith Jackson or Jack Buck.

For several years, Bobby worked part time in the *Telegraph* sports department. He also helped at local TV stations on Friday nights, gathering scores.

It wasn't unusual for Bobby to track down a missing score by calling the deputy sheriff in a nearby town.

His father, Bob, accomplished his goal of traveling with his son to every major-league stadium in the country. Often, they would join former big-league umpire Harry Wendelstedt, a longtime family friend.

Mercer baseball fans won't soon forget the time Bobby couldn't get his tape recorder to play the national anthem before a game. So he grabbed the microphone and sang it himself.

That was Bobby. He always had a song in his heart.

Once, a visiting reporter from Jackson accidentally left his sunglasses in the press box at Luther Williams Field. The reporter called the Macon Braves office to report the lost item. A search of the press box turned up empty.

That's because Bobby had taken the glasses and was on his way to Jackson to deliver them personally.

Gosh, we're going to miss him.

I guess heaven needed someone to help keep score.

Maybe even sing the national anthem.

Mama Clara, We'll Miss You

March 13, 2002

The good Lord gives you a mama. Then he blesses you with more "mamas."

A mama brings you into the world, smothers you with kisses,

tucks you in at night and still bakes for you long after you leave the nest.

Guardian moms are the sugar-sweet surrogates who watch after you when your own mother isn't there.

They remember your birthday. They call when you're sick. They leave thoughtful notes.

Clara Eschmann was one of my "mamas." I'm proud to say I was one of her "chillun."

That's why my heart is especially heavy this morning.

I cannot believe Mama Clara is gone.

I last saw her Sunday. She dropped by the office to finish her "Remember When?" column for today's newspaper.

As always, the gracious Southern lady greeted me.

"Dah-ling."

In the 23 years I knew her, everybody was her darling.

We hugged. We talked. She was worried about her sister in West Virginia, who was in poor health. She had planned to leave Tuesday to see about her.

I held the newsroom door open for her. She had walked with a cane since an automobile accident two years ago. I wondered how many times she had passed through that door in her storied career as the newspaper's food editor.

Sadness swept over the newspaper offices Tuesday when we learned of her death. Outside, it was damp and drizzly. I tried not to think about what it's going to be like without the lady who spread so much sunshine.

Searching for adjectives to describe Clara is like putting everything you love into a favorite recipe.

Sugar and spice and everything nice. ...

And maybe a little Tabasco, too. Miss Clara was feisty. Live wires were loose inside that little woman.

Although she retired from the newspaper almost 15 years ago, she must have taken an eraser to those retirement papers. She came down here just as much as she ever did.

She was a widow who lived alone. But she never let herself get lonely.

She stayed busy in volunteer work and community service. She was very active at Christ Church.

On weekends, when I stopped by the office, I often would find her typing those nostalgic words and recipes that thousands of readers looked forward to each week.

I became one of her "chillun" the day I began work here.

At first, I thought she favored me only because she had a son named "Ed." Then I realized she simply loved people, and people loved her back.

I'll never forget my first New Year's Day in Macon. I had to work and would miss all the bowl games on television.

To add to my misery, it occurred to me that I had never missed eating black-eyed peas on New Year's Day — a Southern tradition to bring good luck in the new year.

My mother was a hundred miles away. What was I going to do?

When I arrived at the office, Clara was waiting with a big pot of black-eyed peas for everybody who had to work that day.

It was something a mother would do.

I'm going to miss my "mama."

Nelson Said It All

July 14, 2004

His students have gone to see Leon Nelson almost every day for the past three weeks.

They gather at the foot of his bed, swallowing hard and reaching for words. They bring along their parents to thank him. Some have brought their preachers to pray for him.

No one leaves without signing the huge get-well card on the wall.

No, this isn't home room at Central High School.

It's a hospital room.

As much as Nelson appreciates the visits, they wear on him. The nurses at The Medical Center of Central Georgia often have to shoo the students out.

The cancer has Mr. Nelson in a full-nelson. True to form, he is fighting back.

Still, his arms and legs are frail. His once-booming voice has been reduced to soft whispers.

Years ago, his father nicknamed him "Porky," after the pig. His diseased body now looks like streaks on a blackboard.

We have this ongoing dialogue on race relations in our city. Blacks and whites can't seem to get along.

There is none of that here.

Most of the students who visit Nelson at the hospital are white. And they love this humble, caring black man who grew up playing baseball against former big-leaguer John "Blue Moon" Odom on the

dusty sandlots of south Macon.

I should know. A pair of Nelson's biggest fans belong to me — my two oldest sons.

"These kids, they don't see color," said Eugene Harper, Nelson's longtime friend and caregiver. "They want to know: 'What can we do for you, Mr. Nelson?' They all have stories about how he has touched their lives. The parents tell about how their children come home and all they talk about is Mr. Nelson."

Nelson grew up the youngest of seven boys. He wanted to be a lawyer because, he said, "I like to talk a lot."

Instead, he used his voice to become a teacher. He taught graphic arts and printing at Northeast and Dudley Hughes vocational school before taking over media technology at Central.

He often held second jobs, working at a print shop on Cotton Avenue and moonlighting as a cameraman for WMAZ-TV.

In August 2002, Nelson went to the doctor. He thought he had been stung by a wasp. It turned out to be cancer in his lymph nodes.

The last two years have been tough. There were times when he couldn't swallow or eat. Despite undergoing chemotherapy, he never gave up going to school or helping care for his 93-year-old father.

Pam Wacter, who retired as Central's principal in May, said Nelson didn't miss more than 10 days during the past two years. She called him a "lesson in courage."

"Regardless of how sick he was, he was there," Wacter said. "He didn't want to let the students down."

Said Nelson: "I told them I would have good days and bad days. They would just have to hang in there with me, and they did."

Bibb County teachers report back on July 30. Although his health may prevent him from returning, Nelson has signed a contract for next year. There is a waiting list of 68 students for his four classes.

Maybe that's why when the school's spirit club sold T-shirts listing the "10 Reasons I Go To Central," one of them simply read: Mr. Nelson.

"It needed no explanation," said Wacter.

That's all it said.

That said it all.

Leon Nelson died on July 15, 2004, one day after this column appeared. I'm glad I was able to honor him while he was still living.

He Never Waved a White Flag

August 20, 2001

I always believed Wayne Bevill was invincible.

If he owned a white flag, he never waved it. He was the gunslinger who dodged every bullet, then climbed on his horse to ride again.

After all, he survived a heart attack, three angioplasties and a knee replacement. In April 1999, they found cancer in his lungs.

Still, I never expected death to take him away, as it did Sunday afternoon.

When life tossed nails in the road, he always kept spare tires in the trunk.

Wayne Bevill was more than director of the Macon Rescue Mission. He was its heartbeat. Its soul. Its inspiration.

He turned 60 years old last month. When his cancer dug deep, he had to retire. The community prayed for him, right up to the end. There was always hope Bevill could climb back on that saddle one more time.

A gifted athlete on the sandlots around Bowden Homes and Memorial Park, he wore No. 10. It was the same number worn by his hero, Fran Tarkenton, the quarterback who loved to scramble.

Off the field, Bevill learned to turn broken plays into big gains, too.

In the early 1960s, he was called into the ministry. When the Rev. Jimmy Waters invited him to preach at Mabel White Baptist Church, Bevill was so nervous he forgot to wear a belt.

On a Friday the 13th in June 1969, he woke up with a sharp pain in his face. He was only 27 years old. The stroke nearly cut him down in the prime of his life. It left him with limited use of his right arm. He dragged his right leg when he walked. Doctors sent him to Warm Springs for rehabilitation and said he would be lucky to ever work again.

Billy Henderson, his football coach at Willingham High, knew the scrambler would never quit, though. "The human spirit," said Henderson, "cannot be measured."

Twenty-five years ago, Bevill arrived at the former Macon Rescue Mission building at the foot of Poplar Street. The interim director's job paid $150 a week. He had no plans to stay more than a few months.

Then one day a young woman and her two children wandered into his office four floors beneath the famous "JESUS CARES" sign.

"When I looked at her, I didn't see her," he said. "All I could see was my own wife and two children, and it scared me. I started crying, and you can only imagine what she must have thought about that."

Bevill would cry every time he told that story. It was the

affirmation of his calling to serve the homeless men, the battered women, and the neglected and abused children seeking shelter from their personal storms. He gave unconditional love to those broken lives that drifted through the mission's doors like flies on a summer day.

In his final years at the mission, he continued to work between the rounds of radiation and chemotherapy. He moved the mission into its new facility at the corner of Hazel and Telfair streets. He led the revival of the Macon Sports Hall of Fame and served as its chairman.

His body, as it turned out, was not invincible.

Only his spirit.

Off the Beaten Path

The Lowdown on Outhouses

September 7, 2003

Over the past couple of years, I've interviewed an entomologist, a U.N. ambassador, a country music star, an undertaker and a Hall of Fame pitcher.

I've also interviewed an old railroad engineer, a television producer, a waitress, a "mad scientist," and the "SHAKE 'N BAKE" twins.

But, until this past week, I had never interviewed a "priviologist."

You might say I had never had the "privy-lege."

I'm not sure I would have known exactly what one was had Claudette Smith not invited me to the monthly meeting of the Forsyth chapter of the American Association of Retired Persons. (No, I am not a member!)

Mary Long of Lawrenceville is an expert on outhouses, and she does more than 50 programs a year on privies. She calls her speech "Privial Pursuit."

Many of the AARP members could relate to the subject. They grew up in the days before indoor plumbing. I'm too young and too much of a city boy to remember those times, although I'll never forget the Porta-Potties of the Great Flood of '94.

(My father tells stories about his family's two-seater outhouse on a farm in the Midwest. They always looked forward to the arrival of the Montgomery Ward and Sears Roebuck catalogs in the fall. That provided their supply of toilet paper for the whole year.)

Long, 71, grew up a country girl from Gwinnett County. She has never forgotten those visits to the little shack out back. When her family moved to a house in Lawrenceville on Luckie Street, she considered herself lucky, too. It had indoor plumbing.

She now is retired after 34 years of teaching, including 10 years in Milledgeville. She serves as president of the Georgia Retired Educators Association.

In 1984, Long longed to write a book on old farmhouses. A publisher suggested that she focus on outhouses. So she and her husband, Dean, traveled the Georgia countryside snapping photographs of every outhouse still standing from Lula to Monticello. (The Environmental Protection Agency has since done away with most of them.)

A book was born, *Old Georgia Privies,* and Long started making speeches about seven years ago. Proceeds from her honorariums

go to scholarship funds at the First Baptist Church of Lawrenceville and the Georgia Retired Educators.

She can tell stories about toilet pioneers John Harrington and Thomas Crapper of England. And explain how Roosevelt instructed WPA workers to build outhouses for a $5 fee.

She can talk about traveling to the Great American Outhouse Blowout in Gravel Switch, Ky., and seeing a two-story outhouse in Montana, built to accommodate heavy snows.

And she can tell you how outhouses have affected the course of history. Take Gene Talmadge, for instance. His gubernatorial re-election bid was derailed when he was bitten by a black widow spider in his outhouse.

Yep, Long is an authority on privies.

She just wants to emphasize that a Ph.D. in priviology does not mean "Piled Higher and Deeper."

Fun, Food and Fellowship in the Shade

August 4, 2002

RHINE — They laugh and call themselves the "Rhine Rotary Club."

Of course, it's not exactly a civic club. They don't elect officers or drop a gavel.

Bylaws are kept simple. Show up with an appetite for food and conversation.

Some of these men have met under the shade trees at Griff Bowen's farm every Thursday for the past 30 years.

They help their plates to fried catfish and Miss Julie's coleslaw. They discuss politics and fret about the weather. They pray for the sick, swap jokes and wait to see who will bite on the biggest fish story.

Do they have any clout?

"Politicians never have any trouble finding us," said Bowen. "Especially during an election year."

Joe Frank Harris launched his campaign for governor from the dirt driveway in 1982. Zell Miller, Lester Maddox, Herman Talmadge, Saxby Chambliss and J. Roy Rowland have made appearances.

There is no guest book, but the Rhiners have broken hush puppies with visitors from all 50 states and several foreign countries.

The tradition began in February 1972. The late Cap Burnham assembled six friends to chew the fat and fry fish at Bowen's place.

"We had so much fun we did it the next Thursday, too," said

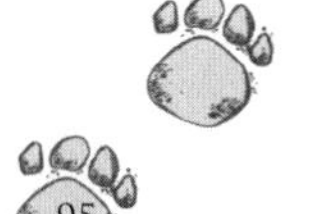

Bowen.

They may have argued about a few things, but they all agreed life was too short not to spend time together. Besides, in those days most of the businesses in Rhine closed every Thursday at noon, so they needed a place to eat "din-nuh."

In 30 years, they've never missed a Thursday. The lone exceptions are Thanksgiving or when Christmas or the Fourth of July falls on a Thursday.

Twice a year, they borrow tables from the Pleasant Grove Baptist Church and invite their wives for Valentine's Day and Mother's Day.

Sometimes the temperature is so cold they can see their breath. Or the afternoon is so hot the gnats pull up a chair at the table.

But they've only had one official "rainout." In 1982, they found themselves ankle-deep in water under a tree. They moved the operation to a shed and set up a large table.

Now, anywhere from 20 to 70 men show up every week.

"We pass the hat and keep cooking until we run out of food," said Bowen.

Said Wayne Hillard: "If there is a big crowd, we just eat less."

There is no dinner bell. When it's time for chow, Wright Harrell bangs a spoon on the nearest appliance.

"If people went to a restaurant and saw a hog or a dog walking through, they probably would get up and leave," said Delton Hillard. "It's commonplace around here."

Bowen, 75, is a jack of all trades — from blacksmith to sawmill operator to farmer. He has lived on this property since he was a tadpole.

Every day, he looks out on 200 acres of peanuts, cotton and corn. But every Thursday he stays and talks until the last diner departs. What keeps them coming back?

"It's not the food," said Bowen. "It's the fellowship."

The Legend of Hogzilla

October 31, 2004

ALAPAHA — Darlene Turner was behind the cash register at Jernigan's Farm Supply when Chris Griffin came by the store on a Saturday in mid-July.

It's not unusual for Chris to stop by Jernigan's several times a day. It's a regular gathering place in Alapaha, a town so small it doesn't have a traffic light.

"He came in to get a log chain," said Darlene. "He said he had

killed a big hog, and they needed it to hoist him up."

Large hogs usually don't raise even the hairiest of eyebrows in these parts. They are quite common in the swamps along the nearby Alapaha River.

Darlene figured Chris had killed something, though.

"You could smell it on him," she said.

Then she laughed.

"I don't know if it was Chris or the hog," she said. "But I know I smelled something."

Something still "smells" about Hogzilla, the 12-foot-long, half-ton feral hog that has given this close-knit community more than just a day in the Georgia sun.

Rumors have been flying it was all a hoax, a tale as tall as the south Georgia pines.

It has been dismissed with other "urban legends," although there's nothing urban about this town on the road from Tifton to Willacoochee.

The wild claims could be a page right out of Ripley's. There hasn't been this much commotion and surrounding mystery since the 1970s, when there were reports of a "peg-legged Bigfoot" along the 5-mile stretch of U.S. 82 between Alapaha and Enigma.

"It has brought a lot of attention to this little town," said Darlene, sitting in the back of the family's store at closing time. "Hey, we're finally going to be on a road map!"

Darlene hasn't allowed herself to get too caught up in the possibility Hogzilla is Alapaha's own version of the Loch Ness Monster.

When her husband, Don, first heard of the super swine, he joined the chorus of disbelievers.

"Yeah, and I killed a 100-pound armadillo in my back yard," he said. "He left a hole so big my Massey Ferguson tractor fell into it."

Only a half-dozen people actually claim they saw the hog. All have signed affidavits swearing to its veracity.

Darlene wasn't one of them. In fact, her only proof is the lone photograph of Chris standing next to Hogzilla that nearly everyone has seen. She now distributes copies of the photograph to curious customers who come by the store.

The photo was published in newspapers all over the world and has been widely circulated on the Internet. In fact, when hotel clerks in Hawaii noticed a local couple was staying there, they told them they were delighted to have someone from "Hogzilla Country."

Folks in Alapaha, seizing the marketability of the moment, are

riding this big hoggy to market.

The theme of this year's 20th annual Alapaha Station Celebration on Nov. 12-14 will be "The Legend of Hogzilla." A crowd of about 8,000 is expected.

"Everybody has an opinion about whether Hogzilla existed," said Sylvia Roberts, one of the festival's organizers. "We're not trying to prove or disprove it. That's why we're calling it 'The Legend of Hogzilla.' People can decide for themselves."

There will be Hogzilla parade floats, a hog-calling contest and a greased pig competition. Elizabeth Moore, of Glory Methodist Church, is going to take 125 pounds of meat, make a 250-foot-long sausage and proclaim it as the "world's longest hogzilla sausage."

"We're going to let the gate open and go hog wild," she said.

At Becky's Beauty Shop downtown, Hogzilla T-shirts are selling like hog-cakes. Owner Becky Davis has sent out orders as far away as Michigan and California.

"I had a man in South Carolina call about buying a T-shirt," she said. "He said his name was Richard Hogg."

No word on whether it was a size XXXL.

Phillip Hoffman, the town's retired postmaster, said he interviewed Chris Griffin for a radio show in Tifton and said he has no reason to doubt his story.

Betty also interrogated Chris while she was cutting his hair.

"I did my best to trip him up, and there weren't any holes in his story," she said.

But tell any story to 100 people and see how many different versions come back to you.

"It's like a fish story," said Elizabeth. "The more you tell it, the bigger it gets."

On the night I met Chris, he was sitting at a neighbor's supper table, wearing a baseball cap and sipping a Mountain Dew.

He is still learning to deal with the unexpected notoriety that comes with bagging a behemoth boar.

He is 31 years old and works as a hunting guide at Ken's Fish Hatchery and River Oak Plantation. Among his many duties is to feed the wild hogs that come up from the river and fatten them up for "sport."

Owner Ken Holyoak brings hunters to the plantation, and Chris feeds the hogs everything from peanut butter to fish pellets to "keep them in the area."

Holyoak asked Chris to kill the large hog roaming the property because he didn't want him to get away and run the risk of someone else

shooting him.

So Chris stuck his rifle in his truck. At feeding time July 17, he noticed the estimated 1,000-pound hog with the 9-inch tusks.

"He came from one of those pig trails coming up from the swamp," Chris said. "He was a big old joker. I had never seen one that big."

It only took one shot, striking the animal behind the shoulder and hitting his heart. The hog ran about 30 yards, then dropped dead in the dirt.

Although the size of the monster hog was only estimated — and therefore subject to exaggeration — it still had to be moved with a backhoe.

It was suspended above the ground with four chains for the now-famous photograph with Chris. When Elliott Minor, a reporter for The Associated Press, wrote a story, people from Dubuque to Delaware were reading about Hogzilla.

"The next thing I knew, people were telling me I was on CNN and that Dan Rather said my name on CBS," Chris said. "In my wildest dreams, I never knew there would be so much interest. You would have sworn I won the lottery."

He wasn't prepared for becoming part of local lore. The Bravo television network recently came to Alapaha to film a documentary. Chris did radio interviews over the phone in places like Seattle, Las Vegas and Boca Raton, Fla.

"I talked to a radio station in Chicago," he said, "and they had banjo music playing in the background."

On the home front, there was a buzz from the Wal-Mart in Fitzgerald to the bowling alley in Tifton, where he was asked for his autograph.

"Nobody had ever asked me for my autograph," he said. "Before all this, I couldn't have given it away."

It would be nice to say Hogzilla was preserved for prosperity, that his remains could be found in a local museum.

Or that a local taxidermist had him stuffed and placed in the town square as a tourist attraction.

Or that he was chopped up to provide enough hot dogs for the Berrien County school system for a whole semester. (Truth is, wild hogs make for mighty tough eating.)

But he was buried on the plantation in a grave marked by a white cross. Hogzilla's massive head was cut off and buried in an undisclosed location, perhaps to discourage grave robbers.

National Geographic magazine is scheduled to come to Alapaha on Nov. 7 and follow Chris around for the week prior to the festival.

Chris said Hogzilla will be exhumed during that time, and DNA testing will be used to determine the size of the hog.

Said Chris: "After *National Geographic* digs him up, if people aren't convinced, they never will be."

Judy Canova's Unofficial Hometown

February 22, 2004

UNADILLA — Before the interstate, there was Highway 41. It was the main drag to Florida, rolling past south Georgia cotton fields and Burma Shave signs into dreamy little towns like Unadilla.

Before there was television, there was radio ... and there was Judy Canova. She was one of America's most beloved comedy queens, a yodeling country bumpkin who became the darling of stage, screen and radio.

Lillian Lewis once owned a dime store in downtown Unadilla. Now 83, she still writes columns for a local newspaper. She remembers, as a young girl, gathering around the radio.

"Between the static, grinding and popping, we were able to hear Judy Canova on the radio each week," she said.

There was a reason for this weekly devotion.

"She made us laugh," said Lewis. "And we wanted to hear what she had to say about Unadilla."

Canova put Unadilla on the map in a way not even Rand McNally could. In her popular radio shows from New York, this sweet-spirited hillbilly claimed to be from "Una-dilly" Georgia.

When she said that, the grins were as wide as the dials on every Zenith back in Dooly County. Depending on which version of the story you believe, Canova may have never set foot in Unadilla. At the very least, she never lived here.

But that was her little secret. The town just winked and embraced its surrogate daughter. In fact, Unadilla was so content to go along for this joy ride that a local automobile dealership in the 1940s actually changed its name to the "Judy Canova Motor Co."

Clint "Boss Hogg" Shugart, the town's former mayor, once worked at a downtown service station. Travelers often would stop to fill 'er up and ask: "Is this the hometown of Judy Canova?"

Shugart would just point to a prominent house in town and tell them that was where little Judy grew up.

Years later, Shugart wrote Canova and sent her a photograph of the house he once claimed was her home place. She sent him a photograph of herself with her famous pigtails. She told him it was what she would have looked like when she lived in the house he told everybody she lived in.

Canova was born on Nov. 20, 1916, in Starke, Fla., near Jacksonville. Her real name was Juliette Canova. Her father was a cotton broker, and her mother was a singer. Judy started performing when she was 10 years old, and sang in clubs and on radio in high school. She had hoped to attend the Cincinnati Conservatory of Music, but the Depression depleted her family's finances.

So she went to New York City with her sister, Anne, and brother, Zeke. The trio sang their hillbilly songs at The Village Barn in Greenwich Village. There, she was discovered by band leader Paul Whiteman, who signed her for his national radio show. She made frequent guest appearances with Rudy Vallee and Edgar Bergen before hitting the big time with her own radio show.

It launched a career that brought her fame as a screen star and radio's "queen of the airwaves." On any given week, she reached a radio audience of some 18 million listeners.

About 3,000 of them were back "home" in Unadilla, where even the folks who didn't have electricity in their homes tuned in on battery-operated radios.

Greg Speight, a Unadilla city councilman and director of the Dooly County Chamber of Commerce, is a sixth-generation Unadillan.

He's only 25 years old. But, like others who grew up here, he listened as Judy Canova stories were passed around front porches like tea cakes in the afternoon.

He said one story claims Canova was on a bus that broke down in Unadilla. She was so enchanted by the local people she "adopted" the town as part of her act. Another version of the legend has her passing through on the train as a child and being amused at the town's name on a sign at the train depot.

"It's a funny name that rolls off the tongue," said Speight.

The story most widely circulated is that Canova had been friends with Robin Ware, whose father, A.R. Ware, ran the local Plymouth-Dodge dealership and later re-named it the Judy Canova Motor Co.

"Between all those stories, who knows?" said Speight.

In April 1939, while making personal appearances at the Roxy Theater in Atlanta, Canova invited a group of about 15 people from Unadilla, including Mayor E.H. "Son" Conner, to be her guests. Canova

met their motorcade at the Atlanta city limits with a police escort and took them to the Roxy, where she treated them like family.

In a way, they were family.

While Unadilla turned out to see Canova, there remains some debate whether Canova ever turned out to see Unadilla.

Willie Joe Goodroe, now 68, swears he once saw Canova at the car dealership for a promotion. And a locally published book, the *Kingdom of Dooly,* has a photo of Canova visiting Unadilla during World War II.

In later years, Canova changed the name of her radio hometown to the fictitious "Cactus Junction."

But the real-life town of Unadilla never forgot her. She was invited to attend the grand opening of the Southeastern Arena on Labor Day 1983, but she died a month before the ceremony.

Today, the legend still lives in a friendly town where the lone stoplight in the county is 10 miles down Highway 41 in Vienna.

"Judy Canova is part of our local folklore," said Speight.

A man named Ernest Christmas is renovating the old Judy Canova Motor Co. building, where he wants to showcase antique cars, soda fountains and an old-fashioned country store display. There are plans to return the Judy Canova Motor Co. sign to the front of the building.

Speight said the city has purchased an old grocery store, with plans to convert it to a welcome center and a display of Canova memorabilia.

He has made several attempts through the Screen Actors Guild to locate Judy's daughter, Diana Canova, who went on to become an actress herself and once starred in the TV comedy "Soap."

"I want to ask her if she remembers anything her mother said about Unadilla," said Speight. "And I want to find out if she has any costumes, props or scripts we could display. We would love to remember our famous 'daughter.'"

Then he laughed.

"If Judy Canova were alive, she probably would think it was hilarious to have a museum for her in the hometown where she never lived."

Old Age is Not for Sissies

At 99, the Judge Looks Back

August 19, 2001

When I asked the wise, old judge the secret to reaching his 99th birthday, he leaned across the morning newspaper.

"Marry the right girl and learn to stay on her good side," he said, reflecting on 72 years of marriage. The walls of his den resonated with laughter.

William Augustus "Gus" Bootle is 36,160 days old today. He has left his mark on most every one of them.

His eyes have charted a remarkable, and often turbulent, course. His heart has championed history's causes — not through advocacy, but with a level-handed gavel of fairness.

In a poll of *Telegraph* readers in January 2000, Bootle was voted Macon's "Person of the Century."

The courageous judge — described by a long-time admirer as "sincere, brilliant and genuine" — has now lived for almost an entire century.

"I once heard a judge say if he had it to do over again he wouldn't do anything differently," Bootle said. "I can't say that. Maybe in a few instances I would."

Calvin Coolidge appointed him U.S. attorney for the Middle District of Georgia in 1928. He took the oath as a federal judge (appointed by President Eisenhower) in 1954, just 16 days after the Supreme Court declared public school segregation unconstitutional in the landmark Brown v. Board of Education decision.

Bootle stood his own ground during the civil rights storm. A year after his appointment, he ordered the names of 122 black voters restored to Randolph County's voting rolls in one of the nation's first voter registration suits.

With a sweep of his pen in 1961, he ordered the University of Georgia to admit its first two black students. A decade later, when he presided over the desegregation of Bibb County schools, there were protests in front of his home.

"Right is right," he said. "I had some people ask me: How could you do it? My question to them was always: How could I not do it?"

As a young boy in Waltersboro, S.C., Bootle would go to the courthouse and watch trial lawyers arguing their cases. "I figured I could do better than some of them," he said.

But his dream of becoming an attorney was a long shot. His father operated a sawmill and moved the family to Reidsville, where he made cypress shingles.

Financially, college was not a consideration until a local businessman, Josh Beasley, offered to lend Bootle $300. Bootle still keeps the original promissory note in a well-worn scrapbook.

He began repaying Beasley $25 a month after he graduated from Mercer's law school and became an assistant district attorney in Bibb County.

"There's no telling where I would be if he had not done that for me," Bootle said.

He has never lived anywhere except Macon since arriving as a Mercer student in 1920.

He met the "right girl," Virginia, while she was at Wesleyan College. Three years ago, the federal courthouse was named in his honor.

At 99, his advice is simple and heartfelt.

"Whatever you're looking for is out there," he said. "Go get it."

Judge Bootle died on January 25, 2005. He was 102.

Happy Birthday, Spare the Candles

October 13, 2004

HILLSBORO — Margaret Sammons' daughters are taking her to the beauty parlor this morning.

They usually go every Friday, but the end of the week has been reserved for cake and ice cream.

Miss Margaret is having a birthday.

I asked her daughter, Saralyn, what she was going to do about all those candles.

"We'll only have one," she said, laughing. "We don't want to burn the house down!"

In two days — Lord willing and the creeks don't rise — Margaret Sammons will be 106 years old. That is 38,717 days, if you figure in all the leap years.

I first met Miss Margaret in December 1999 when she was 101. I interviewed her for a series of stories called "Eyes on a Century."

Not too many people can claim to have lived in three different centuries.

What should I tell you about her? That she once made the best lemon cheesecake in Jasper County?

Or that if you challenged her to a game of Scrabble, she usually would have you begging for mercy?

Or that the closest she ever came to profanity was when she uttered "darn" a few years back?

She was born Margaret Greer on Oct. 15, 1898, in a house on the same property where she now lives with daughters Saralyn and Jane.

While the Wright Brothers were giving us wings and Henry Ford was giving us wheels, she was busy playing hide-and-seek on her family's farm.

She joined Hillsboro Baptist Church in 1910, when she was 12, and was baptized in a pool near a local cotton gin.

She never owned a "store-bought" dress until she attended college at Wesleyan. Her daughters can count on one hand the number of times she hasn't worn a dress in public.

She met her husband, Dick Sammons, at a "prom party" in Round Oak. They married in 1918.

When Dick was in France during World War I, she would address his letters to "Richard Johnson Sammons." A soldier from Virginia with the same name received some of them by mistake, but he was kind enough to return them.

I could tell you plenty of other stories about Miss Margaret. Like the time a neighbor's cows kept wandering into her yard and her patience began to run thin.

She marched down to church, where she was supposed to teach Sunday school that morning, and announced: "Today's lesson is about loving your neighbor, but I just don't think I can teach it!"

Audrey Ezell, whose late mother-in-law, Yulyn Ezell, was Miss Margaret's sister, calls her "Aunt Rite" and hails her as one of "God's earthly angels."

"When you walk in the room, you just know there is something special about Miss Margaret," said Judy Dills, who has spent 11 years as a caregiver for the Sammons family.

As 106 approaches, Miss Margaret uses a wheelchair. She battles arthritis, and her hearing and eyesight obviously aren't as keen as they used to be.

She's still the oldest living person I know.

"She is so lovable," said Gwen Catchings, the family cook. "As broke as I am, I wouldn't take a million dollars for her."

Great-Granny Goes to College

January 11, 2002

Irene Sharp is not your typical sophomore at Macon State

College.

She doesn't fret about the prospective job market for the Class of 2004.

"I don't know anybody who would even hire me," she said.

She has no reason to be concerned about long-term job security. Internships, life insurance and health benefits aren't on the radar screen.

You certainly look at the future through a different set of lenses when you are 81 years old.

Yes, Irene Sharp is 81 going on 18.

It's easy to admire her better-late-than-never spirit. You simply don't find that many octogenarians on college campuses. Unless, of course, it's homecoming weekend.

Never mind that she is a great-grandmother. Or is blind in her left eye. Never mind that she is older than any of the buildings at Macon State, which opened as a junior college in 1968.

Never mind that David Schwaber, a student in her math class this semester, happens to be her grandson.

Never mind that she might have to abbreviate her weekly bridge games Thursday nights, depending on how much homework she has.

"I always said I wanted to graduate by the time I was 65 years old," she said.

She laughed. "I'm a little behind."

No one could have blamed her if she had closed the book on her dream. Often, the odds seemed stacked against her at every intersection.

But here she is, closing in on her two-year certificate while admitting she probably has to study twice as hard as any of her classmates.

"My memory isn't what it used to be," she said.

As with most commuter colleges, Macon State draws heavily on older students from a seven-county area.

Still, more than half the 4,500 students enrolled this past fall were recent high school graduates.

The average age for a Macon State student was 27, with about 40 percent between the ages of 17 and 21.

Although there were 89 students over age 50 last semester, Sharp knows she is in a class by herself.

"I'm sure I get some curious looks," she said. "But I can't see very well, so I don't notice them."

An automobile accident cut short her freshman year at Georgia State College for Women in Milledgeville in 1941. Later, World War II interrupted her academic plans. Then she got married and started a

family.

After a 20-year career in real estate, she finally got back to the classroom five years ago when she enrolled in a computer class. Her own health problems, followed by the death of her husband, Jim, in November 2000, delayed her pursuit.

She has taken advantage of a state program for seniors (over 65) that pays for college tuition costs, excluding books. She is working toward a degree in journalism. She wants to become a writer.

I asked where she plans to hang her diploma.

"Oh, I won't have to put it on a wall," she said. "I'll know."

Mrs. Sharp attended Macon State College until she was 83. She died in October 2004.

Forsyth Barber Still a Cut Above

August 10, 2001

FORSYTH — Folks around here have been watching W.C. "Bill" Roquemore sweep hair off the floor at the City Barber Shop on East Johnston Street for the past 63 years.

Roquemore turned 95 years old this past January and still flips the switch on the red-and-white-striped barber pole at 7:45 a.m. five days a week.

The only time he has ever missed opening was after he had gall bladder surgery last fall. He closes every Sunday and Wednesday. Sundays are for church. Wednesdays are for cutting the grass.

Amazing.

One of 10 children, Roquemore left the family farm in 1927 to become a full-time barber in Juliette. In 1938, he moved to the "big" city of Forsyth.

He opened his shop near the square in an empty building the telephone company used for storage. He bought most of his furnishings from a barber shop that closed on Broadway in Macon.

Six decades later, the decor has barely changed. When you climb the two steps, you also step back in time.

Three of the four barber chairs are still bolted to the wooden floors, although he is the only barber remaining. A shoeshine stand is a landmark in the front corner, but it has been 20 years since the last spit shine.

Once upon a time, you could take a shower in a wooden stall in the back. Talk about one-stop shopping. Shave. Shine. Shower.

Roquemore uses an old iron cash register from the era when

haircuts cost 35 cents. It is in the middle of the room, next to the rotary-dial phone.

Joe Chambers remembers those five-and-dime days. He was 10 years old when he first sat in Roquemore's barber chair in Juliette. He is 84 now and is Roquemore's longest-running customer.

Today, the hand-written sign on the mirror reads: Haircuts $5. Flat Tops $6.

Roquemore charges Chambers the regular price for a haircut. He breaks down the cost.

"Four dollars to cut it," he said. Then he laughed. "And a dollar to find it."

In the old days, the wait for the barber's chair could be as long as two hours on Saturdays. Roquemore usually stayed open until almost midnight to take care of all his customers.

Everything from local politics to farming to Mary Persons High School football has been discussed around the seats around the shop. The antique radio on the counter has tuned in to many a World Series game.

Roquemore has no plans to retire. He prefers to take it one day at a time.

His friend Henry Foster, who is 91, just can't see that day ever coming.

"He'll be cutting hair until his toes turn up."

Miss Lois at the Polls

November 4, 1998

PITTS — In honor of her 90th birthday last week, Lois Humphries became the 90th voter Tuesday morning at the Pitts Community Center.

The moment almost slipped up on her. The turnout was a bit heavy, and the symbolic gesture arrived sooner than she anticipated. She managed to jump in line between Nos. 89 and 91. There were only two voting booths at the precinct, and longtime poll worker Bennie King said it had been one of those mornings when they sure could have used a third.

Humphries pulled the booth's curtains behind her and darkened the ovals on the ballot with a No. 2 pencil before sitting down for a lunch of cornbread and stew.

She has become something of a local institution on election days in Pitts.

She has watched generations of Wilcox County voters make

every election a special election for her.

She was born 12 years before women were awarded the right to vote in 1920. She went to the polls for the first time herself and helped put a rookie named Franklin Roosevelt in the White House.

Hey, did anyone remember that Tuesday was the 50th anniversary of "Dewey Defeats Truman?"

Her father, James Henry Smith, was the town's justice of the peace. He ran local elections for two decades. Her husband, Roscoe Humphries, handled the tiny town's primary elections until his death in 1990.

Now, at age 90, Humphries carries on the family tradition and is believed to be the oldest active poll manager in the state.

You can count on one hand the number of elections she has missed in 66 years of dispersing ballots, writing down names and enduring a few recounts and recalls.

Once, she fell ill on election day.

Said King: "We spent more time explaining why she wasn't here than anything else we did that day."

On Tuesday, she was up with the sun, arriving early at the small, cinder-block building that also serves as City Hall and the fire station. The first raindrops in more than three weeks had fallen during the night.

But, by mid-morning, the sun had broken through the clouds. Miss Lois wondered if opening the double doors to let in the fresh air was such a good idea. After all, November's holdover flies and gnats were filing in, along with the registered voters.

But that was easy to overlook. Her heart was racing. She was as wide-eyed as a child on Christmas morning. She gave out just as many hugs as she did those peach-shaped "I'm a Georgia Voter" stickers.

"I love every minute of election day," she said. "You get to see some people you haven't seen since the last one."

By early afternoon, she had greeted local ministers, farmers in overalls and ladies she had once taught in the first grade at the old Pitts Elementary School. Some of them recalled her beautiful handwriting — she was a real stickler for penmanship in 42 years as a teacher.

I was not surprised to learn she has lived in the same house and attended the same church for more than a half-century. Or that she never has bought anything on credit. Or that she makes the best sweet-potato souffle this side of Seville.

She didn't particularly care for a new state regulation requiring poll workers to ask voters to produce some identification. Especially when her own son, Jimie Jink Humphries, came by to vote and she had to

"card" him.

"I feel kind of stupid because I've known most of these people all their lives," she said.

But some things have improved since the old days, when she had to stay late and count ballots. Election day never ended until well past midnight.

Technology has helped poll workers get a better night's sleep. They simply drop off the results at the courthouse up the road and often are home in time for supper.

"When the polls close, we say amen," said Humphries. "Then we pack up the ballots and head for Abbeville."

GUIDEPOSTS

The Preacher on the Roof

April 27, 2003

MONTEZUMA — When he went to the Kiwanis Club last week, someone approached Ken Myers and said:

"You realize the whole town is talking about this!"

Myers smiled, then swallowed hard. The pastor at Montezuma United Methodist Church has caused quite a stir over on North Dooly Street.

Excited? Nervous?

"A little of both," he admitted.

A week from today, Myers will honor a pledge he made to his congregation.

He promised if 200 or more people attended the worship service March 16, he would deliver his sermon from the roof on May 4. The Methodists put 222 in the pews that Sunday. They've been anticipating the preacher's ascent ever since.

One slight problem.

He's afraid of heights.

Oh, well. We shall overcome.

Folks next door at First Baptist Church have been so intrigued with their neighbor's spiritual high they've called off their own services.

After Sunday School, they will join the Methodists for a combined worship and dinner on the grounds.

No word on whether anyone who joins the church must climb the ladder during the hymn of invitation.

I've heard of one minister who preaches from a horse's saddle and calls it a "Sermon on the Mount."

But I've never witnessed a "Sermon on the Shingles."

Myers is leaning — careful, now — toward a sermon about Zacchaeus, the diminutive tax collector who climbed a tree to see Jesus.

"Zacchaeus is a story of determination," he said.

Myers, 38, was an associate pastor at Perry United Methodist from 1995-99 and St. Mark United Methodist in Columbus from 1999-2001. He moved to Montezuma on Jan. 5, 2002, and made his pulpit debut the following day. His sermon was titled "Get Out of the Boat."

Myers never dreamed "Get Out of the Boat" would one day lead to "Get Up on the Roof."

The church has 239 members. On a typical Sunday, about 80 to 100 attend.

Earlier this year, Myers issued his challenge during the morning

service.

"There was silence," he said. "They looked at me like I was nuts."

The congregation was thrilled, though. The initial head count on March 16 was 217. However, the ushers forgot to count four folks in the nursery and one late-comer.

Church member Frank Lester insisted if attendance was stuck on 199, he would run out the front door and recruit somebody off the street.

Myers will preach from the roof of the fellowship hall. Because of the incline, he will be perched on a modified deer stand.

Acrophobia? Myers visited the World Trade Center as a high school senior. "The elevator doors opened on the observation deck, and my knees turned to Jell-O," he said.

Myers is laid-back and soft-spoken. Reading from the Book of Roof is by no means a publicity stunt.

"Totally out of character for me," he said.

I asked what he might do for an encore.

"I don't know," he said. "A hot-air balloon?"

Halo the Great

October 31, 1999

BUTLER — The black hearse is parked in the dirt. It is not going anywhere. It needs a new carburetor and set of spark plugs and heaven only knows what else.

The other hearse — the one you cannot see at first glance — has been laid to rest a few feet behind the tiny house.

It is not going anywhere, either. Even if you could turn the ignition and pump the gas pedal, it is impossible to drive away in something buried 6 feet underground.

The Rev. Halo the Great dug the hole, rolled the hearse into the ground and piled the dirt high.

He can swing open the back door, as if he were rolling away a stone at a tomb, and crawl inside. Nothing luxurious, but there is a portable toilet, a telephone, a supply of drinking water, a can of Lysol and a foam mat.

Halo the Great says he's willing to be buried alive inside the hearse.

He is convinced he could go underground for as long as 30 days, working his body into a deep trance and engaging himself in a death-like state of mind.

Just have someone bring him breakfast (in bed) every morning. Then, maybe the donations will start pouring in, and he can raise the necessary building funds for the First Baptist Church for All People.

Don't laugh. The man has plenty of experience at this.

Claustrophobics need not apply.

He has spent nearly 40 years being "buried alive" in metal caskets and pine boxes. There was a time when he took his road show up and down the Eastern Seaboard and across the deep South.

He has preached sermons from open caskets in small churches all over Georgia. He has been placed in coffins and buried alive at drive-in movie theaters from Macon to Hawkinsville, where he was part of a double-feature attraction of horror films.

Folks have lined up to file past his "grave" at auditoriums from Brooklyn to Baltimore to St. Louis.

No, Halo is not your everyday pulpit preacher. He wears a turban. It never leaves his head.

Everywhere he goes, he gets strange looks. He has been stuffed inside a casket and has parachuted out of an airplane. He has been submerged in water while resting in a glass coffin. He once spent 45 days buried beneath sandy soil near Tampa, Fla.

He insists the promoter there never paid him even though some 7,000 people coughed up $2 a head, as if he were some sideshow at the fair.

As a minister, he has even married people. Yes, the bride and groom were in coffins, too. (So much for opting out of the "til death do us part" vows.)

You might have missed it — and I actually hope you did — but the Rev. Halo the Great was in a closed casket for two days leading up to an appearance on the Jerry Springer Show in 1996.

He shared the television stage with a man who claimed to be Elvis, a psychic couple who communicated with dead celebrities and a woman who said Jesus appeared to her in a painting while she was watching her favorite soap opera, "One Life to Live."

Halo flailed his arms when Springer lifted the top off the casket. "You have been in this coffin for two days?" Springer asked him.

Then the TV guy deadpanned: "I bet that cuts into your social life."

Halo returned to his old stomping ground in Macon nearly 30 years ago.

He arrived driving a hearse with an empty casket in the back. He hired a lawyer and changed his legal name (whatever it was, it remains a

secret) to Halo the Great.

Now, his only stable source of income, a monthly Social Security check, comes made out to "Halo the Great." His driver's license reads: "Great, Halo."

But things aren't so great these days.

He arrived in Taylor County three years ago, moving his roadside ministry from the old Midway Truck Stop north on U.S. 19 near Thomaston.

Great now lives somewhere below the poverty line in a one-room shack that has no water or indoor plumbing. He must drive four miles into Butler to bring buckets of water back with him. His refrigerator stays mostly bare.

The fuel tank in his car always seems to hover around empty. He has fallen on hard times.

To make matters tougher, his home has had to double as his church building. There are no stained glass windows, only windows stained with dust.

Lately, there haven't been many in attendance at the First Baptist Church for All People, a denomination he founded. As many as 15 people used to crowd into his living quarters to hear him preach. They entered the "church" only after Halo first moved the bed, chairs and table out into the yard to make room for the congregation to sit down.

He claims that most of them eventually got tired of not having a sanctuary, so they all quit coming. He has a sermon prepared every Sunday, just in case they return. He once thought church members were going to dig him a well, but they never did.

He expects it to take about $150,000 to build a new church. The hand-painted sign along the dirt road lets the outside world know that $10 donations are accepted for preaching and counseling. Every little bit helps.

If only he could resurrect his act.

"What I need is a promoter," he said. "If I had a promoter, I could really go places."

The demand for a casket preacher isn't quite what it was in the old days, when Halo the Great was a prime-time player.

He tells his life story in sketches, and some people may contend that he doesn't have all his eggs in one casket. As unbelievable as his stories are, he swears they are not divisible.

His father, a merchant seaman from Calcutta, India, married his mother, an African-American woman from Macon. He spent his

childhood shuffling between relatives in both New Jersey and Byron. He graduated from a technical high school in Cleveland, Ohio, and later joined the merchant marine.

He traveled overseas, and even played baseball in Japan. He claims he could hit a fly ball, drop the bat and then run catch it.

His spiritual journey as Halo began with a near-death experience in India. He collapsed from the heat, had no pulse and was taken to a funeral home, where he was presumed dead for 16 hours.

He woke up from his trance just as he was about to be embalmed. Scared the holy cow out of some folks, too.

Those visions of living and dying convinced him to begin his unique ministry. He had to "rent" his first coffin — a used casket that had once transported corpses.

"I've never thought it was strange," he said. "It's a gift from God. It's not evil. Whatever you do in life, be real. Don't false pretend."

Halo never stayed very long in one place, enduring his share of dishonest promoters and flim-flam artists who crossed his path.

He once was accidentally locked inside a casket and left behind at a funeral parlor. Fortunately, someone discovered the mistake.

Another time, a man threw a bucket of snakes on him. He was dropped by four drunks trying to carry his casket.

"The top flew off," he said. "I went one way and the casket went the other way."

In Macon, he was buried in a swimming pool as part of a publicity stunt at the old Weis Drive-In in south Macon.

He also may be remembered for making front-page news when his car was stolen from his home at Broadway and Hazel Street in 1980.

The car thief obviously didn't realize Halo had left his 4-foot-long pet cobra in the vehicle for protection.

The snake was never found. Nor the thief.

Today, he lives an almost hermit-like existence in rural Taylor County.

He keeps two of his old caskets in a storage shed. He still has his share of curious people stop by. As much as he wants to welcome them, they sometimes invade his privacy by taking pictures and asking lots of questions.

A gentle, non-threatening man, the Rev. Halo the Great walks the line between preacher and freak show.

He wishes the church-goers would come back, so he could deliver his message to something besides the four lonely walls.

He is pushing the years on the backslope of life, but he refuses to hit the brakes.

Said Halo the Great: "I'll retire when I'm in the graveyard."

It shouldn't be a difficult transition.

Just Call Him 'Uncle Sam'

July 1, 2001

BYRON — The Rev. Sam Lamback Jr. will be 8 feet tall today.

He will have to stoop to walk through doorways. He will have to endure jokes asking him about the weather up there. He will probably hear a few wise cracks about being picked in last week's NBA draft.

The dress code for ministers will be relaxed at Byron United Methodist Church this morning.

After all, Uncle Sam is preaching.

Lamback will play his banjo, weave in a few patriotic stories and strike a modern-day analogy about the Promised Land in a sermon from the book of Hebrews.

Uncle Sam will be allowed to look down on his congregation because he has no choice. He will be standing on 18-inch stilts and wearing red striped pants that make him look like a giant peppermint stick.

If he's not careful, his star-spangled top hat might bump into a few light fixtures. Chandeliers, beware.

There are plenty of reasons Lamback has stepped into this larger-than-life role as Uncle Sam over the years.

Mostly, it is a love of God and country.

It is not a gimmick. It is a message that needs to be taught to children and reinforced to parents and grandparents.

Lamback, 58, is a retired Army chaplain who has been minister at the Byron church since 1995. His congregation has been fortunate to get to shake hands with his Uncle Sam character several times each year. He has also shared his message with other churches, civic clubs and American Legion posts.

Depending on his audience, his routine is flexible. But the foundation never changes.

Uncle Sam's stories promote America as the greatest country on earth. He believes people are its best natural resource and history is its most honored teacher. He emphasizes that we should never take our freedom for granted.

His parents, Sam Sr. and Mary B. Lamback, made certain their son appreciated those fundamental freedoms while growing up in Macon. The Lamback family members were not fanatical flag-wavers. They were law-abiding and community-minded folks with a deep love of country.

Sam was a product of the much-revered ROTC program at old Lanier High School. He graduated from West Point in 1964, then had two tours of duty in Vietnam — the first as a field artillery officer and the second as a chaplain. He graduated from Yale Divinity School in 1970.

While stationed at Army bases around the country, Lamback became involved with a clown ministry. He also began developing an act with stilts.

In 1992, while living at Fort Monmouth, N.J., he asked his wife, Gini, if she would design an Uncle Sam outfit for him to wear at a community-wide Fourth of July celebration. Gini found a local seamstress who agreed to make the costume.

Although Lamback did not perform during the festival, he walked around in his new threads. That planted the seeds for future Uncle Sam opportunities.

"I still wear the same costume," he said, laughing. "I'm due for a new one. It's a little beat-up."

After he retired from the military and moved back to Macon, his mother asked him if he would entertain the "Young at Heart" seniors group at Mulberry United Methodist.

He pulled together some stories and songs with all-American themes. When he showed up in his dress blues, reds and whites, he wasn't so sure the crowd knew what to think.

"I grew up in that church, and I bet some of those folks thought I had gone off the deep end," he said.

Hardly. Uncle Sam grew by word of mouth. Soon, he was being contacted by other churches and civic groups.

"I ended up on the (speaking) circuit," he said.

Today, Uncle Sam will preach and teach and sing. He has always been fascinated with how music can tell the story of America. He will spin a few tales about Betsy Ross, Francis Scott Key and others.

Following the service, church members will have a picnic, toss a few games of horseshoes and thank Uncle Sam for a message we can never hear enough.

One Mile, One Meal Milestone

May 1, 2002

By 7:48 Tuesday morning, Otis Andrews had earned his breakfast.

A few minutes past 8 a.m., he had bagged his lunch. Seventeen minutes and several laps later, sweat equity had delivered his supper.

Otis calls this his "Mile-a-Meal" daily fitness program. He should carry a sign: "Will Walk for Food."

The math is simple. One mile equals one meal.

"If you don't walk, you don't eat," he said.

Don't worry about Otis.

He hasn't been going around hungry.

In fact, today's miles are a "milestone." He began these daily walks May 1, 1992. He hasn't missed a step in 10 years.

That's 11,011 miles. That's hundreds of days like Tuesday, when the lightning popped, the thunder rolled and he splashed through countless puddles.

Not even the most devoted mail carrier delivers this kind of commitment.

Otis has braved freak snowstorms and blistering pavement. He has worn out 18 pairs of walking shoes, been mistaken for a homeless man and skinned his knees after a few nasty tumbles. He has taken his regimen through crowded airports, deserted streets, hotel lobbies and church aisles.

Nothing — not even outpatient surgery — has stopped him from his appointed rounds of three miles a day.

"My goal is to walk around the world," he said.

That would be a distance of 24,901 miles, so he's not quite halfway there. He already has done the calculating, though. He will be 73 years old.

Otis is a Baptist preacher at Glenwood Hills and a family counselor with the Macon Baptist Association. He wears a variety of hats, from author to "shade-tree mechanic."

His journey began a decade ago at age 50. While looking for motivation, he found his carrot-on-a-stick.

He loved to eat, and tipped the scales at about 300 pounds. By the end of his first week of exercise, he already was up to three miles. He once attempted an "advance," walking six miles in a day. He vowed never to cheat himself again. He has had three square miles/meals a day ever since.

He started out walking around his neighborhood in Wimbish Woods. After several narrow escapes with cars, he figured it was time to relocate. After all, he was supposed to be doing this for his health.

Otis then began walking at two shopping centers on Northside Drive. His latest strolls are at Kroger and Kmart on Tom Hill Sr. Boulevard. The covered walkways offer him no excuse for skipping a day.

He keeps a stopwatch around his neck. The first 40 minutes are

"personal time," followed by 15 minutes of "social time" inside the stores.

Tuesday morning, he chatted with Kroger employees as he cruised from the produce to the pork rinds.

It takes dedication, determination, discipline and a supportive wife, named Deigie, who once urged him to be careful as he left their motel room to go for a walk in a strange city early one morning.

"Don't worry," he told her. "Not many folks will be getting up at 6:30 a.m. to go out and mug a 300-pound man."

40 Years of Sunday School Lessons

November 29, 1998

DRY BRANCH — When the bell rings this morning at Stone Creek Baptist Church, the 11 women in the Adult III Sunday School class will take their seats.

There are only a few things in life that are certain, but the presence of Virginia Wood must be one of them.

She has not missed Sunday School in 40 years.

Perfect attendance. Through rain, snow, tornadoes, heat waves, aching bones, flat tires, torn panty hose and runny noses.

"If she wasn't here," said Daisy Fountain, who teaches the class, "I'd be out there looking for her."

Last month, Sunday School superintendent Mac Land praised her dedication and presented Wood, who is 82, with a plaque to honor her attendance.

"I think you can probably count on one hand the number of people who have this kind of record," said the Rev. Donnie Sutton of Stone Creek. "It's really a remarkable feat. I've been in the ministry for 35 years, and I've never heard of it, nor do I know of anyone who has heard of it."

The venerable Southern Baptist Sunday School Board in Nashville, Tenn., (now known as Lifeway Christian Resources) makes attendance pins available all the way up to 70 years. Obviously, it isn't necessary to keep many of the higher numbers in stock.

Forty years is 2,080 straight Sundays. Forty years is the Biblical account of how long Moses stayed in the wilderness. The last time Virginia Wood wasn't in Sunday School, Alaska and Hawaii weren't even states.

"I just tell everybody that I have to give God all the credit," she said.

Wood grew up on a Dodge County farm and attended Sunday School almost every week, even though her small church only had a worship service every fourth Sunday.

She was 22 years old when she looked off her front porch and laid eyes on Raymond Wood, who had come down on a visit from Dry Branch. It must have been love at first sight, because she married him a month later, after only five dates. (On Dec. 24, the couple will celebrate their 60th wedding anniversary.)

"We got married on a Saturday, didn't go on a honeymoon and started going to church at Stone Creek a week later," Wood said. "I always tried to go to Sunday School as much as I could, but it wasn't easy to be there every week with four young children."

In 1953, Stone Creek Baptist was destroyed by a tornado. Services were held at a nearby schoolhouse until the church could be re-built. Whenever Wood went out of town to visit, she would attend a local church and bring back papers to certify she had attended Sunday School.

She never thought about any streak. She just let the power of the word keep pulling her back every week.

"I've been a lot of times when I didn't feel like going," she said. "I just made myself go because I didn't want to miss."

Her friends tell her that, if she ever fails to show up, they are "going to have to go hunt for me." She plans to keep going "as long as I live — or unless I'm flat on my back."

Nothing has stopped her. Not even a tardy run on a newspaper route one Sunday morning some 30 years ago. She and her daughter, Evelyn, didn't finish delivering papers until late.

"What are we going to do, Mama? It's five minutes until 10!" asked Evelyn when they returned home.

She already knew the answer.

"We're going in the house, wash our face and hands and put on our Sunday clothes," said Wood. "If we hurry, we can still make it to Sunday school."

And they did.

BOOK OF LIFE

Coming Home to Kiss Mama Goodbye

May 11, 2003

The letter arrived six months ago from a man in California I did not know.

He told me about a September morning in 1963, when he was 19. He looked out the rear window of a Greyhound bus leaving Macon. His parents were waving goodbye.

Thus began four decades of self-isolation from his family in Warner Robins. He never wrote letters. Never sent photographs. There was an occasional phone call from his sister. But he totally withdrew. He severed all ties.

He served in Vietnam. He married and had two children. His mother-in-law became his "surrogate mom." He lived his life with no tether to his past.

His father died nine years after he left Georgia. His mother, sister and brother became distant relatives — strangers on a dark continent 3,000 miles away.

A few months ago, his sister called. His mother, now in her 80s, was in declining health and had made a request. She wanted him to come home and say goodbye. I'll think about it, he said.

Then he read a column I had written for Mother's Day five years ago: "Never Too Old to Kiss Mama." It is the first chapter in my most recent book, and I had posted an excerpt on my Web site.

"I'm going home to see Mom," he wrote to me. "I'm a blessed man to have this last chance. I'm going home to say goodbye. But I'm going home. Thanks for the encouraging push from your words."

I will always marvel at how something I wrote five years ago would have such a profound impact on someone living so far away.

I responded to his letter by asking if I could tell his story. But other painful details began to surface. We agreed many of them were too private, too traumatic to put on public display.

So I never wrote the column.

But hardly a day has gone by in the past six months that I haven't wondered about his reunion with his mother. Did it ever take place? How was he received?

And I never gave up on the idea of telling his story. As Mother's Day approached, I contacted him. This time, he consented to let me share it.

He requested I use only his first name, Lamar, to protect his relatives from public scrutiny.

"Since going home I have become quite emotional when talking about the life-changing event," he said. He thanked me again for the "inspiration you gave me to make the trip to see my mom. ... The healing of my own soul has been the result."

He returned to Warner Robins after four decades and enough tears to fill an ocean.

"For me, it was akin to going back into a dark room to find something you didn't think you would ever need again," he said.

Lamar is 59 now, married, with a 31-year-old daughter and 27-year-old son. He has one grandchild and another on the way. He is an electronics technician in San Francisco. For 15 years, he has worked in the Bay Area's rescue missions, trying to bring hope to those in a broken world.

But in many ways, his own world was fractured by stubbornness and pain the day he left Georgia. He vowed never to return home.

"When my wife and children asked me why we could never go back to Georgia, I would always tell them there was nothing there," he said. "If there had been something there, I would have never left."

Growing up, he certainly never felt love. He never remembers being hugged or kissed. He remembers only the years of physical and mental abuse his parents inflicted on each other and their children.

"I moved away at the first opportunity I could," he said. "Even if it was to fight a war in Vietnam."

He left with only the clothes on his back, riding a trail of Greyhound bus fumes. His parents were so angry they threw away all of his possessions.

But when he returned this past February, his brother embraced him and said: "I saved these for you." There were two oil paintings Lamar had painted when he was 14.

He wept.

With his brother and sister at his side, Lamar returned to the Warner Robins house where they had lived. It was empty, an unhappy past still part of the residue.

They showed him the hole in the wall from one of the two shots his mother fired from a .22 pistol in self-defense when their father, in an alcoholic rage, tried to harm her on a Sunday morning in August 1972.

For her, it was either kill or be killed.

Lamar didn't come home for the funeral.

He stood there three months ago with his brother and sister, staring down the pain from the past.

And then they slowly began to put that pain to rest.

He went to see his mother. She was in a rehabilitation hospital in Macon, recovering from multiple strokes and a broken hip. Her speech was limited to only a few words.

He walked into her room, followed by his wife, daughter and granddaughter. For a moment, he and his mother just stared at each other.

"At first I thought she wasn't recognizing me," he said. "Then her eyes watered up and she nodded her head at me and simply said 'yeah.' "

Everyone smiled. He walked over to her bed. "Mom, do you recognize this man?" his sister asked.

Without breaking her stare, his mother answered "yeah" again.

Every time he visited her during the days he was there, her blue eyes followed him around the room. And each time he left, she would turn her cheek to be kissed.

"Mom," he would say, "all is forgiven. I truly love you."

On the day he left to return to California, he told his mother goodbye, promised to pray for her and bent over to kiss her cheek.

"But she refused a kiss on the cheek," he said. "She pressed her lips up and waited for me to kiss her on the mouth. ... I was moved to tears as I kissed her and stepped away from her bed.

"I looked back at her as I walked to the door of her room. She continued to stare at me. I paused and wiped my eyes clear of tears. She attempted a smile, then winked at me, giving me the assurance she was still my mom. And that she still loved me."

It was a "soft" look, he said. "A look I never saw when I was growing up."

Since he returned to the West Coast, his mother has been slowly dying.

She requires 24-hour care. She weighs just 78 pounds. Her face muscles are paralyzed by the strokes.

She won't lift her head, and there's no sparkle left in her eyes, his sister tells him.

His mother no longer remembers anyone, not even her children. Doctors were unsuccessful in trying to install a feeding tube this past week.

Today is Mother's Day.

Lamar will walk from his house to a cliff overlooking the Pacific Ocean. There he'll remember that look in her eyes and a simple "yeah" that spoke volumes.

Lamar's mother died in June 2003.

Wind, Rain and the Naked Truth
September 15, 2004

The lady woke up last week to the sound of wind and rain lashing against her bedroom windows.

There was nothing soothing about this storm. No soft patter of raindrops against the sill. No gentle breeze nudging the boughs of the trees.

The storm arrived in the middle of the night — fast and furious. Hurricane Frances had been downgraded to a tropical storm, then a tropical depression when it moved inland. But, as the elements whipped the September night into a frenzy, even a tamer Frances was frightening.

"It sounded like the wolves were at the door," the lady said. "When I looked out, I thought the eye of the hurricane was coming right in."

The lady lives alone in a two-story townhouse in Macon's intown historic district. When she first heard the storm, she checked around the edges of the window air-conditioning unit near her bed. Sure enough, rain was seeping through.

"I need to cover it with plastic from the outside," she thought. So she opened her other bedroom window, and was prepared to crawl onto the roof with a plastic garbage sack when she remembered.

She chuckled to herself. Had she forgotten what happened the last time she tried such a stunt? She vowed there would be no curtain call.

I've changed the lady's name here to protect her identity, especially since her story is so embarrassing she has dared to tell it to only a handful of people over the past three years.

She asked that I simply call her "Pauline."

And her saga?

"The Perils of Pauline," she said, laughing.

During that storm of three years ago, she attempted to plug her leaky window with towels. When that didn't work, she had no choice but to cover it with plastic from the outside. So she raised the other window and stepped out on the roof.

But, before she did, she slipped out of her nightgown.

Let's just say there was more than one moon over Macon that night, despite the poor visibility.

"I didn't want to get my nightgown wet," she explained. "So, there I was ... in my birthday suit."

"Pauline" had moved only a few feet away when she heard an

awful noise. No, it wasn't the clap of thunder or the snap of a tree limb. It was the sound of the storm window, slamming shut behind her and locking her out. About that time, the wind blew away the plastic.

Now, here's the dilemma. She couldn't knock on her neighbor's upstairs window. How does a naked lady justify being on the roof at 2 a.m. in the middle of a gale?

She couldn't leap from the roof, either. She was at least 20 feet off the ground. Besides, she had no spare key. And no pockets to carry a key, even if she had one.

"I was panicked," she said. "I realized I had to take control."

After what seemed like an eternity, she found a loose brick at the other end of the building, smashed the window and climbed back to safety. Exhausted, she went downstairs and fell asleep on the floor.

Now, as another hurricane threatens the midstate, you can bet Pauline is ready with a moral to this story.

"Never climb out the window," she said, "... without your clothes."

Purple Rock of Ages

May 29, 2002

When the Little League season was over, we had won nine games.

We had scored more runs in one game (33) than some teams do in an entire season. We chewed 577 pieces of bubble gum in slightly less than seven weeks. (We had plenty of help from younger brothers and sisters, of course.)

These are the joys of baseball season. You learn about catching, throwing, hitting, sliding and blowing bubbles.

You learn that, while success is the residue of hard work, sometimes it is beyond your control.

The ball will be rolling along. You may be in perfect position to field it. Suddenly, the forces of gravity are yanked like a rip cord. The ball leaps over your head or whizzes past your ear.

Bad hops are a part of the game. In baseball vernacular, the ball hit a pebble.

Or maybe a purple rock.

Our season bumped into a purple rock last week. It caromed over our hats sooner than we had hoped.

Its finality was whiplash. Our bats were rusty. Our gloves were in cold storage. Our hearts were broken.

It was tough to hide our disappointment with losing in the tournament.

We wiped a few tears and fumbled with the regrets still stuck in our throats.

As their coach, I huddled with these young boys after the game. I dug deep for what to say in our last meeting as a team.

"How many of you watched 'Survivor' the other night?" I asked. Most raised their hands.

"Well, we had a purple rock day," I explained.

It wasn't an excuse. When you're 7 or 8 years old, you don't have a full grasp of life's ups and downs. Even when you're an adult, the lessons from an accumulation of purple rock days are a work in progress.

I've seen my share of red flags, green monsters and black widows. But I had never encountered a "purple rock" until last week's final episode of "Survivor."

Thomaston's Paschal "Pappy" English was gone with one unfortunate reach into a bag.

But with it, this gracious Southern gentleman taught us more about class than we ever could have learned from a textbook.

If anyone didn't deserve the kiss-of-death purple rock from that bag, it was Pappy.

He didn't receive a single vote against him during his stay on the island. The two women who drew the "immune" yellow rocks from the bag each went before him, so he had no choice. He had to take what was left.

This will be Paschal English's legacy. He did not allow the purple rock to become his tombstone. He didn't whine or complain, cry foul or call names. He didn't threaten a lawsuit or blame a right-wing conspiracy.

Instead, he came away with a new twist on an old lesson.

When life gives you lemons, make lemonade.

When the world hands you a purple rock — and it will — that's no excuse for throwing in the white towel.

We must accept that some days are going to be colored.

It's what we do with them that counts.

Thanks, Pappy, for your gift.

The purple rock of ages.

The Longest Death Row
March 7, 2001

I sat in a courtroom for the first time when I was an intern for *The Columbus Enquirer* during the summer of 1977.

No college journalism class or episode of "Perry Mason" could ever have prepared me for my week in Muscogee County Superior Court.

Ronald Keith Spivey was in that courtroom, too. He was 37 years old. He grew up in Macon. He had dark, wavy hair and a haunted look on his face.

I will never forget that face.

At 6-foot-6, he towered above the others. He was tall, just like his brother — the famed "Georgia Pine."

Bill Spivey played on a different court. He had been an All-America center on Kentucky's 1951 national championship basketball team, coached by the legendary Adolph Rupp.

Ronnie Spivey had made newspaper headlines in his own way. He was described by prosecuting attorneys as a man whose mind was "eaten up by meanness."

Trouble followed him into every dark corner of his life. His lawyers claimed Spivey walked a tightrope between sanity and insanity.

Just three days after Christmas in 1976, he shot and killed an off-duty Columbus police officer. He then kidnapped a waitress and fled to Alabama before he was captured. Less than 24 hours earlier, he murdered a Macon man over a $20 bet at a pool table.

His crimes left a trail of heartache and broken lives.

Pain is what I remember the most about that courtroom. It cut a swath from wall to wall, sparing no one.

The slain police officer left behind a wife and four children. He was moonlighting as a security guard at the Peachtree Mall when he was gunned down. He had been baptized seven months earlier, and had just returned from Central America, where he helped build a church.

But there were other victims. The trial took its toll on Spivey's parents. His father, Oscar Spivey, and his mother, Tommie, were tragic figures, too.

I realized that, regardless of Ronald Keith Spivey's fate, he would not be the only one to suffer. In another sense, his own family was part of the wreckage.

For reasons still unclear to me, Oscar Spivey approached me during a court recess. He spoke of his relentless efforts to spare his son from the electric chair.

He was 77 years old and a retired electrician from Robins Air Force Base. He had spent six months visiting prisons and awaiting court dates. It had taken much of his life's savings to pay for his son's legal fees.

The elder Spivey was remorseful. He said his son had "obviously caused a lot of people a lot of sadness." I followed him to his car in a nearby parking deck. He opened the trunk and showed me copies of letters he had written on his son's behalf. One was addressed to Jimmy Carter, requesting a presidential pardon.

Then, the father handed me a letter of confession, written by his son. Ronnie Spivey blamed "demons" for stalking him since he was 10 years old. He wrote that, unless those demons could be eliminated or controlled, he "should be removed from society permanently or eliminated as society sees fit." The text of that letter appeared on the front page in Columbus the following morning.

It took the jury less than a half hour to return a guilty verdict and recommend that he be put to death. Ronald Keith Spivey leaned into the courtroom microphone and told the jury: "If a God exists, then we shall live together in eternity."

The judge sentenced him to die in the electric chair five weeks from that summer afternoon. That was almost 24 years ago, an eternity in itself.

His mother died two years after the trial. His father was killed in a traffic accident 10 years ago. His brother passed away in 1995.

And Tuesday afternoon, just hours before Spivey was scheduled to have his last meal of Wendy's hamburgers and sweet pickles, the Georgia Supreme Court issued a stay of execution.

I never realized death row could reach so long.

Ronald Spivey was executed nine months later, on Jan. 24, 2002.

The List of All Lists

July 30, 2001

I have been compiling lists my entire adult life. Things that need fixing around the house. Phone calls I must return at work. A grocery list. A reading list. Lists of places to go and people to see.

So it should come as no surprise that these lists have produced offspring. The grocery list has spawned a list of places to eat when the cupboard is bare. The reading list has prompted a list of story ideas.

One of these days, I'm going to find a hammock and start

devising — and revising — the list of all lists.

It would contain plenty of joy. And a few regrets. ...

Vegetables I'm glad my mother made me eat. Sunrises and sunsets I have admired. Songs that will be stuck in my head forever. Roads I did not take. Detours I wish I had made.

Contraptions I wish I had invented. (I would be rich.) People I am fortunate to know. (I am rich in blessings.) Jokes I can still remember. College parties I can't remember.

Restrooms between Macon and St. Simons Island. Hats I have worn. Shoes I have filled. Advice I wish I had taken. Dares I wish I had not taken.

Floors I have needlessly paced. Train wrecks I could have avoided. Second chances I'm glad someone gave me. Roller coasters I have ridden. Teachers I have loved. Tests I wish I could take over again.

Stores where the salespeople act as if they appreciate my business. (A short list, unfortunately.) Cute things my children have said. Motel room keys I have forgotten to return. Family stories that have been worth repeating.

Days when it has paid to get out of bed. Toasts I was honored to make. Friends I wish I had stayed in touch with. Names I wish I could remember. (Except that I can't list them.)

Movies that have never failed to choke me up. Books that have made an impact. Sermons that have made a difference.

Santa Clauses I have known. Grinches I would like to forget. Items I would love to find in a yard sale. Automobiles I wish I could afford. Girls I wish I had kissed. (Before I married, of course.)

Directions I should have read carefully before I opened the box. Passwords I need to memorize. Streets in Macon that should be renamed. Warnings my father gave me that turned out to be true.

Dogs I wish could have lived forever. Press boxes where I have written stories on deadline. Signs that made me chuckle. States I have visited. (Thirty-nine at last count.) "Jeopardy!" questions I have actually answered.

Ice cream flavors I have tasted. Baseball cards I regret trading. Closets, drawers and medicine cabinets I have snooped around in. Bible verses I have committed to memory. Hymns I have loved since I was a kid.

Politicians I would like to show the door. Things I wish I had never bought. Things I am glad I bought. Exotic places I would like to visit. Buildings that should be condemned. Policies that should be condemned, too. Laws that need to be changed.

Newspaper readers I would like to thank.

Time on Our Hands

Where Every Room Tick Tocks
October 27, 2002

The sound follows you everywhere you go in Bill and Dot Anderson's house.

Over your shoulder. At your fingertips. Under your nose.

Tick. Tick. Tick. Tick. Tick.

On the mantel. Against the wall. Flanking the door.

Tick. Tick. Tick. Tick. Tick.

"It's the heartbeat of our home," said Dot.

In the logbook of life, few people keep minutes like the Andersons.

At last count, they had 94 antique clocks under their roof. From the parlor to the pantry to the powder room, every room is the Tick Tock Room.

I must admit I was feeling sorry for anyone who had to change that many clocks when daylight-saving time officially ended today at 2 a.m.

Although it is no small task, the Andersons have this timely subject down to a science. Saturday, they paused the nearly eight dozen clocks, waited one hour, then started them again.

Yep, it's much easier to "fall back" than to "spring forward."

When daylight-saving time begins in April, they have to manually move each clock's hands ahead, stopping to allow for any series of chimes. Otherwise, it fouls up the clock's timing mechanism.

Bill has grown accustomed to the duties of clock management. Every eight days, he swings like a pendulum from room to room, manually winding each time piece.

It takes him about four hours.

He is much like the gardener who loves to grow flowers but loathes pulling weeds.

"I love clocks," he said. "But I hate winding them."

Dot took over the clock-winding duties one day. The next morning, she looked at her fingers. They were bruised from all the twisting and turning.

This all began in 1966, when Bill was returning from a business trip and stopped at an antique clock shop in Roberta.

He had never been too keen on antiques. In fact, he used to stay in the car when Dot insisted on browsing in an antique store.

But something intrigued him enough to park at the curb that day, and he ventured inside. The scene was a canvas right out of Norman

Rockwell. The shopkeeper wore gold wire-rimmed glasses, and the room smelled of oil.

"I was fascinated," said Bill. He took home three clocks.

"Now," he said, laughing, "it's a case of collecting gone awry."

The Andersons have owned hundreds of clocks over the years. Some have expired and gone to minute-hand heaven. But most are still ticking. The oldest clock, made in France, dates back to 1620.

There are five grandfather clocks, one grandmother clock and four cuckoo clocks. There are clocks from ships and locomotives. There are courthouse clocks, dome clocks, keyhole clocks, steeple clocks and hand-painted china clocks.

"They are all like members of the family," Dot said. "Each one has its own personality."

There are clocks shaped like banjos and clocks displaying old-time advertising such as Orange Crush, Calumet Baking Powder and Sauer's Flavoring Extract.

The Andersons hunt for their clocks through the classified ads, estate sales, antique stores and word of mouth. Bill has been known to develop an affinity for someone's clock and make them an offer, even if they have no intention of selling.

They do their house guests a favor at night, too. They call a cease fire on every clock in the guest bedroom. Seems that some folks have a difficult time sleeping with so much ticking.

"I can be lying in bed at night and, if one of the clocks is off, I know which one," Bill said.

They love their clocks.

Tick. Tick. Tick. Tick. Tick.

Those hearts never stop beating.

Postcard from a Summer's Day

June 29, 2001

You don't have to go to the beach to send a postcard. You don't have to lick a stamp from Disney World or scribble a few "wish you were here" lines with a postmark from the Grand Canyon.

Sometimes, postcards can be delivered from your own back yard. They are the mental snapshots and slices of everyday life.

I took a "mini-vacation" in my hometown this past week and sent myself a "postcard." It wasn't a holiday. It was a special day for no other reason than it was another great day to be living in Macon.

I drove around for hours. I went sight-seeing and people-watch-

ing. I had fun.

I watched three young boys walking on the sidewalk along Napier Avenue. They had just bought bottles of soda from the store. They were giggling because one of them had opened his, and it was spewing everywhere.

On Bond Street, I saw a mail carrier walking across lawns to mailboxes near the front doors. No faxes. No e-mail. Just letters (and a few postcards) delivered the old-fashioned way.

In a yard along Macon Avenue, I watched two cats stalk an unsuspecting bird in the tall grass. At the corner of Jeff Davis and Plant streets, I observed a dozen men playing checkers in the shade of an old oak tree.

As the afternoon rose to a slow broil, I drove past the gates at Luther Williams Field, where the Macon Braves were promoting the upcoming fireworks show July 4. It's hard to believe that, on a hot day like this 10 years ago, I went to the same ballpark to watch a young firecracker named Chipper Jones play shortstop.

I drove past a young woman pushing a baby in a stroller along College Street. I watched a woman open an umbrella on Poplar Street, not to deflect raindrops but for the portable shade of a summer's day.

I saw a lady who had stopped to rest on the front steps of a downtown church. I strained my neck to watch a few kids thump their baseball gloves while playing a game of catch at Henry Burns Park. I watched as three Mercer law students tossed a Frisbee at the top of Coleman Hill.

I noticed giant sunflowers propped against a front porch on Forest Avenue, and a child bouncing a basketball down Maynard Street. An American flag was flying in a patriotic gesture on Euclid Avenue.

I passed the new Bruster's Ice Cream place on Forsyth Road, where people were lining up for a scoop of peach. It was an ice-cream kind of day.

But not for everyone. A city bus driver was eating Cheetos while waiting for his passengers to board.

I noticed a man delivering propane tanks to a convenience store in midtown. Getting ready for the Fourth of July, I guess. I passed by Marty Willet's "beachcomber" house on Walnut Street. I observed a man walking into the thrift store on Emery Highway with a sweaty towel over his head. I watched a youngster on a bicycle near Birch Street carrying a sack between his handlebars.

All in all, it was a nice trip. I had a great time.

Wish you could have been there. Maybe you were.

He's Made Every Second Count

June 23, 2002

In his own way, Raymond Hamrick has kept life moving along in Macon for the past 67 years.

He has gotten folks to their jobs for shift changes. He has kept the trains running on schedule. And he has helped brides and grooms get to church on time.

We often take those clocks on the wall and straps on our wrist for granted.

We just assume they won't let us down when it's time to cook the meatloaf or catch the school bus.

But while time keeps marching, our timepieces do not. They slow down or stop. Second hands quit sweeping. Cuckoos cease to cuckoo.

Hamrick is believed to be the only full-time watch repairman in Macon — and for miles around. At one time, there were more than 30,000 watch repairmen in the United States. Now, there are only about 3,500.

He turned 87 years old a few days ago, and he still clocks in for work six days a week.

He's one of the most remarkable men I've met in a long time. He's as dependable as a Rolex and, at 6-foot-4, as tall as a grandfather clock.

He keeps time to music, too. Hamrick is nationally known as a composer and singer of Sacred Harp music — historical, "shaped-note" songs and non-denominational religious compositions. (Sacred Harp singing is performed in four-part harmony and unaccompanied by harps or any other instruments.)

Since he began at Andersen's Jewelers in 1935, Hamrick estimates he has repaired more than a half-million watches. And that doesn't count the ones where he simply replaced a battery or made a minor repair.

George Andersen was a neighbor who lived two doors down from Hamrick's family on Napier Avenue in the 1920s. He opened a jewelry store on Cotton Avenue in 1929, then moved to the location at 361 Second St. in 1933.

He convinced Hamrick to join him in the business two years later. Except for a four-year stint as an instrument specialist in the Army Air Corps during World War II, Hamrick has been there ever since.

Hamrick was urged to keep the name of the store after Andersen

died in 1963.

"People still come in and call me Mr. Andersen," he said. "I always answer to it."

To step into his store is to step back in time. The decor hasn't changed much since Hamrick was an apprentice jeweler. The walls are the same pale green. The cases have remained unchanged. If you really want to get nostalgic, there's a hand-cranked cash register that's been there since Jefferson was on the head of a nickel.

"A lot of people are entranced with the way the store looks," he said. "I've always said if Mr. Andersen came back, he would be right at home."

Watches, clocks and other timepieces arrive in need of repair from every time zone in the country. Hamrick has had watches shipped to him from as far away as Alaska.

Yes, he even keeps the Eskimos on time, too.

Magic Moments

Yard Where the Fairies Live

June 8, 2003

There are fairies on Overlook Avenue, and they live in Howard and Paula Knight's back yard.

They lurk beneath the river birch and tall pines. They hide behind rocks in the garden. They seek shelter inside the "Fairy House" at the end of the long path.

If you don't believe in fairy tales, you should be lucky enough to sit on the terrace when the curtain falls on a summer's day.

That's when the fireflies come out, and there are almost as many of them as there are stars on a clear night.

Howard loves to tell the neighborhood children about how he and Paula went to Ireland and brought back two fairies in their suitcases. He watches their eyes grow wide.

Although a stone wall surrounds their back yard, imagination knows no boundaries here.

"The fairies are the guardian angels of nature," Paula said.

It's somewhat fitting a family named Knight lives in a house that resembles a castle. The back gate of the property leads through dense woods to the Grotto, a rocky area once used as a retreat for the monks at nearby St. Stanislaus College.

Paula is a native of Soperton. Howard is from Dublin. They moved to Macon 46 years ago and found a slice of heaven outside the back window of the home they bought in 1989.

Years ago, Paula would drive past the English Tudor — the oldest house on Overlook (built in 1928) — and feel its magical tug. "It was enchanting," she said.

When the house went on the market, they were first in line. From the beginning, the garden has been a refuge and sanctuary. Six years ago, their son Paul was married there.

It has lifted them through difficult times and provided a landscape of expression and creativity.

"We find that, in gardening, we are always looking ahead," said Paula. "And that is good, we think."

Two years ago, they had the collective inspiration for the Fairy House.

While driving through north Georgia, they came across an ordinary playhouse, built by the Amish. They brought it home in seven pieces, mentally moved it five times in the yard and spent two years building and decorating the tiny, one-room cottage.

"We should rent our house and live here ourselves," said Paula, laughing.

If there is a single inspiration behind the fairy house, it is their 8-year-old grandson Austin Meitz, who lives in Loganville.

Austin has a neurological disorder known as Sturge-Weber Syndrome. He has never walked or talked.

He is most content when he is in his grandparents' back yard, surrounded by trees, waterfalls, Koi ponds ... and fairies.

The Knights keep Popsicles in their freezer for the neighborhood children who drop by the Fairy House.

"Although it's an expression of our feelings for each other, it wouldn't be as much fun if we didn't share it with others," said Paula.

I've never been absolutely sure how a fairy is supposed to look.

I now know where to find one.

Give Me a Day Like Saturday

March 28, 2004

Give me a day when the sky is blue and the sun smothers you with kisses.

Give me a day when the dress code is pink — not red, purple or chartreuse — but shades of pink.

Give me a day when you can hardly find a parking place downtown. And it's the weekend!

Give me a day when the cherry trees clutch their blossoms for as long as they can, then gently release them in the warm afternoon breeze, where they float to the ground like pink snowflakes.

Give me a day when winter legs come out of hibernation and a few brave toes go skinny dipping in the grass.

Give me a day with a good excuse to come down with an incurable case of spring fever.

Give me a day when it doesn't matter if we are rich or poor, black or white, Republican or Democrat. We realize we've all been blessed with the same day, and we share it.

Give me a day when a visitor from Louisville, Ky., asks if Macon is this pretty all the time. You laugh and tell her, "Of course it is!" And you really do wish it could be.

Give me a day that even though the pollen jumps down your throat (cough), up your nose (sneeze) and uses your head for a punching bag, you convince yourself there is no way you're going to stay inside and miss all the fun.

Give me a day when mothers push baby strollers and dads snap photographs to preserve the memories, even though it's the kind of day no one is likely to forget any time soon.

Give me a day when crowds gather to eat pink pancakes in Central City Park, save room for pink cornbread at the Willow on Fifth and stand in line for a scoop of pink ice cream in the Third Street Park.

Give me a day when the Jones family sets up a lemonade stand in their front yard on Oxford Road, with signs that read "Free Lemonade" and "Tour Buses Welcome."

Give me a day that inspires poetry, lifts words and keeps them fresh, a day when you run out of time and space before you run out of adjectives.

Give me a day when people move elbow-to-elbow at the Mulberry Street Arts and Crafts Festival, where there are long lines, but very few long faces.

Give me a party after sundown on Cherry, where people dance in the street while others gather to watch the fireworks from Coleman Hill.

Give me a day when the score of some basketball game takes a back seat to the Cherry Dazzle at Central City Park. Who cares about March Madness when you have March Gladness?

Give me a day when this community takes pride in ownership and rolls out the pink carpet for its guests.

Give me a day with something for everyone and everything for some.

Give me a day when there is no other place I would rather be than Macon in the springtime.

Give me a day when I wave, everybody waves back.

Yes, give me a day like Saturday.

The Elvis Babe – Warts and All

August 15, 2004

CORNELIA – Joni Mabe was washing her car the day Elvis died. The local radio station was playing a musical tribute to the King, so she had a hard time getting Elvis out of her head.

She has spent the rest of her life keeping him in her heart.

She is now known as "Joni Mabe, the Elvis Babe." In downtown Cornelia, she owns what she bills as the "largest and most unique Elvis exhibition in the world."

If you want to see Presley's famous 1955 pink Cadillac, you'll have to go to Graceland.

But if you're itching to see the Elvis Wart, a vial of Elvis' sweat and the Maybe Elvis Toenail, the Loudermilk Boarding House Museum at the foothills of the north Georgia mountains is a must-stop for your blue suede shoes.

Five years ago, Joni turned her family's old boarding house (built in 1908) into "Joni Mabe's Panoramic Encyclopedia of Everything Elvis."

For 14 years, she took a traveling exhibit to museums in places like Los Angeles, New York and London. "Like P.T. Barnum," she said.

Elvis eventually settled at the boarding house that has become a final resting place for more than 30,000 artifacts. Upstairs, where the ceiling fans keep rhythm to the sounds of you-know-who on the stereo, four rooms and a hallway are a shrine to every Elvis item imaginable.

There is a gift shop, too, and Joni is converting the basement into a B & E — a Bed & Elvis — with King-sized mattresses, no doubt.

The toenail and the wart are still the main attractions, though. She keeps them locked in a glass case at the top of the stairs.

The toenail came straight from the floor at Graceland on her visit there in 1983. When her tour group went through Presley's famous "Jungle Room," she purposely lagged behind to "skim the area beyond the ropes."

"I just wanted to touch where he had touched," she said. She got down on her hands and knees and discovered the toenail clipping in the green shag carpet.

She can't be sure it came from the King's foot, though. That's why she calls it the "Maybe Elvis Toenail." She's even less certain about the small vial of Elvis sweat she bought from a man in New York. (Could be snake oil, you know.)

Joni is more convinced about the authenticity of the wart, which she purchased from a Memphis doctor in 1990. He had removed it from Elvis' right wrist when Presley enlisted in the Army in 1958. It is kept in a tube of formaldehyde. She won't reveal how much she paid for it.

Since then, she has heard from a nurse who claims to keep some Elvis blood in her refrigerator. That wouldn't work for Joni, though. "I faint at the sight of blood," she said.

Another man told her his father-in-law, who was a dentist, had saved some of Elvis' fillings, but she didn't bite on that one.

She said there is an organization that calls itself Americans for Cloning Elvis (ACE). She is opposed to cloning but admitted it might be intriguing to put the King back together, "piece by piece."

She has come a long way since Aug. 16, 1977, the day Elvis was

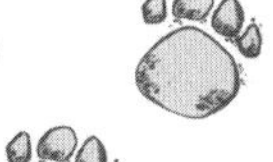

found dead on his bathroom floor at Graceland. At the time, she was a 19-year-old art major at the University of Georgia and nearly a generation younger than most Elvis fans.

In fact, she had turned down a chance to attend an Elvis concert in Atlanta the year before. She went to see Lynyrd Skynyrd instead.

"(Elvis) was campy and overweight," she said. "A friend of mine who went said he kept forgetting the words to the songs and kissing all the women. ... Now I wish I had gone."

She did her master's thesis on Elvis, then started collecting many of the Elvis essentials that would later provide the foundation for her museum. In 1995, she wrote a book, *Everything Elvis*. She has been featured in national newspapers and magazines and has been interviewed by the likes of Montel Williams, Howard Stern and Bill O'Reilly.

This past week, she hosted the fifth annual "Big E Festival" in Cornelia, which attracted more than 1,000 fans and a host of Elvis impersonators.

Even though Monday marks the 27th anniversary of Presley's death, the weekend has mostly been quiet around the museum.

"Everybody has gone to Memphis," she explained.

So Joni Mabe the Elvis Babe will sit on her front porch swing and pay homage to a man she never met but whose presence she feels in every room.

The boarding house, which is listed on the National Register of Historic Places, sits across the street from the local Methodist and Baptist churches.

In a way, the museum is sacred ground, too.

"Elvis?" she said. "He's like a part of my family."

Pick of All Trades

August 31, 2003

GRAY — Folks used to think Ed Thornton must have been born with a toothpick.

He always seemed to have one clenched between his teeth. It was part of his dress code to have a stick of wood protruding above his chin, as if his lips were walking the plank.

This toothpick habit started after he quit smoking. He had to satisfy the fixation of having something in his mouth.

He went from a pack a day to a pick a day.

"I was more worried about termites than lung cancer," he said, chuckling.

At the time, he never could have imagined carving and painting ballerinas, lighthouses, giraffes, angels, turkeys, windmills and Christmas trees — all on the heads of toothpicks.

He now practices a craft that almost defies belief. I watched him whittle a hummingbird. (It rated about a 9.9 on the Gris Whiz Scale.)

Thornton uses a single bristle to paint each toothpick. The attention to detail is so extraordinary you can take a magnifying glass and see the white ivory keys on a baby grand piano.

Not to mention a two-legged lady standing on a three-legged table holding a four-legged chair above her head and wearing a wristwatch.

When it comes to craftsmanship, Thornton, 70, is somewhat of a stick of all trades.

He retired after 19 years as the superintendent of public works for the city of Gray.

Now his occupation is piddler, according to his wife, Margaret Anne.

He has done leather work, painted nature scenes, carved dogs, boots and birds out of bass wood, and sculpted chain links out of pool cue sticks.

Seven years ago, he was introduced to the art of toothpick sculpting by a son-in-law. He showed Thornton a toothpick carved by a Florida man named Michael Drummond, who later was featured in *People* magazine.

If anything, it was convenient. Thornton already had the supplies. After all, he usually was walking around with a toothpick in his mouth. (He has since given that up.)

"I tried a flower the first time, and I must have gone through 15 toothpicks before I got it right," he said. "I cut my fingers several times."

Now he has perfected the art. He works a couple of hours every night at the kitchen table with a pair of trifocals, a magnifying glass and two steady hands.

A box of 800 Diamond round toothpicks and a razor knife can produce an "assembly line" of magic.

Every sculpture is carved from a single toothpick. There are no moving parts. There is no glue. (The paint serves as an adhesive.)

Thornton gives them to friends, sells them at arts and crafts festivals and carries a tackle box full of his creations practically everywhere he goes. He's had waitresses chase him down in parking lots trying to buy them.

He showed me a toothpick with a blonde woman wearing an evening dress. I squinted.

"It's Dolly Parton," he said.

Then he laughed. "Turn it sideways."

I did.

It was definitely Dolly.

Yellow Brick Road

August 3, 2003

VIENNA — When you arrive at Fred Causey's house, you get the feeling you're not in Georgia anymore.

Maybe it's the red Chevrolet in the driveway with the license plate that reads: "WIZ OZ."

Or maybe it's the yellow-brick sidewalk that leads inside the house, where every room is painted a different color of the rainbow.

Around this town where Fred Causey grew up and has been a media specialist in the local school system for nearly 30 years, they call him the "Wizard of Vienna."

No, the tornadoes that roared through four years ago didn't plop his house down at the corner of U.S. 41 and Third Street.

He has lived here for all of his 53 years, and his love of "The Wizard of Oz" has been filling rooms for parts of four decades.

His mother, Delia Causey, used to tell him his collection was OK, just as long as he left her a clear path to the kitchen and the bathroom. She died two years ago, and those paths are no longer as wide as they once were.

At last count, Fred has more than 3,400 Oz-related items filling every nook, cranny, corner, wall and mantel of his home.

Friends in his Oz network tell him he probably has the largest such collection in the South, if not the universe.

"People are amazed when they see it," he said. "When I tell them I collect the Wizard of Oz, they think I might have it all on one bookshelf. Then I start leading them from room to room!

"Now I'm running out of space," he said, laughing. "I have to be more selective about what I get."

I've always been a huge fan of one of the most beloved movies of all time. So I met with Fred last week to take his "Over the Rainbow Tour."

I learned to be careful, though. If you don't watch where you sit down, you might crush a Tin Man or squash a Scarecrow.

And Toto, too.

The "tour" begins in the same room where Fred watched the movie as a 6-year-old boy when it debuted on television the night of Nov. 3, 1956.

He saw it on a black-and-white TV, of course. It made history by becoming the first movie shown annually (CBS) on commercial TV.

"It's hard to find anyone who hasn't seen it at least once," he said. "It's so much a part of our culture."

Fred owns more than 500 books on Oz and even has videotapes of the movie in French and Spanish. There are Oz dolls, neckties, snow globes, Christmas ornaments, collector's plates, doormats, pillow cases and puzzles. He has original sheet music of "Over the Rainbow" sung by everybody from Judy Garland to Willie Nelson. Yes, he even has some 17 autographs from original "munchkins."

He also is the proud owner of a pair of ruby slippers. Actually, they are made from some 2,000 red sequins. But they are Dorothy's correct size (5 ½), and there is a reproduction of the original shoe label.

Fred satisfies his Oz appetite by shopping at flea markets and yard sales. He swaps and sells so much on the Internet, his middle name could be "eBay."

He has displayed his collection at schools, theaters and libraries. He enjoys talking with people about their memories of the film.

Everyone, it seems, has a rainbow connection.

His interests have spilled into other areas, too. He also has shrines to Tarzan, Harry Potter and the old "Dark Shadows" soap opera.

But his main allegiance is to the great and powerful Oz.

"There is something about the movie that makes it different than anything I've ever seen," he said. "It will never be duplicated. It was the right script with the right actors with the right songs."

The yellow brick road must run right through Vienna.

For Fred Causey, there really is no place like home.

Good Sports

Championship Was in the Cards

June 27, 2003

The sign went up before the dew had time to dry along Forsyth Street.

"I BELIEVE!"

Bob Berg has been posting clever messages on his marquee at Sid's Sandwich Shop since 1984. He's a real ham-and-cheese on wry. Sandwich buns with puns.

(Berg's wit once sold some wheels. His sign advertised a roast beef sandwich for $2,800. He threw in a truck for free.)

But he's never had more fun than the three consonants and five vowels that were posted on the sign one week ago today.

He has every right to be proud. The 9- and 10-year-old boys he coached at Vine-Ingle won the minor league championship. The Cardinals came out of nowhere and went everywhere, a team with cleats on the bottoms of Cinderella slippers.

Berg just might have to run a special on hero sandwiches.

On the last day of May, the Cards had a 2-11 record. They had been outscored by a whopping 54 runs.

Although they won their last three games of the regular season, most folks expected them to exit stage left field when the league tournament began on June 10.

Even Berg had his doubts about his team's staying power. He had treated his players at Dairy Queen after each victory, but that didn't exactly break the bank on ice cream.

At the team party, he blurted out he would take them to White Water, a popular water park north of Atlanta, if they won the championship.

"I don't know why I said White Water. It was just the first thing I thought of," said Berg. "I could have promised them Fort Knox and never dreamed I would have to pay it off."

The Cardinals struck gold, though.

Back in spring training in March, Berg and his coaches — Monte Kellam and Scott Murphy — were simply wishing for a break-even season.

After lopsided losses in their first four games, they revised that goal.

"We were just hoping to win a game," said Murphy.

Admittedly, the Cardinals weren't always focused on winning. The chemistry didn't seem to be there. Once, the coaches had to break up

a fight in the dugout. The losses piled high.

"You need to play with enthusiasm," Berg told his troops.

"What does enthusiasm mean?" asked one player.

The Cardinals might not have been able to define enthusiasm, but they soon began to demonstrate it. Berg began huddling his players between innings — looking them in the eyes, patting them on the backs and issuing them challenges.

"I believe!" he screamed. "Do you believe?"

One by one, the tournament Goliaths began to fall. First it was the Angels, then the Mariners and Expos.

The Cardinals were making believers out of nonbelievers, including themselves.

"We were underdogs, so everybody was pulling for us," Berg said.

In the championship game, the Cards played the Tigers, a team that had won 16 straight games and had whipped them 17-1 a month earlier.

It was rumored someone on the Tigers was going to phone in an order at Sid's — for a "roasted Cardinal sandwich."

The Cards fell behind 8-2 in the second inning. Berg urged them not to quit believing.

There were plenty of heroes that night. But when little Farris Thomas, who hadn't gotten a hit all season, led off the fifth inning with a single, there was magic in the air at Turner Field. (That's Turner, as in the late Jim Turner, a longtime coach at Vine-Ingle.)

The Cardinals scored five times in the inning to take the lead. They held on to win the game 11-9.

"I watched Rice win the College World Series on TV the other day," said Kellam. "So I knew exactly how they felt."

By the next morning, Berg had put up the sign in front of Sid's and had started a "shrine" to the Cardinals inside the restaurant.

Sid's may have been named after poet Sidney Lanier, but Berg was practically at a loss for words in describing his emotions.

He believed.

They all did.

Caskets for the Die-Hard Fan

June 6, 2001

The caskets are on display in a showroom in the back. Some are made of 18-gauge steel. Others are mahogany, oak or maple. All have

hand-sewn velvet interiors.

What gets your attention are the colors. Red. Blue. Black. Silver. And bright orange.

If the Tennessee Volunteers are your favorite team, this is where you might choose to spend eternity.

Scott Walston has taken a novel idea and turned it into one of Macon's most unique businesses.

Coffins and cremation urns for, er, die-hard fans.

"There are three things people will tell you about themselves when you meet them," said Walston. "Who they married. How many children they have. And where they went to college. There is great pride and loyalty to their school."

Collegiate Memorials is not listed in the phone book. There is no sign on the door of the old mill building on Lake Street.

It is a subsidiary of Southeastern Casket Distributors, the parent company Walston founded. It shares office space with All Pets Go To Heaven, a pet cremation service Walston opened in 1996.

Although this casket personalization business may be a well-kept secret in Macon, it has developed a national reputation.

Walston has been interviewed by CNN, ESPN, the BBC and newspapers in Columbia, S.C., Raleigh, N.C., and Atlanta. He has been on radio talk shows in Chicago, Los Angeles, Orlando, Fla., Tallahassee, Fla., and Madison, Wis., and "live" on TV in Birmingham, Ala.

He has been featured in a European magazine and by the Canadian Broadcasting Network.

Last week, he was listening to Paul Harvey's radio commentary on his way to work. "Pomp and Circumstance" was playing in the background. At first, he thought it was a commercial. Then Harvey started talking about caskets for college fans. ...

Walston was driving down Napier Avenue just a few blocks from his office, and his business was being plugged on car radios from Bangor, Maine, to Aberdeen, Wash.

He came up with the idea three years ago after noticing a trend. Personalized caskets — with inscriptions of everything from praying hands to the 23rd Psalm — were outselling conventional models. Since people show their school pride on everything from cars to mailboxes, he wondered if he might market that display of loyalty on a celestial level.

After jumping through all the legal and financial hoops with collegiate licensing companies, Walston now has contracts with more than 40 schools. He sold his first casket to a local family. The deceased was a devoted Auburn fan.

Nebraska and Tennessee are his best sellers. He gets orders from as far away as New Mexico. The company also offers headstone memorials and visitation registries.

The caskets are not tacky. It is important that they maintain dignity. Even though they involve death, Walston calls them a "celebration of life."

Dearly beloved, we have gathered here today to pay our last respects. ... and Roll Tide!

Bobby Keeps Air Fresh in Football

October 15, 2004

HAWKINSVILLE — Bobby Jackson never played a down for Hawkinsville High School last season.

He never threw a touchdown pass or made a saving tackle.

Instead, he washed dirty uniforms, fixed broken chin straps and did a little dance on the sidelines when the Red Devils scored.

After Hawkinsville won the Class A state football title five days before Christmas, one question still loomed large.

"Everybody wanted to know about Bobby getting his championship ring," said head coach Lee Campbell.

Bobby is such a breath of fresh air, they should use him to pump up every football in Pulaski County.

"Players have come and gone, and coaches have changed, but Bobby has been a fixture in the program," said Mike Henry, a former Hawkinsville quarterback in the 1970s whose son Jim is a backup quarterback on this year's team.

Bobby is 45 years old, never married and doesn't drive. He walks five miles to the school, where he works in the cafeteria. After he finishes cleaning the lunch trays and emptying the trash, he reports to his "other" job.

He is a volunteer team manager.

"I do it because it's in my heart," he said.

Said Henry: "I've never seen him without that Red Devils cap on his head. It doesn't matter what time of year it is. And you always see him walking on the streets. Everybody knows him, so he usually can get a ride."

To say Bobby grew up in a family of 11 children is an understatement. He never "grew" much at all.

When he showed up for football practice as a ninth-grader in 1975, he was only 5 feet tall and weighed 100 pounds.

"I kept thinking I would grow, but I never got big," said Bobby. "Coach Gentry was doing me a favor when he asked me to be a manager."

Bobby Gentry is a legend in Hawkinsville. The high school stadium is named in his honor. He coached for 28 years, retiring in 1977. He won three state titles in the 1950s.

The state championship Hawkinsville won last year was the school's first since 1959.

"That's the year I was born," said Bobby.

It was Gentry who started calling Bobby "Mr. Clean." The nickname has stuck to Bobby like pay dirt for almost a generation.

"It was great Bobby could be part of the team," said Gentry. "He's like clockwork, a jack-of-all-trades. This whole community thinks the world of him."

Bobby's not going anywhere, either. Sometimes, he even gets the idea he's part of the coaching staff.

"One of our assistants laid down his headset during a game," said Campbell. "I turned around, and Bobby had picked up the headset and had it on. He was walking down the sidelines, agreeing with the play we were calling."

Bobby said being measured for his championship ring last year was the "biggest thrill of my life."

At the end of this season, Campbell hopes to award Bobby a letter jacket.

Might need to free up another finger, too. Unbeaten in seven games, the Red Devils remain the top-ranked team in Class A.

"In a small town," said Bobby, "high school football is big stuff."

Bubble Gum, Basketball and Johnny

March 5, 2004

The Southwest High School letter jacket still hangs in his closet at the nursing home. On a nearby table, he keeps a bucket filled with his traditional bubble gum.

Johnny Higdon has always been known for bubble gum and basketball.

Twenty-five years ago this week, the Southwest Patriots put the finishing touches on a 28-0 season by winning the Class AAAA basketball championship.

A capacity crowd of 8,300 jammed the Macon Coliseum to

watch the Patriots beat crosstown rival Northeast for the title.

It's rare when the state's two best teams stand shoulder-to-shoulder in the same city. They met four times during that memorable season.

Five days after winning the title, Southwest was named national high school champions by *Basketball Weekly* magazine.

Johnny was such a fixture at Southwest games, the coaches later gave him the designation of "school spirit director."

With his megaphone in his hand, he would walk as if he were falling forward. His pockets were stuffed with gum, and he handed out Super Bubble to everyone within arm's reach. The dentists in town must have loved Johnny.

The fans sure loved him. His strained voice would rise above their own cheers.

Gooooooo Southwest!!!!! Gooooooo Patriots!!!!!!!

Johnny no longer hears the sound of bouncing balls in crowded gymnasiums or the squeaking of sneakers cutting against the planks of the hardwood floor.

The only squeaking he now hears is the wheels of the meal cart in the hallway, bringing him a supper of Salisbury steak, mashed potatoes, peas and milk.

Johnny is 56 years old. His health has declined. He has a difficult time remembering the last game he was able to attend.

"I miss going," he said. "But everything is different now."

There was a time when just about everybody in south Macon knew Johnny.

But not many of them still go by and visit with him at the nursing home.

He doesn't get much mail, either.

"The cable bill," he said, laughing.

He fell a few weeks ago and was moved to another room. He has to wear padded headgear when he walks the hallways.

Johnny was a promising athlete at Willingham High School, which later became Southwest. As a sophomore in 1963, he was a strapping 6-foot-1, 185 pounds.

One day, while climbing a tree to retrieve a kite for his brother, he fell headfirst to the ground. He stayed in a coma for several months. The accident left him physically and mentally impaired.

Johnny once inspired his coach, Billy Henderson, to call him the "greatest high school sports fan in America."

On the eve of the anniversary of Southwest's national championship, I must admit my thoughts are with Johnny.

One of my proudest moments was on stage at the Grand Opera House in 1988, when I presented Johnny the *Telegraph's* annual Sam Burke Award for sportsmanship and service.

I can't think of anyone who has ever deserved it more.

Haley wins biggest race of all

Nov. 14, 2004

Her parents knew she was fast on the soccer field.

It was as if Haley Tidwell's legs were in a hurry to get there before the rest of her did.

Her brother, Cam, also realized she had a fast motor. He bet some friends his little sister could beat them in a race. Easiest $5 he ever made. When they asked for a rematch, she beat them again.

So when Haley started the fourth grade at First Presbyterian Day School this fall, Ty and Denise Tidwell encouraged her to run on the elementary school cross-country team.

Every time she ran against children her own age, she needed a rear-view mirror to locate them. It didn't matter whether she was running against the girls — or the boys.

"She smoked 'em," said Denise.

Haley's comet.

Late in the season, Joe McDaniel, FPD's volunteer coach, moved Haley up to the junior varsity, grades 6-8. She suddenly found herself competing against kids two-heads taller, with longer legs and more experience.

They wouldn't talk to her on competitive runs, and would try to elbow her out of position on the winding trails.

And, when she outran them all, too, one older girl lamented.

"I got beat by a fourth-grader," she moaned.

"Yeah," said her coach, "but this one's special."

How special?

Haley ran in the GISA state meet three weeks ago at Stratford and finished sixth among all girls.

Her parents had no idea what to expect. She was so young. Maybe middle of the pack?

At the start, they watched her disappear into the woods, barely coming up to the armpits of the older children, as she tackled the challenging trail.

Then, at the end, there was Haley coming out of the woods among the leaders.

Ty and Denise Tidwell cried.

And cried.

Not a drop of rain fell in Macon that day, but there were puddles at the Tidwells' feet.

"We were more emotional about it than anything she has ever done," Denise said. "When she came running out of those woods, we both just lost it. It was like a flashback of her life, and all she has been through."

Seven years ago this week, Haley went through her last round of radiation and chemotherapy. When she was 2, doctors found a tumor on her kidney the size of a small football. It was suspected the cancer might have spread to other parts of her tiny body.

But six hours of surgery brought the best possible news. The tumor was confined and removed. Haley lost one of her kidneys and there remains so much scar tissue her lungs are still only at about 80 percent capacity.

During Haley's radiation treatments, she lost her hair. Ty shaved off his curly locks so his daughter wouldn't be self-conscious about being bald.

Haley's sandy brown hair now falls to her shoulders.

Ty laughs. His hair never came back.

But neither has Haley's cancer.

She celebrated her 10th birthday one month ago today. The Tidwells will never forget their bounty of blessings. They live their lives with faith, not fear.

Haley has already won the biggest race of her life.

The Ultimate Fan

November 24, 2000

MILLEDGEVILLE — The jersey is neatly folded across a chair in the living room.

Outside the window are the remnants of a late autumn day. In the back yard, a dog named "Buzz" is barking in his pen.

The Saturday after Thanksgiving is so close at hand Alton Rogers can almost anticipate the coin toss.

It can mean only one thing.

The Georgia-Georgia Tech game.

Rogers will wear his special Georgia Tech jersey to Saturday's civil war in Athens. It is No. 74, with "ROGERS" across the back.

On the Tech roster, No. 74 belongs to freshman offensive

lineman Leon Robinson.

But, in the stands, No. 74 — as in years — is clearly the possession of Alton Rogers. It was recently assigned to him by Georgia Tech athletic director Dave Braine in recognition for his remarkable longevity and loyalty.

After all, this will be Rogers' 74th consecutive Georgia-Georgia Tech football game.

He has braved cold winds, rain, sleet and fog. He has endured night games and 10 a.m. kickoffs. He has witnessed blowouts, overtime victories and controversial fumbles. He has heard the frenzied pitch of Bulldog fans and the roar of the Rambling Wreck hitting on all cylinders.

Rogers is 91 years old. Arthritis and old age have gang-tackled his legs. He will attend his 74th Georgia-Georgia Tech game in a wheelchair.

But why should that stop him? Four years ago, he went to the game just two days after being released from the hospital.

He had suffered a heart attack.

Rogers has lived through a rivalry that has divided loyalties between families, neighbors, co-workers, stockholders and church deacons.

He has not missed a game since 1927. He was a freshman at Tech that year and played saxophone in the marching band.

That was the same year Charles Lindbergh made his historic flight across the Atlantic and Babe Ruth socked 60 over the fence.

It was just two years after the Jackets and Bulldogs resumed their rivalry following an eight-year feud. It was two years before Sanford Stadium, site of today's 95th meeting, was dedicated.

Naturally, Rogers is proud of his attendance mark. He also is humble.

"I just take them one year at a time," he said.

If there is anyone who could eventually break his record, it is his son, Al, who lives in Macon. Al Rogers has not missed a game since 1955, and is hopeful a touch of the flu this week won't prevent him from continuing his own streak.

"Not many people could do what my dad has done," he said. "He has persevered."

Alton Rogers' wife, Frances, had an impressive streak of her own before she died in 1994. The couple was married in 1941. Not long after their marriage, Rogers purchased season tickets. That way, he could guarantee that his family would always have seats at the biggest game of the season.

Rogers doesn't claim to have a favorite game in the series.

Every Tech victory has a special place in his mental scrapbook. He still remembers his first visit to Sanford Stadium on Dec. 7, 1929. That was the year the stadium opened and came just 44 days after the stock market crashed to trigger the Great Depression.

Georgia won that day, 12-6, but that was only half the misery. Rogers and the rest of the Tech band had to ride the train to Athens, unload at the depot and march to the stadium through the cold rain, ankle deep in red mud.

The closest Rogers came to having his streak snapped was in 1996. As he lay in a hospital bed in intensive care the week before the game, he pleaded with doctors and family members to let him attend.

"He kept telling us he had to get to the game," said his daughter, Patsy Tripp. "And I kept thinking to myself: If he doesn't get to go, it would be like cutting a lifeline. It is something that keeps him going."

Rogers was released from the hospital on a Thursday — Thanksgiving Day — under strict doctor's orders to stay home. On game day, after other family members had departed for Athens, Rogers stayed behind with Patsy.

When the house was quiet, he looked at her. She looked at him. "How are you feeling, Daddy?" she asked.

"What have you got in mind?" he replied. Patsy, who lives in Athens, asked if he would like to ride up to the game and make a cameo appearance, just to keep the lofty string unbroken.

"I could see that gleam in his eyes," she said.

"Do you think we could do that?" he wondered.

Patsy managed to talk her way through four police barricades near the stadium and was allowed to park near Gate 1. She got out, purchased a game program and grabbed her camera. She took her father's picture holding his tickets and the program.

They listened to the opening kickoff from outside the stadium gate. After the first series of plays, they went back to the car and returned to Milledgeville.

"We giggled about it the whole time," she said. "It was like we were pulling something off — and we were."

The streak lives on.

Just how high do those jersey numbers go?

Alton Rogers died in June 2001.

Getting Back On

March 29, 1998

WARNER ROBINS — Ray Cowan cannot remember the name of the horse. He can only remember the fall, and then trying to pick up the pieces.

This wasn't just another race on just another day. It would be the last one.

When the horse's left leg shattered and collapsed beneath him, Cowan's tiny body, twisted and helpless, went flying at the mercy of gravity and the ground.

He stayed in the hospital for 18 months. His back had been broken in four places. His leg had been crushed.

The horse with no name was put out of its misery.

There were times when Ray Cowan must have wondered if his own misery ever would end.

He never raced again, of course, but that wasn't the only thing that almost killed him. His life, like his backbone, had been broken in too many places.

His memory of that day, and others, has been blotted by the wear and tear of alcohol. His money disappeared through tough luck and bad marriages.

Occasionally, he could catch a glimpse of the pain that brought him a measure of fame, riding as a jockey at Hialeah Park in Miami. The horrible crash of 28 years ago was played and replayed in the opening sequence of ABC's "Wide World of Sports."

"I couldn't believe it when I first saw it," Cowan said. "And every time I saw it after that it would still scare me."

The popular sports television program, now in its 35th year, would show a former Yugoslavian forklift operator named Vinko Bogatj, hurdling out of control down a ski ramp.

The opening credits would evoke the narrator's "thrill of victory" followed by the "agony of defeat." For many years, the bone-breaking ski wipeout was followed by Cowan's mishap at the racetrack.

"The one thing I remember about that show when it came on was watching the horse throw him off," said Bob Mochrie, of Bay City Mich., who befriended Cowan 13 years ago in Warner Robins. "I never imagined the day would come when I would meet the guy in person."

The diminutive "celebrity" now lives in a trailer park in Warner Robins. The only thing resembling a horse is the horseshoe-shaped Porkie Drive, the address he now calls home. It is far from the

fast lane that took him on his near-fatal ride into life's gutters.

His close friends know his story, but others would be hard-pressed to believe he once took the saddle against Willie Shoemaker, Eddie Arcaro, Bill Hartack and other famous jockeys of that era. Or that he once had a part in the movie, "The Champ" with Jon Voight and Faye Dunaway.

It is difficult to fathom that a man who was a "millionaire several times over" is now living on a fixed income, painting houses to stay busy and, at age 56, learning to read by taking night classes at the Middle Georgia Technical Institute.

Ray Cowan is living proof.

"At one time, there were guys living under the Spring Street Bridge in Macon who had more going for them than I did," he said. "But I think I had to take the path that I took. It's like being caught in a forest. You have to take the path that will get you out."

No, he cannot remember the horse's name.

He just remembers that it took too many years to break his fall.

He grew up on Front Street in Warner Robins, a child trapped in a dysfunctional environment. He was a third-grade dropout who shined shoes, hawked newspapers and sold packages of peanuts just to make a few bucks for his family.

Life with his stepfather was, in his own words, "brutal." Though Ray Cowan was his legal name, the young child was forced by his stepfather to carry his last name, Rogers.

Ray Rogers, unlike the cowboy Roy Rogers, had never seen a horse.

That changed when he eventually went to live with his real father in Johnson City, Tenn., assumed his God-given name again, and stayed with a family of bootleggers. Cowan worked for a vending machine business, traveling the Tennessee hills in a '53 Plymouth. He later was hired to do odd jobs.

"I never could work at the service station because I was 4-foot tall and weighed 70 pounds," he said. "Some of those tires weighed as much as I did. I just didn't have enough lead in my britches to do heavy lifting."

His course would change when he met a man named Roy Faircloth.

"He was drunk, and sitting in a coffee shop," Cowan said. "He had grass stains all down one leg and his shirt tail was out. He looked like he just crawled out of a ditch. He was rough, really rough, and his hair stuck out like Dagwood."

Faircloth had a reputation for putting down a few bets at the track, and he knew a jockey when he spotted one.

"I was a little bitty thing, and he asked if I would like to be a jockey," said Cowan. "I said: 'Sir, I wouldn't know which end of the horse to feed.' I had never been on a horse, never seen one, really."

But the next day, he found himself waiting for Faircloth at a Chevrolet dealership so large it stretched a city block. Cowan remembers waiting in the lobby, listening to the footsteps of people shuffling across the marble floors.

He saw Faircloth, the owner of the dealership, appearing nothing like the disheveled man who had approached him a day earlier.

"He had on a fresh, dry-cleaned suit, and he looked like a thousand-dollar bill," said Cowan. "He wanted me to go to Maryland and train to become a jockey. Next thing I knew, I had signed a five-year contract with him for $50 a week."

He spent several years as a stable boy, learning to overcome his shyness of horses and culling the wisdom of old grooms who had watched their entire lives run circles around the racetrack.

"You don't just let a mechanic fly an airplane," he said. "If you've never been around a horse, it can scare you. But once I started riding, it fit me like a glove. Thoroughbreds aren't like riding those old plow horses. It was like getting out of an old Ford and climbing into a Cadillac."

Success did not come with the first competitive ride, or even the second. He went to the well 270 times before he finally won on the circuit. He crossed the finish line first more than 7,000 times before his career was through.

He rode horses for Campbell Soup Co., Wells Fargo and entertainer Dean Martin.

He rose to near the top of his profession. It didn't seem to matter that he couldn't read. He simply had to learn to sign his name on the checks. He had bookkeepers, agents and valets.

"All I had to do was suit up and show up," he said.

But that wasn't always easy. There were the marriages, and the children.

Everything got too complicated before it settled into just plain sad. He married a woman from Kissimmee, Fla., then a go-go girl from Maine, who divorced him when he was in the hospital. There would be two more brides, two more weddings and two more divorces.

He now knows why none of it seemed to work. The hangovers began to mount.

There are details of his life he still cannot recollect because the effects of alcohol emptied those bottles of time and flushed them down.

He said he would never drink and drive the horses. Then the spill that ended his career nearly ruined him. He lay in the hospital bed in traction and in a body cast. One machine was pumping blood in, another pumping blood out.

But because he had money, he also had friends. They would bring booze to his hospital room, and Cowan often would pay the orderlies to sneak miniature bottles of whisky to his bedside.

"I was a mess," he said. "Alcoholism is a terrible, terrible thing. It's not just the idea of being drunk or in bad shape or having a hangover. It's a way of life. It happens. But you can't always explain it to someone who has never been there. It's not a moral issue. It's a disease that can kill you."

The problems didn't stop when he moved back to Warner Robins in 1976. In many ways they accelerated. Then, he pulled the reins before it finally consumed him.

"Fifteen years ago, I was living in a roach-infested apartment with all my possessions in a paper bag," he said. "I got into a lot of trouble because I had so many DUIs. I finally realized how much I was hurting myself."

He now lives alone in his trailer on a steady diet of coffee and cigarettes.

But Ray Cowan is a changed man who now knows the lay of the land mines. He hasn't had a sip of alcohol since 1983. A Bible rests on his coffee table and, thanks to his classes at the local vocational school, he can read it. He attends church on Sunday mornings.

"I know that God is working in my life," he said. "Some people say this thing about God has to be something they can see or touch. Well, sometimes I need a God with skin on him, too. I get that through spiritual people."

Bad days still raise their heads. He has suffered a heart attack and had two brushes with cancer. He manages to survive on his monthly social security check and working at odd jobs as a painter. He has "grown" to 5-foot-3, 140 pounds.

"To know Ray is to love him," said Mochrie. "He's the type of guy who would give you the shirt off his back, even if it was the only piece of clothing he owned. He was a millionaire at one time, but he doesn't look down on anybody."

Mochrie laughed.

"Well, at his size, he may look up at most people."

On a recent spring morning, Cowan walked to the front of his trailer and leaned against the sign in the front of his yard that reads: "Ray's Place."

"Yeah, there's a lot I wish I could do over again," he said.

He cannot change the past. But this new saddle has a different look, a different feel.

The agony of defeat has found its own private victory.

Blue Skies for Tommie Gray

December 4, 2002

WARNER ROBINS — Tommie Gray III won't ever run like Michael Vick or win a football game with the swing of his foot.

He plays football on two stumps he calls legs.

In the trenches for the Northside Eagles, it's easy to lose track of No. 52.

After all, he's only 3 feet tall — the equivalent of a single yard on a football field.

"One of our biggest fears," said Northside coach Conrad Nix, "is stepping on him."

Wearing his artificial legs, Tommie is 5-foot-11, 180 pounds of pure heart.

But the Georgia High School Association does not allow prosthetic limbs. So, without them, the sophomore noseguard is even dwarfed by opposing offensive linemen in their three-point stances.

When he was 4 years old, Tommie contracted meningitis. Both legs had to be amputated above the knee.

It just about broke his mother's heart. His father's heart, too. Tommie Gray Jr. played running back for Northside in the early 1980s. Now his young son was facing life in a wheelchair.

But Tommie was a kid bent on moving every mountain in his path.

His cousins strapped his artificial feet to his bicycle pedals and taught him to ride. He swam competitively and played T-ball at the recreation department. He participated in wheelchair soccer and basketball.

"Nothing held him back," said his mother, Daryl Gray. "He believed he could do anything."

Still, Tommie's doctors would not clear him to participate in contact sports.

As a ninth-grader last year, Tommie finally passed his physical.

At first, Nix was concerned Tommie might be a "distraction," a high-maintenance player with minimal contribution to the program.

Tommie proved otherwise

"He's one of us now," said Nix. "He's an inspiration. He is determined to be out there. His teammates don't pamper him. He gets knocked down, just like everyone else. He just doesn't have as far to fall."

He does, however, have higher to climb.

Early in the season, defensive line coach Kevin Smith was hesitant about putting Tommie through rigorous drills. "But he didn't want to be treated any differently," said Smith.

Now, when he watches the young man who barely reaches his teammates' thigh pads, Smith gets chill bumps.

"It's emotional for me just to see how much effort it takes for him to get on his gear and get to the field," Smith said.

Don't expect Tommie to play a major role in Northside's rematch with two-time defending Class AAAAA champ Parkview on Friday night. He has played in only two varsity games.

But against Effingham County a few weeks back, he lined up and made a tackle. Northside fans chanted his name. In a junior varsity game against Jones County, he sacked the quarterback.

Tommie still has a bit of dreamer in him.

"I want to try out for the basketball team," he said, laughing.

The sky's the limit.

The Old Man in the Ring

May 28, 1994

The world is full of might-have-beens.

Jackie Cranford has his own story.

His boxing career took him to within a single fight of meeting Joe Louis for the world heavyweight championship.

In his prime, he was compared to a young Gene Tunney. His career as a heavyweight contender in the 1940s was marked by only nine losses in 101 fights.

His memories fill five scrapbooks at his south Macon home. Even now, as he tugs on a cigarette with the same huge hands that knocked out 25 opponents in 51 professional fights, he can't help but wonder how much different his life might have been had he gotten his shot at the Brown Bomber.

Still, there are no regrets. Absolutely no regrets. He knew his limits.

"Oh, I would have liked to have fought him for the honor and all that," he said. "And I think I could have kept him away from me and

out-boxed him for a few rounds. But I'll be honest with you. I don't think I could have beaten him."

Cranford is 73 now and Macon's most famous boxing legend since the late W.L."Young" Stribling. (Stribling lost to Germany's Max Schmeling for the world heavyweight championship in 1931.)

Cranford still gets letters from boxing fans seeking autographs and pictures from as far away as Oklahoma and Alaska. It seems they haven't forgotten him, even if he was a might-have-been.

He spends many of his afternoons at the L & W sports bar on Pio Nono Avenue, shooting pool and shooting the breeze. A story and photograph from a 1946 issue of *The Boxing News* hang at the far corner of the bar.

"People still come up to me and say, 'Hey, Jackie, how are you doing? Please don't hit me!' " said Cranford. "And I say: 'Man, are you crazy? I don't go around hitting people any more.'"

All he throws now is a friendly left jab — his trademark in the ring — to show the instincts haven't been kayoed after almost 50 years.

"He can still hurt you with that little punch in the shoulder," said Will Hammock, owner of the L & W. "For a guy his age, he can still wallop you. And you feel it for a day or two."

He was hired as a lifeguard at a Washington, D.C., swimming pool after his family moved there from Macon in 1934.

"A man at the pool came up to me one day and told me I looked like I would make a good fighter," Cranford said. "I didn't know anything about fighting. I had never hit anyone."

He fought only 11 times as an amateur before turning pro in 1941. "If I was going to get hit, I wanted to get paid for it," he told fight promoters. "And my family was desperate for money."

When World War II came, Cranford spent 40 months in the Coast Guard, losing only one time in 45 bouts in the military. Jack Dempsey, who refereed one of Cranford's fights in the service, compared him to Tunney, the man who had beaten Dempsey twice for the heavyweight titles in 1926-27.

Cranford married his wife, Wanda, after she sent him a romantic telegram — "I love you like a hog loves slop" — and resumed his pro career after the war under manager Chris Dundee. His corner man was Dundee's brother, Angelo Dundee, who later gained fame as Muhammad Ali's manager and who also married Cranford's cousin.

Cranford achieved a measure of notoriety in boxing. With his rugged good looks, he was pictured in a four-page fashion feature in the May 1948 issue of *Sport* magazine, one with Babe Ruth on the cover.

But he missed his best chance to face Joe Louis when he lost to Italy's Gino Buonovino, the European champion, at Madison Square Garden on Jan. 2, 1948.

After eight more fights, he retired and moved back to Macon, telling the national press: "It's a tough road on the way up, and I sort of got the idea that I might never make the grade. A few years from now, I'd be through with nothing to show for my efforts but a beat-up body and no future."

Louis defended his heavyweight title 25 times. When he had run out of well-qualified contenders, his opponents were collectively known as the "Bum of the Month Club."

He retired one year after Cranford, but climbed back into the ring in 1950 and fought in an exhibition in Macon at Luther Williams Field.

Cranford went and re-introduced himself.

"I told him I almost got to fight him in 1948," said Cranford. "He was so big I had to look up at him when I said it."

And what was Louis' response?

"He just laughed," said Cranford, laughing himself at the memory of what might have been.

Jackie Cranford died in May 2002.

The Hurt Is Always There

August 27, 2004

The graves are side by side, on the slope of a hill at Macon Memorial Park, their final resting place in the shade of a tall pine tree.

Part of Billy Henderson is buried here, too.

"It gets easier with time," he said. "But the hurt is always there."

The old coach pulled a handkerchief from his pocket and brushed the pine straw from the two headstones.

His mother, Jewell Henderson, was his hero. His oldest son, Brad Henderson, was his heart.

Jewell was the center of his universe, the unselfish mama who made countless sacrifices for her children.

His father had died when Henderson was 8. He grew up on the proverbial other side of the tracks in a neighborhood where "only way out was to be able to run fast."

William Bradford Henderson Jr., was named after his father/ coach – a chip off the old block.

Two weeks ago, on Aug. 15, Brad Henderson would have

celebrated his 56th birthday. Labor Day weekend will mark the 40th anniversary of his death.

Coach Henderson has long been a legend in his hometown of Macon. Hundreds, if not thousands, of lives have been influenced by one of the winningest high school football coaches in the state at Willingham, Mount de Sales and Athens' Clarke Central.

His name evokes a deep reverence, especially in South Macon, where every dusty sandlot and corner store holds some special memory.

He is 76 now and retired in Athens. He still sports what newspaper columnist Lewis Grizzard once called "one of the last crew cuts in captivity."

Henderson is working on a book about his life. His health is still good, although he no longer can hear in his left ear and battles the dragons of vertigo. (In 1996, he went through six hours of surgery to remove a benign tumor from behind his left ear.)

I never played sports for Coach Henderson, but I'm fortunate to have learned enough from him over the years to have his positive attitude and eternal optimism rub off on me.

Thursday afternoon, as I rode through Macon reminiscing with him, I continued to learn.

He showed me where he used to race his friend, Louis Wanninger, to the drug store. Louis would call Henderson on the telephone and they would run out the door to see who arrived first.

"He started beating me every time," said Henderson. "It was years before I found out he was calling me from the drug store."

He showed me where a girl broke his heart when he was 15 years old. It was in front of the Navarro Apartments on Orange Street. He showed me what he called the "mystic wall" near the parking lot at Mount de Sales.

And we saw where he played football at Tattnall Square Park on Saturdays, often after starring in the backfield for the Lanier High Poets on Friday night.

He talked about growing up so poor he would pretend to be asleep on the team bus because he didn't have enough money to buy snacks after a game. He talked about meeting Fosky, his wife of 58 years, on a blind date. They went on a hayride at Lakeside Park.

He talked about how, even when he broke into coaching, he had to moonlight to make ends meet. He worked extra jobs at bowling alleys, convenience stores and skating rinks just to keep enough food on the table for five children.

And he talked about taking his children on weekend outings.

Fosky would always count heads when he got home to make sure he hadn't left one behind.

He talked about players he still loves from Willingham High, folks like Eddie Battle who love him tenfold in return. We went to see one of them, Johnny Higdon, now in a nursing home.

He talked about how he never believed in cutting players. (He once suited up a squad of 105 to play Valdosta.) And he talked about how when he left Mount de Sales in 1973 for Clarke Central in Athens, the nuns called a meeting to pray he wouldn't go.

But, mostly, he talked about Brad.

We went to the baseball field on Anthony Road, where Brad led Macon Little League to the state championship in 1960. Then we crossed the street to the football stadium, dedicated in 1965 as Brad Henderson Memorial Stadium.

Brad was born in 1948, a few weeks before his dad started his junior season with the University of Georgia football team.

Billy Henderson was playing semi-pro baseball in Wrightsville that summer. When he arrived for a game one night, he was summoned by a message from St. Mary's Hospital in Athens. He had better hurry home. He was about to become a father.

Brad was a gifted athlete. When he was in sixth grade, one of his baseball coaches explained to the team that a runner at second base was considered to be in "scoring position."

Confident, but never cocky, Brad interrupted. "Coach," he said. "whenever I'm at the plate, I'm in scoring position."

His heroes were astronaut John Glenn and President John F. Kennedy. On opening night of football season — Friday, Sept. 4, 1964 — junior quarterback Brad Henderson set a Willingham school passing record in a 21-0 victory over Warner Robins.

Who was the opposing quarterback that night? Gov. Sonny Perdue.

The following Monday morning, Labor Day, the team watched game film. Henderson gave his players the rest of the day off. Brad, 16, went with some friends on a picnic to High Falls State Park.

Henderson remembers Brad appearing at the doorway to the coach's office. He tossed him the keys to the family station wagon. It was the last time he saw his son alive.

On their way back to Macon, Brad and his girlfriend, Diane Driggars, were at a stop sign at Wesleyan Drive and Riverside. A speeding car driven by a 62-year-old Macon man hit them head on. All three were killed.

Henderson became restless when Brad didn't return to pick him up at the school at 3 p.m., as he promised. They received word that two teenagers had been killed on Riverside Drive. Henderson turned to his coaching staff and said: "Brad is never late."

Then Sheriff Ray Wilkes showed up at Henderson's door. "He didn't have to say a word," Henderson said.

The funeral was on Wednesday. Henderson showed up at the Willingham practice field later that afternoon.

It was Henderson's way of letting his players and coaching staff know that life goes on, no matter how heavy the heart. Parents who have lost a child will tell you there is no greater grief. For years, Henderson would cope by involving himself in dozens of community activities. He wanted to be tired enough to fall asleep at night.

The memories, like the ones he shared Thursday afternoon, are what keep him going.

"Brad lived life to the ultimate," he said. "He loved his family, his school, and he loved sports with a passion."

Is there a greater lesson? A better sermon?

The old coach has never put down his clipboard.

Critters

Bug Man Creates a Buzz
July 9, 2003

MUSELLA — There are people with highways and bridges named in their honor.

Others have gardens, baseball fields, deli sandwiches and church pews that bear their names.

Jerry Payne has a beetle, spider, protozoan and millipede named after him. An isopod, too. Or, as we call them in the South, a roly-poly.

If you ever encounter a *nesticus paynei* (spider), you now know where it got its name. Same goes for a species of beetle called the *pseudanophthalmus paynei.*

Although Payne has been retired for almost 10 years as a research entomologist, nobody ever said anything about downshifting.

The work is never really done, but that's the fun part. There's always something to learn. And discover.

He's married to a Rose and spends his days traversing 80 acres of woods in a corner pocket of the world where Bibb, Crawford and Monroe counties come together.

He and Rose jokingly refer to their property as "Tick Hill Estates." It even says so on their business card. He's right at home among the bugs, even the ones that bite.

The Paynes have identified 175 different species of birds and 73 species of butterflies on their "estate."

You can't walk away from Jerry Payne without congratulating yourself for meeting an interesting character.

He's perhaps the only guy on his block — or any block — with a resume' that includes academic pursuits and training in the fields of medicine, mammalogy, speleology, forensic entomology, radiation ecology, radioactive waste disposal and wildlife biology.

It all makes for fascinating conversation at the dinner table.

He worked for the U.S. Department of Agriculture for 27 years, including the Southeastern Fruit and Tree Nut Research Laboratory in Byron. There, his main focus was on the production problems caused by insects and mites on peaches, blueberries, pecans and other crops.

He also has been involved with identifying and labeling plants utilized by wildlife and establishing a native wildflower planting for bees, butterflies and hummingbirds.

Since there are no rocks on his land, he makes stone and brush escape/thermal cover for reptiles, birds and amphibians. He also builds lizard fences, trellises and tadpole ponds, among other contraptions.

But for all his activities and accomplishments, he is perhaps most noted for something he did 41 summers ago while he was a graduate student at Clemson.

It was a project that earned him entire chapters in nearly a dozen books, including *The Case of the Mummified Pigs and Other Mysteries of Nature* and *A Fly for the Prosecution: How Insect Evidence Helps Solve Crime*. In 1966, he was featured in both *Time* and *Scientific American* magazines.

Payne said there aren't too many folks in Middle Georgia who know about his now-famous experiments with insects and decaying animal carcasses.

So the locals probably were not aware he was a pioneer in this kind of forensic research with pigs that inspired an episode of television's top-rated show, "CSI," last year.

In the summer of 1962 at Clemson, going against the advice of his professors, Payne set out to prove insects played a major role in the decomposition of dead animals.

"If they didn't, we would be up to our necks in dead deer and other animals," he said.

He also was curious about determining the patterns of insects for establishing the time of death. After considering a variety of roadkill for his project, he settled on pigs because their skin most closely resembled that of humans.

Payne convinced farmers to save their dead pigs for him. He placed the carcasses in the South Carolina woods, with some of the pigs screened against insects and the others fully exposed to an invasion of bugs.

He monitored and identified 522 species of what *Time* magazine referred to as "insect morticians." Their arrival and departure were much like a shift change. Within 10 days, all that was left of the exposed pigs was bone, cartilage and dry skin.

When the national magazine article appeared, Payne said he received more than 1,000 letters from all over the country.

Today, he is more involved with such passions as bird and butterfly counts for the Department of Natural Resources.

Still, part of him remains curious about the complexities and cycles of nature.

Said Rose: "We can't walk past a dead animal without Jerry poking it."

And, of course, he's never met a bug he didn't like.

Especially those with a Payne in their name.

They're practically part of the ... er, family tree.

If the Dog Answers, Don't Hang Up
September 5, 2001

I'm not sure how to say "hello" in poodle. But it must have been what Nick was trying to tell me last week when I called the south Macon home of Dub and Nina Simmons.

The Simmonses usually apologize to first-time callers, who aren't accustomed to having a poodle pick up after the first ring.

Who needs Caller ID when you've got Collar ID?

Dub and Nina have no idea who taught Nick to blitz the telephone, grab the receiver with his teeth, place it on the sofa and begin barking into the mouthpiece.

He was already trained when he came to live with them seven years ago.

Said Nina: "None of our other dogs ever paid attention when the phone rang."

That's not the case with Nick, the K-9 with K-911 savvy. Answering the telephone has become his life's, er, calling.

"Our friends know to wait until we can get there," Dub said. "A lot of times, we'll pick up and they'll be talking to Nick."

This curly, black answering machine arrived on Rice Mill Road one week before Christmas in 1993. They named him Nick, after St. Nicholas.

Dub and Nina have been married for 53 years. They have no children, so their poodles have always been important to them. First, there was Chipper, then Onyx and Chico.

Chico got his name from one of their favorite TV shows, "Chico and the Man." He developed cancer in 1991 and had to be put to sleep.

"It takes a long time to get over something like that," said Dub. "We were without a dog for two years before Nick came along."

A friend in Smarr, Eddie Bowdoin, was driving to work when he noticed the miniature poodle walking on Rumble Road from the direction of Interstate 75. He wondered if the dog had been lost in the vicinity of a rest area.

When Bowdoin returned home that evening, the dog had taken up residence in his yard. He ran ads in local newspapers, but the owner never came forward.

After about a month, Nina's brother, Bob Land, called to tell them about the dog.

"(Nick) had been living outside, sleeping under the porch,

chasing the chickens and had so much red mud on him you could hardly tell what he was," Dub said. "(Bowdoin) was going to have to take him to the pound if he couldn't find him a home."

Nina and Dub are convinced it was divine intervention. "We believe God sent him our way," Nina said. "We couldn't have searched the world over and found a better dog."

A local veterinarian estimated that Nick was about 2 years old.

Nick immediately began answering the phone at his new castle. Dub and Nina were amazed — and amused. The humor was not lost on Nina, who is retired from Southern Bell.

They speculated that Nick's previous owner might have been hearing impaired, and the dog was trained to signal when there was a ring.

Experience has taught them to unplug the phone by the couch whenever they leave the house.

Nick may know how to answer a call, but he still needs some work on hanging up.

Happy Tails: Gus Has Come Home

May 7, 2004

Gus came home through the back door, his tail wagging like a windshield wiper blade switched on high.

He headed straight for his food and water dishes. They were exactly where he left them a month ago.

He had lost a lot of weight, dropping from 75 pounds down to 58. (Such is life on the lost-dog diet.) The veterinarian had pulled enough ticks from his brown fur to start a small colony.

All that didn't matter now, though.

Gus was home.

If you love stories with happy endings, this is your lucky day.

John Orlando, a man practically at death's door a month ago, is back at his River North home. He has made a remarkable recovery.

And Gus, the dog he adores like a second son, has returned to take his familiar place at the foot of John's recliner.

Five weeks ago today, no one would have thought this reunion would have been possible.

John is a single father raising two children. He moved his family here five years ago from Lancaster, Pa., to take a management position with Armstrong World Industries.

On Friday, April 2, he had planned a weekend camping trip to

the Okefenokee Swamp with his son, Andrew, a senior at Jones County High School.

His daughter, Maggie, a junior at Mount de Sales, was celebrating her 17th birthday that day and had traveled to Duluth for the state Key Club convention.

While taking Gus to a local veterinarian's office for boarding, John was involved in a serious automobile accident at the intersection of Riverside Drive where Arkwright Road becomes Bass Road. He suffered severe head injuries.

He spent five days at The Medical Center of Central Georgia before he was transferred to the Shepherd Center in Atlanta.

Gus slipped out of the car and away from the accident scene, still wearing his leash.

John has been home for two weeks now, and is undergoing rehabilitation to help fill the gaps in his April memory banks. His father, Joe, is staying in Macon to help the family.

John is showing few outward signs of the crash that nearly claimed his life. He is regaining those fuzzy pieces of memory — except for the week between the accident and meeting his doctor at the Shepherd Center.

Of all his injuries, a heavy heart inflicted the most pain.

After all, Gus has been like a member of the family since John got him from a Pennsylvania breeder. His parents were both show dogs. His father, Fangtasm Dakota, has been featured in a book about American Staffordshire Terriers.

The registered name for Gus is "Mountain View Chief of Staff." But, when John was taking him home, he took one look at his new dog's facial features and said: "You look like a Gus."

Gus sleeps on the bed and controls just about everything in the household, including the remote. He loves to jump in the recliner with John and is a big fan of all the televised dog shows.

Upon returning home, John said his spirits were lifted when he learned about local efforts to find the missing dog. The family began receiving dozens of calls after I wrote a column April 16. Andrew and Maggie placed signs in neighborhoods near the accident scene.

There had been several "Gus" sightings from New Forsyth Road to Wesleyan Drive. John even spotted Gus himself, walking on the side of the road.

"I called to him, but he just looked at me and walked into the woods," John said.

John was worried since Gus has always been an "inside" dog. He

was afraid his pet would not survive in the wild. He was concerned Gus would not know how to cross busy streets and highways.

Several families on the north end of Wesleyan Drive began leaving food for a wandering dog they believed to be Gus.

Stephanie Jordan, a veterinarian with Brantley and Jordan Animal Hospital on Thomaston Road, tried to reassure John that Gus was going to be fine.

"He's just having fun," she told him. "People are feeding him. His instincts have kicked in, and he is enjoying himself."

Ralph Whitehead was very involved in reuniting Gus with the Orlando family. Whitehead lives on Wesleyan Drive, and was among those leaving food for the dog.

John pondered a plan to put a sedative in the dog's food, but ruled it out. He also consulted with a professional animal trapper about using a dart gun to sedate the dog, but eventually decided against it, too.

John took the advice of Sgt. George Meadows, a Bibb deputy sheriff and coordinator of the county's "Neighborhood Watch" program. Meadows suggested allowing animal control to set up a trap. They baited a cage with hot dogs.

On Thursday, May 29, Whitehead called the house. Joe answered the phone.

"I think we got him," said Whitehead.

While John went to Florida for a few days with Joe, Gus spent six days at Brantley and Jordan for medical observation.

"Gus needed some transition before he came home," said John. "He needed a halfway house for dogs."

He still can't believe the "celebrity" status of his dog in recent weeks. And he has been touched by the outpouring of support from Macon and Middle Georgia.

Strangers have called to say they were praying for the family. Parents from Mount de Sales have sent meals. Neighbors have come over and cut the grass.

"Somehow, saying 'thank you' isn't enough," he said. "I knew there were good people here. But I didn't know there were so many of them. It just amazes me. I know it sounds terrible, but I'm fortunate the accident happened here. Even though we've only lived in Macon a few years, the community responded to us."

Gus might have nodded in agreement, but he was sound asleep. The den floor sure felt good.

A Dog's Life in the Pink

March 24, 2001

My name is Casper. As you might guess, I am as white as a ghost for most days on the calendar.

But this is the week of the Cherry Blossom Festival, so I've had my hair done for you.

Surely, you have seen a pink poodle before.

This is my time for a little canine shine. Of course, you could cover me in anything Sherwin-Williams or Baskin-Robbins has to offer, and I would never recognize the difference.

Like all dogs, I'm colorblind. I do, however, know the third week of March like the back of my paw. It is my favorite time of the year.

I don't just bask in all this attention during the festival — I glow.

It's like I've "dyed" and gone to heaven.

My owners — Paul and Alice Williams — love to show me off. One year, for the Georgia State Fair, they colored me blue.

But pink is my color.

Even though I'm a guy dog.

Today, you will see me walking around the Mulberry Street Arts & Crafts Festival. Or strolling my curly locks through the Third Street park. Or turning heads down at Central City Park.

Paul recently took me to the bank, where the women made their annual fuss over me. He also drove me up to Wal-Mart, but we had to wait outside.

There is a "No Pets Allowed" sign on the entrance. We never would have made it through the front door without getting a "pink" slip.

When he walks me in the yard at his business, Tradebank, I have been known to stop traffic along Pio Nono Avenue. People will turn around in their cars to come back and see me.

Ever rubberneck a pink poodle?

I'm not just pink — I'm fuchsia. To be more accurate, it's neon hot pink.

I don't answer to the name Spot, although you can spot me a mile away.

If you must ask, it is food coloring.

Paul and Alice did not "spray paint" me, as folks often speculate. Years ago, they started out by experimenting with a coating of cherry Kool-Aid mix. That got me into some pretty sticky situations.

Now they've switched to professional food coloring, just like

you will find in cakes and cookies from the bakery. It's still a little messy, and Paul's palms usually stay pink for most of the week. He has learned to mix it with a little vinegar.

Got the idea for that from dipping Easter eggs. At the arts and crafts festival two years ago, one of the vendors gave me a pink flamingo hat.

Last year, she presented me with a matching pink leash. I can't wait to see what she has for me this year.

I've been doing this pink gig for 10 years now, from about the time I was a pup. (I'll be 11 in June.) My friend, Teddy, is another poodle seen around Macon wearing a fashionable pink coat.

Teddy and I have been often imitated, but rarely duplicated. Teddy is taking a sabbatical for this festival after owners Paul and Delise Knight moved to Fort Valley.

If you want to know my life story, here it is — in dog years, of course. I was born in Pittsburgh, and Paul and Alice drove 14 hours from Macon to adopt me. They made the lady promise not to sell me before they got there. They snuck me into a motel on the trip home — my first big adventure — and they have always given me lots of attention.

They love poodles. I'm the fifth one they've owned in the 33 years they've been married. They once ran a dog grooming business called Paul's Pet Palace and Grooming Salon. The floodwaters of Rocky Creek forced them to close in 1994.

It's difficult to earn a living washing dogs when you don't have running water.

In the Third Street Park Friday, people were coming up to me every couple of steps. I met a man from Panama City Beach and a few other exotic places. I am used to all the attention. I've posed for photographs with people from Japan, England, Germany, France, Australia and a few places I can't spell.

I'm prepared for even more attention this weekend. Sometimes it takes me hours to circle the two blocks at the arts and crafts festival.

If you see me, please stop to say hi.

I'll be the pink poodle.

No way you can miss me.

MARGINS
OF LIFE

No Home for the Holidays

December 13, 2000

Ike goes wherever his size 9 ½ sneakers take him.

Sometimes he heads for the hills. Fort Hill. Pleasant Hill. College Hill.

Other times, he wanders down by the river. Or gives his regards to Broadway.

"I'm always thinking about where I'm going to go next," Ike said. "I just don't know where I'm going to spend the night."

Nights are the toughest when you're homeless. That's when the cold jumps on you like white on rice. The nicotine and caffeine at your fingertips can't warm the chill, calm the fear or cure the loneliness.

"You get scared," he said. "You don't really sleep. You cat-nap. You have one eye closed and one eye open."

His name is Isaiah, like the prophet, but most folks just call him Ike. He is not a prophet. He doesn't always know where his next meal will come from or where he will rest his head for the night.

For 15 years, he has had no address. He has slept on front porches and in back alleys. He has sought refuge inside shelters at the Macon Rescue Mission and Salvation Army.

A friend or relative may take him in for a few days before he is back on the streets again. He once slept in a box. He has holed up in empty shotgun houses and crawled inside abandoned storefronts.

"See that broken window up there?" he said, pointing to the second floor of a ghost lounge on Third Street. "I've been up there in the dark. You may think you're the only one there, but you can hear other people moving around you."

Although Ike is 46 years old, the time lines on his face are worn. He has been unable to soften life's hard edges.

He was raised by his grandmother in rural Jones County. They buried her on his 14th birthday, and he went back to his mother. He never knew his daddy.

They moved to Macon. He quit school. Either he found the streets or the streets found him. Ike has been in and out of institutions and clinics for depression and alcoholism. He has been in jail for fighting, drinking and disorderly conduct.

The scrabbled details of his life make him shiver like a dip in the mercury. He has lost his share of jobs. "When you don't show up for work, you will find yourself out of a job," he said.

He once lived with a woman. They were not married. He still

wears a wedding band on his left hand, but don't let that fool you. He was walking the streets and stepped on it. He has no idea whom it belongs to or where it came from — just that it fits.

Sometimes, the police stop and ask him about the sack he is carrying, even if it is only some warm clothes from the Loaves and Fishes Ministry downtown.

People have thrown things out of car windows and hit him. Others yell obscenities. He doesn't know why. He carries a knife for protection.

"I'm not bothering anybody. I know people are tired of seeing me on the streets," he said. "I'm tired of seeing them, too."

Ike has been asked many times what it is like to be homeless. He said it is nothing like the description given by a man once interviewed on local TV, who was homeless by choice.

"He called himself a pioneer, like Daniel Boone or Davy Crockett," said Ike.

Although he carries a small watch in his pocket, he has no schedule to keep. His only upcoming social engagement is to attend the annual Christmas Party for the Homeless at Christ Church.

The season sometimes makes Ike sad. The downtown streets he walks at night are decorated with lights.

He has no Christmas tree waiting at home.

"Are there miracles?" he asked. "I don't know. I ain't ever had one. I haven't given up."

The Homeless at Thanksgiving

November 24, 2004

I see them more often than I see some of my closest friends.

I pass them on the streets, their earthly possessions stuffed in some plastic sack, shuffling their shoes but with no real place to go.

I think about them when I head home to my family, where there is food on the table, flannel sheets on the bed and the love flows like warm air through the vents on an autumn night.

I see them pushing shopping carts and garbage cans. These are their wheels, and they don't really own them. They have "borrowed" them from some parking lot. These are not the same kind of tires that will carry an estimated 1.2 million Georgians on the road this Thanksgiving holiday.

I wonder who they are and how they arrived at this dead end. Are they homeless because of hard luck or by choice?

Life's blessings, like gravity, keep most of us grounded. The homeless have dropped off the map and are living somewhere in the margins.

From my office window, I see them come up from the river. They cross busy Riverside Drive and traverse the downtown alleys, avoiding eye contact with the world.

Sometimes, they have a dog on a leash or a rope. I watch them disappear along the narrow trail across the railroad tracks and navigate the gentle slope to the riverbank. I wonder if they go downtown to the soup kitchens. And if their dogs are hungry, too.

I rarely notice the clothes they wear, except they are probably the same ones they were wearing the last time. It is a mismatch of plaids and dots, faded by time and discarded by fashion. They always seem two sizes too large or too small. I don't understand their logic when I see them wearing heavy coats in summer, thin cotton in winter.

Every day, there is another layer of stubble and pain on their faces, some of it self-inflicted. I wonder if they know there are people out there who would help them, but they don't know how. Society guards its walls.

They have no welcome mat, no mailbox in the cardboard yard they call home. When the newspapers we read this morning become yesterday's news, they may use them to cover themselves like a blanket at night. The empty boxes we throw away during the holidays may be their new shelter.

Every city has a homeless population and a relentless uneasiness about where to hide it. We have churches, missions and agencies that help feed and clothe them.

But even a giving heart spouts its theories. By showing compassion and providing, do we also attract them like moths to the light? And where do we draw the line between giving a hand and a hand-out?

I struggle with this almost every day. I have been taught not to judge people.

But, when they get too close at the traffic light, I lock my doors.

I have given them money just so they will leave me alone.

I can't say I always know the difference between a panhandler and someone who needs a lifeline.

How do I know they will work for food? Do they really need money for a bus ticket? Can I be sure the $5 I gave them won't end up in the cash register at the liquor store?

They have their ways of keeping a lump in my throat.

Footsteps of a Simple Man

October 20, 2000

BLOUNT — They say Carroll Dickerson walked these roads as if he owned them.

When he hit stride, his shoulders reached so far back it almost was like he was walking downhill.

He navigated the well-traveled routes to Jackson and Forsyth. He roamed every backroad from High Falls to Indian Springs. He knew every step along Brownlee Road.

But his favorite was a 10-mile stretch of asphalt on Ga. 42 north to Jackson. He was a familiar sight walking in the shadows of tall pines and double lines.

People who did not know him sometimes would stop and ask for directions. Carroll never had the ability to tell them or even understand their questions.

He was a man of few words. He was mentally challenged.

"Like talking to a 3- or 4-year-old," said his longtime friend Jimmy Pettigrew.

Pettigrew and others begged him to stay out of the busy road, but Carroll could be stubborn. Last year, he was hit by a car, broke his arm in two places and had to be hospitalized.

Judy Pettigrew often became frustrated with the 72-year-old man who lived alone in a trailer on their property.

It rained two weeks ago today, and she urged him to stay home. As soon as she left, though, he took off like an old dog who still knows how to jump the fence.

"He walked a lot of places, but Jackson was his favorite," Judy Pettigrew said. "He loved to be around people. That's what drew him there. He always would find his way home."

Carroll made his usual rounds that Friday. He was a regular at the Mason Jar restaurant, where owner Bobby Mackey had been feeding him two or three times a week for the past 20 years.

No one really knows what happened after Carroll ate his last free lunch.

He left the restaurant, crossed the highway and stepped onto the railroad tracks.

He never saw the train. He never heard the whistle.

They buried him two days later in the cemetery at Pleasant Grove Methodist Church, not far from the farm where he was born.

At the funeral, whites and blacks both paid their respects to this

simple man, affectionately known as the "Mayor of Blount." (His only surviving relative is a sister, who lives in Barnesville and also is mentally challenged.)

Some folks were afraid of him. He chain-smoked cigarettes and chain-drank Coca-Colas. His hygiene and social skills were limited. Had it not been for a man named Robert Freeman, Carroll most certainly would have been institutionalized.

When Freeman died three years ago at age 97, the Pettigrews stepped in as caregivers. They arranged to have a small trailer placed on their property and helped Carroll enroll in programs at the Monroe County Retardation Center.

"Bringing him here was the right thing to do," Judy Pettigrew said. They took him to church at Paran Baptist. He survived on a diet of potted meat, Vienna sausage and honey buns. Judy would make him toasted cheese sandwiches. He always wore a coat, even on the hottest days of the year, and slept in his clothes.

Carroll never was one to watch TV. He was convinced every single song he heard came from the Grand Ole Opry.

Although the Pettigrews have a photograph of him with a fishing pole, Judy said she doubted he even knew how to bait a hook.

But they cared for him, which is more than most folks might do.

They loved him. And now they miss him.

Heaven's backroads surely must be hearing footsteps.

War & Remembrance

One Was One Too Many

October 26, 2003

When the telephone rang in the wee hours of the morning, David Carter knew it was going to be a sad day.

He would dress in his Army uniform and slip into the dawn's first light.

Most mornings, he might have been on his way to Macon's old Lanier High School. He was the commanding officer of 1,300 cadets in the largest Junior ROTC program in the country.

But, on those days the phone calls came, he knew he would be traveling backroads and standing on front porches in Macon, Dublin, Warner Robins and Forsyth.

He knocked on doors with the grim task of informing families that their son or husband had been killed in action in Vietnam.

Carter had seen death before. He spent seven months in combat in Korea.

But nothing compared to this.

"It was worse," he said, "than being in battle."

Carter is now 73 years old. He served his country in the military. He served his city in public office. He was a councilman for 17 years, including eight as council president. (In 1995, he finished the term of Mayor Tommy Olmstead when Olmstead left office to head the state Department of Human Resources.)

Not long after he came to Macon in 1963, Carter was assigned the duties of a "notification" officer. There was no formal training.

"I don't know why I was picked. I guess I was better prepared than some of the other officers because I was combat-hardened," he said. "Every case was different. Every family was different."

He had wives and mothers faint in his arms. He had tears fall at his feet. Sometimes, family members were angry and bitter. Other times, they were so grief-stricken they could not speak.

"They looked at me as the government," he said. "Some saw me as the commanding officer. Or the person who drafted their son. Some of them blamed me, and I didn't even know them."

During World War II, families often were notified by the cold hard type of a Western Union telegram.

In Vietnam, the policy was to send two officers to the home, usually early in the morning, to inform the family their loved one had either been killed or was missing in action.

"We would usually stay 30 minutes to an hour," said Carter. "But

we would always stay as long as the family needed to talk."

The duties did not end there. Carter was responsible for making arrangements for the military funerals, from the color guards to the pallbearers to the bugle players who played "Taps."

He remembers one funeral when a preacher had car trouble and missed the service. Carter was asked to stand up and deliver a eulogy for a young man he did not know.

"You had to be everything," he said. "Minister. Commanding officer. Psychologist. Lawyer."

Now, when he goes to funerals, especially the ones with flag-draped caskets, those memories come rushing back.

How many times did that phone ring before dawn? How many doors did he knock on? How many hearts did his words break?

He lost count.

One was one too many.

Now They Will Never Be Forgotten
November 11, 2001

ABBEVILLE — A sense of duty sent some to war. Some simply waited for Uncle Sam to wave his finger and order them halfway around the world.

They came from small towns like Rochelle and Pineview. And from bumps in the road along rural mail routes, like Sibbie and Double Run.

When their country needed soldiers, it pulled them from the cotton fields and cantaloupe patches of Wilcox County. It recruited them from the backwaters of Folsom Creek and Oscewichee Spring, and issued them uniforms almost as soon as they turned their tassels at high school graduation.

Some came home heroes. Some returned crippled and scarred, changed forever by their experiences.

Others came home in pine boxes. Their final resting places were the cemeteries at churches where they were baptized as young boys and took brides as young men.

Friday morning, they were honored here on the small lawn of the courthouse, at the intersection of the only traffic light in the county seat of Abbeville.

Large granite monuments, imported from Elberton, displayed names of the 64 native sons who died during the nation's seven previous armed conflicts.

All were somebody's son. Somebody's brother. Somebody's father.

At their feet, granite bricks carried names like "Tot" and "Cap" and "Skeet." They served their country honorably, then were blessed to breathe the pine-scented air of home again.

Now, many of them have passed on, too. They were not there Friday to read the inscription at the heart of the Wilcox County Veterans Memorial: "Freedom Is Not Free."

They were not there to see the placement of a wreath. Or hear the prayers, pledges and anthems, or the keynote speech by Ret. Brig. Gen. John C. Bahnsen, a native of Wilcox County. At the end of the ceremony, the bugle softly played "Taps."

It took more than a year to pull this together, to rally the citizens, raise the money and research the records of every veteran for 380 square miles.

"We're about 50 years late," said Bill Sutton, chairman of the veterans committee. "Some of these boys are gone. Their mothers and fathers are gone. Their families are gone."

Better late than never, though. From the beginning, Sutton reminded folks of the sacrifices made by those they were seeking to honor.

"They didn't quit," Sutton told them. "Neither can we."

Sutton is a businessman in Rochelle who opened the town's first Dairy Queen. He spent a year in Vietnam in 1968. He is the baby of a "Band of Brothers" who served in World War II, Korea and Vietnam. Twenty years separated George Henry (deceased), Charles Otis, Bobbie, Johnny, Floyd, James and Bill Sutton.

The 43 deaths listed from World War II include brothers, too. Marcus and Luther Miller are buried at the cemetery in Pitts. John D. and Wilson E. Jones, of Seville, were killed in action two days apart.

"I knew most of them, or knew their families," said Sutton, his eyes moving across the granite.

Now they can be assured they will never be forgotten.

The Man Who Made the Armies March

January 13, 2002

SANDERSVILLE — Willie Lee Duckworth lives with his wife, Edna, in a blue house along Highway 242 as it edges east toward Riddleville and Bartow.

The rural mail carrier brings the usual assortment of envelopes addressed to "Occupant" and "Resident." There are circulars from the

Food Lion, applications for credit cards and sweepstakes entries from faraway places.

But every couple of months, a special letter will travel the time-worn path to his door.

It is a royalty check. The royalties make him feel like a king. There were years when those checks brought more money than he made hauling pulpwood in Washington County.

In many ways, they have been gifts that keep on giving. They have helped put food on the table and buttons on his shirts.

In 1944, Willie Lee Duckworth, an unsuspecting buck private from Georgia, authored one of the most popular marching cadences in Army history.

At first, it simply was known as the "Duckworth Chant." It later gained fame as "Sound Off."

Ain't no use in goin' home.
Jody's got your gal and gone.
Ain't no use in feelin' blue.
Jody's got your sister, too.
Sound off!
One, two.
Sound off!
Three, four. ...

With those words, and others, Duckworth made the journey from foot soldier to footnote in military history.

"Sound Off" became the title of a song performed by big band leader Vaughn Monroe. And this year marks the 50th anniversary of the movie by the same name, starring Mickey Rooney.

"It made me famous for a while," Willie Lee said. "And it put some money in my pocket."

He celebrated his 78th birthday this past Tuesday. Although many folks in Washington County are aware of his contribution, the march of time has delivered a generation of others who know little or nothing about Duckworth's serendipitous fame.

He was raised by his grandparents in a sharecropper's house not far from where he now lives. He was working in a sawmill when he was drafted during World War II. It was the first time he had been more than 100 miles from home.

Duckworth was assigned to a provisional training center in Fort Slocum, N.Y., in March 1944. On orders from a non-commissioned officer, he improvised his own drill for the nine black soldiers in the unit. Soon, all the ranks were buzzing and keeping rhythm.

Col. Bernard Lentz, who was the base commander, approached Duckworth and asked where he developed his unique chant.

"I told him it came from calling hogs back home," Duckworth said. "I was scared, and that was the only thing I could think of to say."

The marching cadence built upon a military tradition developed to keep soldiers in step and their spirits high.

Over the years, many variations have been added to the original 23 verses Duckworth wrote with the help of Lentz and others.

"Sound Off" is still making noise, with the blessings of the old soldier who dreamed it up.

Willie Lee Duckworth died in February 2004.

The Day Cole Was Taken Away
September 11, 2002

She first noticed his blue eyes.

They were radiant, like the man behind them.

Wallace Cole Hogan Jr. was the kind of person who made you glad to be in the same room.

Pat Phermsangngam was in the same room on a September day five years ago. It was a doctor's office at Howard Air Force Base in Panama.

Cole had been battling a stomach virus for a week. He had traveled more than an hour from the Army base at Fort Sherman to seek medical assistance. An internist, she was the doctor who saw him.

They talked for an hour, not just about his symptoms, but everything under the Panamanian sun. She filled him with so much joy he practically forgot what ailed him. He made her laugh — and late for her next appointment.

When she asked for his medical history, including information about a past injury to his back, he began thumbing through the pages of a black book. He quickly produced a copy of his MRI.

Only the book was much more than his medical file. It contained names, phone numbers and appointments. There were contacts and prospects, personal goals and history.

Some of the information was written in pencil. As people moved away or passed away, an eraser had made way for the necessary changes. There were permanent spots reserved for others.

"This is my book of life," he told her.

Before he left, he asked her for a date.

She was added to his "book of life."

"That book went wherever he went," Pat said.

He placed it in his military backpack when he left for work the morning of Sept. 11, 2001. He rolled out of bed at 4:45 a.m. and had one foot out the door at 5:10.

He kissed Pat, who had become his wife. He told her he loved her. He left to catch the commuter train to the Pentagon.

He was at his desk next to the general's office by 6 a.m.

The book of life was with him when the airplane hit.

Pat Hogan thinks a lot about the day she looked into those blue eyes for the first time. It was Sept. 19, 1997.

Fate had brought them together from different worlds.

She was an Air Force doctor an ocean away from her native Thailand. He was in the Army, stationed 1,658 miles from his home in Macon.

She was a Buddhist. He was a Methodist.

But, for all their differences, they had much in common. They were both outdoor enthusiasts who enjoyed exercise and traveling. Their energy was as boundless as their love.

Cole, an Army major and Green Beret, had spent time in Thailand on one of his deployments. While there, he bought black, star sapphire rings for his mother, sister and niece.

He purchased an extra ring and kept it in a drawer as he moved from post to post with the military. He told friends he was saving it for when he met his "special lady."

Two weeks after Pat came into his life, he gave her the ring.

It was a perfect fit.

Yes, Pat thinks a lot about the day she met Cole. The date, Sept. 19, 1997, now haunts her memory.

That's because on Sept. 19, 2001 — eight days after the terrorist attacks on the Pentagon and World Trade Center — Army officers from Fort Benning knocked on the door of Cole's parents, Wallace and Jane Hogan of Macon.

Pat was there. The officers had come to tell her and other family members that Cole's body had been identified.

In the end, the death toll would stand at 125 people killed at the Pentagon and 64 confirmed deaths of passengers and crew on American Airlines Flight 77.

"I ask all the time why it had to happen," said Pat. "Gosh, we had waited so long to find each other. In a way, I guess the date was symbolic. It was four years to the day we met.

"Would I have preferred that the news had come on a different day? I would have preferred that there hadn't been a day. ..."

Growing up, three of Cole's closest friends were Larry Williams, Rusty Bean and Andy Greenway.

Williams, a Macon attorney, knew Cole because their fathers, Wallace Hogan and Al Williams, were in business together at Sanco Products, an industrial cleaning business on Seventh Street.

Their fathers often took them dove hunting together. They began working at the business during the summers.

Although Williams was two years older and they attended rival high schools (Williams went to Stratford and Hogan attended First Presbyterian), they still remained close friends.

In high school, Bean and Hogan were practically inseparable. Bean, now a veterinarian in Gray, played noseguard on FPD's football team. Hogan was a defensive end.

"We both loved the outdoors, and we were always doing something together," said Bean. "We used to drive his '71 Wagoneer around to see if we could get it stuck somewhere. One time, we sank it so deep on the power line behind Wesleyan that Mr. Hogan had to hire a Caterpillar (tractor) to get it out."

They were freshmen together at Valdosta State in the fall of 1978. That's when Hogan became fast friends with Greenway, who was his "big brother" in Sigma Alpha Epsilon fraternity.

"I was older and had gone to Mount de Sales, but I knew of Cole," said Greenway, now a real estate agent with Fickling & Co. "Our friendship just clicked. That's what I liked about him. He was genuine. He had that vibrant personality that made him fun to be around."

Bean was studying in the Valdosta State library one day during summer school when Cole approached him.

"We're joining the National Guard tomorrow," he told Bean.

It was July 13, 1980. They signed up at the same time and stayed together through basic training.

"He always remembered that day, because he would send me a card every July 13," said Bean. Fifteen years later, Bean graduated from vet school on the same day.

Bean stayed in the Guard for more than 20 years. From the beginning, though, he knew Cole was going to be a career military man.

After college, Cole's sense of adventure took him to Colorado, where he worked at a ski resort, and Hawaii, where he was a police officer in Honolulu and was employed at a dive shop in Maui.

His military career in the Special Forces carried him all over the

map, then eventually to Panama with the Army Jungle Operations Training Battalion at Fort Sherman.

Williams remembers the phone ringing early one morning. It was Cole, calling to tell him about meeting Pat.

"He told me she was 'squared away,' " said Williams. "It meant that she had drive and vision."

Pat and Cole dated for two years, working out transfers to Washington so they could be together. Cole took a job at the Pentagon. Pat worked at the hospital at Andrews Air Force Base.

They were married Oct. 9, 1999 — Cole's 39th birthday. The wedding was in the back yard of the home they bought in the Alexandria suburbs.

"Our marriage was more than I thought it ever could be," said Pat. "He was so perfect. I probably shouldn't say this, but he would get up on Saturday mornings and clean the house. He would tell me to relax."

Cole was an early riser. He wanted to maximize every minute of every day.

"He busted his tail at everything," said Williams. "I never was around him when he wasn't productive. He loved working hard. He was the most disciplined and well-organized person I've ever met. He always had a 'to do' list tacked somewhere."

Physical exercise and training were his passion. In his early days working at the Pentagon, he would ride his mountain bike 15 miles to work. But he would not stop there. He would sometimes continue for another 25 miles through the pre-dawn streets of Washington before arriving at his desk at 8 a.m.

That changed in July 2001, when he began working for Gen. Philip Kensinger in the office of the deputy chief of staff for operations and plans.

His hours were longer. His workload became heavier. He would arrive at the Pentagon at 6 a.m. and often not return home at night until 8 or 9.

So he and Pat began to cherish their time together on the weekends. He loved military history and enjoyed visiting battlefields. One of his favorite places to hike was at historic Harper's Ferry, located at the confluence of the Potomac and Shenandoah rivers.

On Labor Day 2001, he completed the Chesapeake and Ohio Canal trail on his bike. The C & O trail follows the route of the Potomac River for 184 miles from Washington to Cumberland, Md.

"I had seen him at a wedding that summer in Macon," Greenway

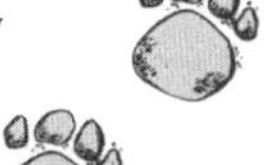

said. "He told me he had been riding sections of the canal. We decided I would go up there in the fall and do a portion of the trail. I bought a book that goes over the trail, mile by mile. He was going to pick out one of his favorite sections, and we were going to ride it together."

The weekend after Labor Day, Cole took Pat to Annapolis for the Georgia Tech-Navy football game Sept. 8. She had never seen a college football game. They also toured Annapolis on their bikes.

At home the next day, Cole wanted to go bike riding again, but Pat told him she was too tired.

"It was a lazy Sunday. I wanted to stay home," she said. "He left about 1 and was back by 3. I asked him why he was back so soon. He told me he had missed me. I don't know why, but it was like he knew something."

Pat Hogan was making her rounds at the hospital the morning of Sept. 11.

Andy Greenway was in a sales meeting at his office.

Rusty Bean was on a veterinary call.

Larry Williams was in court in Houston County.

"My client pleaded guilty, so I was out early," Williams said. "I was going to get some breakfast, and I was listening to the radio in the car. It was one of those comedy guys in the mornings. He made the comment that some idiot had just flown a plane into the World Trade Center. I kept listening, but then another plane hit. I knew we were being attacked. I decided to skip breakfast."

Before Williams could return to Macon, the Pentagon had also been hit by a commercial airplane hijacked by terrorists.

In the spring, Williams had visited Cole in Washington and had toured the Pentagon with his buddy. At that time, Cole's offices were located in the basement.

Cole took him to the large courtyard at the center of the Pentagon, one of the largest office buildings in the world, covering almost 3.7 million square feet.

"He said something about the courtyard being the most secure place on the planet," Williams said.

There was a feeling of military invincibility.

But Pat Hogan knew better as she stared at the TV in disbelief. Three weeks earlier, Hogan's office had been moved to a remodeled part of the west wing of the Pentagon.

She knew Cole's new office was near the helicopter pad. Her eyes searched the television screen for signs of the helipad.

"When I saw all that smoke, a light went out inside me," she

said. "In my head, I was saying that Cole was probably OK. In my heart, I knew something bad had happened."

She called his office. No answer. Back home in Macon, Greenway and Williams also tried to call. The phone kept ringing.

Pat later dialed Kensinger's home number. Six minutes before the plane hit, the general had been talking to Cole at his desk. Then he left for business in another part of the building.

He had phoned his wife to let her know he was safe. He did not mention Cole, but the general's wife tried to reassure Pat.

"I'm sure he's all right. He goes everywhere the general goes," she said.

Said Pat: "I thought about the reasons I might not hear from him. He might have been taken to the hospital. He might be busy helping others. The phones weren't working. That was probably why he hadn't called.

"I decided to call the Hogans in Macon. Pop (Wallace Hogan Sr.) is always home. That was our backup when we were traveling and couldn't get in touch with each other. We would call the Hogans, and they would relay the message."

When the Hogans told Pat they had not heard from their son, a feeling of doom came over her.

Greenway went to the Hogans' house that night. When he walked in, Jane Hogan was on the phone with someone from U.S. Rep. Saxby Chambliss' office. Cole and a 38-year-old secretary in his office, Diane Hale-McKenzy, were unaccounted for.

"I was still thinking he was OK," Greenway said. "There was just so much chaos, we couldn't reach him. I thought if anybody would survive that, Cole would. He would get out of there."

Bean was thinking the same thing.

"The guy was a warrior," he said. "He wasn't about to be taken out by somebody like that."

By Friday, Pat had asked to go to the Pentagon as part of an emergency medical personnel team.

She stood about 25 yards from the building, not far from the rubble and smoke.

Cole's office had been at the point of impact.

"I knew he was in there," she said. "I wanted to be close to him."

There are daily reminders. They may recall something he said. Or did. They guard those memories closely.

For Bean, the lasting image is a torn photograph of the two of

them taken during basic training 22 years ago at Fort Benning. He keeps the framed photograph in his bedroom.

"I have a wife and six kids. But if we get deep in a war, I'm going," Bean said. "Put the gear in the truck. It's personal now."

Williams remembers his friend as being positive, smart and an avid reader with an intellectual curiosity.

"We had that in common. He was a great conversationalist, and most of our phone calls over the years lasted an hour or more," Williams said. "He was a great listener and really focused on you. When you asked his opinion on something, he was always honest without being judgmental. He appreciated when I disagreed with him and respected it. I don't believe we ever got mad with each other. He had a great sense of humor with a booming laugh.

"He finished in the top of all the classes he took in the military, yet never bragged. Cole never said anything bad about anyone. He seemed to see the best in everyone."

There are times Williams catches himself reaching for the phone to call his friend. They had been roommates when Cole lived in Colorado and Hawaii.

Cole's military duty in recent years had separated them by miles and time zones.

"Because I wasn't used to seeing him every day, it sometimes seems like he's just away on another assignment," he said. "... It still hits me when I can't wait to tell Cole something. Then, I remember."

Cole's death, he said, has "created a gap in my life."

Pat Hogan has moved from Washington. In May, she transferred to Okinawa, Japan, where she is a flight surgeon. She asked Greenway to come to Washington to help with the move.

"She told me she had never done anything with Cole's clothes," Greenway said. "She thought she could pack his stuff, but she couldn't. I went up there to help her."

In June, a year of grieving grew even more difficult. Pat's father, Dhavi Phermsangngam, a commercial airline pilot, died after an extended illness.

She spent this past Labor Day weekend in Macon visiting with Cole's family and friends. She plans to attend today's memorial services in Washington.

"I can't say how I'm going to feel that day," she said. "I may just want to forget it and lock myself in a room."

She shared her life with Cole for only four years. She's 35 years old. She isn't sure if she will remarry.

"He changed my life, for sure," she said. "He made me a better person and a better military officer. He showed me how happy you can be. I know Cole would want me to be strong, to go on and live life to the fullest. I want to make him proud of me."

Pat has started her own black book, filling it with names, numbers and dates.

She calls it her own "book of life."

She remembers having a conversation about death with Cole in January 2001. A close friend had been killed in a car accident. They talked about what would happen if something ever happened to the other.

Cole died nine months to the day after his friend's untimely death. He was buried Oct. 12, three days after what would have been his 41st birthday and his second wedding anniversary.

He was laid to rest with full military honors near a stand of oaks in Arlington National Cemetery. In the distance, down the hill and through those same trees, you can see the Pentagon.

Sometimes, Pat hears strangers talking about Sept. 11. It may be in a store, a park, a terminal at the airport. She catches herself stopping to eavesdrop.

"Most of the time, they say how things have changed since 9/11," she said. "I want to say something, but I don't. I want to tell them they have no idea. It was the day Cole was taken away from us."

The Father He Never Knew

October 25, 2003

When you ask 3-year-old Maddie Jackson about the young man in the photograph, she will tell you it is her daddy.

One day, she will understand that it isn't.

For Maddie, it is the grandfather she never knew.

For her daddy, Terry Kent Jackson Jr., it is a framed picture of the father he never knew.

He is 34 years old now, and there are times when he must feel like he's walking around in another man's skin.

Family members tell him he's the spitting image of his dad, who was killed in Vietnam Feb. 13, 1969, two months before Terry Jr. was born.

Strangers have stopped and asked him if he is Terry Jackson. Or tugged at his arm in the emergency room at The Medical Center of Central Georgia, where he works as a nurse.

I knew your father, they tell him.

He was a great man, so you must be, too.

"I respect my dad because so many people respected him," Terry said.

The pride is there. So is the pain.

"I think about what it would have been like if he had been in my life," he said.

Terry is the son of one elementary school principal and the husband of another. His mother, Sherrell Cherry, is principal at Rosa Taylor. She remarried 17 years ago to Sid Cherry, the head of the Macon-Bibb County Urban Development Authority.

His wife, Donna Jackson, is principal at Porter Elementary and the youngest principal in the Bibb County school system. (Besides Maddie, they have a son named Terry Shaw Jackson. They call him Shaw.)

When he married Donna, he used his father's wedding ring as his own.

"From the beginning, Terry looked so much like his father it was almost scary," Sherrell Cherry said. "He has the same mannerisms. He has the same discipline and focus. And Terry is a family man, a great dad — just like his father would have been."

Terry Jackson Sr.'s parents, Carl and Belle Jackson, still live in Macon. Carl Jackson often looks at his grandson and sees his oldest son.

"He favors him," Carl Jackson said. "They are alike in a lot of ways."

Sherrell Cherry met her future husband while swimming at a Macon lake when she was a sophomore at Hawkinsville High School. They married after she graduated from high school in 1966.

Terry Jackson's middle name was Kent. He was named for an uncle who had been killed in World War II.

Terry was a popular student and a football player at Willingham High School. He joined the Marines in 1967.

He had an aptitude for language. He was trained in linguistics and spoke Vietnamese fluently. He was sent to Vietnam to serve as an interpreter for the military and civilians.

He left for Southeast Asia in August 1968. He was killed seven months later.

"It was devastating," Cherry said. "If it hadn't been for my mother, Catherine Sapp, I never would have made it. She held me up and told me everything was going to be OK. She said she would help me through it, and she would be there for me when it was over."

He was buried near her family's plot at Orange Hill Cemetery in Hawkinsville. The words of a theme on courage he had written a year

earlier are inscribed on his grave.

Terry Jr. was born in April of that year. He was named after his father.

But Sherrell Cherry said if the baby had been a girl, she had planned to name her daughter Terry, too.

Terry Jr. participated in the ROTC program at Central High in Macon and at North Georgia College, where he was part of a group effort to bring the traveling Vietnam Memorial wall to Dahlonega.

While he was in college, his mother was principal at Union Elementary. She asked if he would serve as a chaperone on the annual sixth-grade trip to Washington, D.C., and help a child with special needs who would be traveling with the group.

In Washington, they visited the Vietnam Veterans Memorial Wall, where they found the name Terry Kent Jackson Sr. on Panel 32W, Row 27.

When the only connection you have with your father is the photographs and memories of those who knew him, a part of you always will be missing.

He had been to his father's grave. The Wall was different, though. He was surprised at its strong emotional pull.

He turned to his mother and said: "Mom, I didn't know I would feel this way."

He Ain't Heavy; He's My Brother

February 1, 2004

EASTMAN — They fought in the same war on different sides of the world.

Jack King built roads and bridges on islands in the south Pacific. Curtis Jones marched across Europe with Patton's Third Army and was on the front lines when the war ended.

After they returned from World War II, they shook hands and introduced themselves.

As Bogart would have noted, it was the beginning of a beautiful friendship.

Jones worked at an automobile dealership in Eastman. King was busy engineering bridges across streams and rivers in south Georgia. He went to Jones to purchase several trucks for his business.

"We leaned on each other," said King. "He needed the business to feed his family, and I needed the trucks to make a living."

They still lean on each other.

Their friendship has stretched across the decades. They swap old war stories. Today, the mutual enemy is the advancing army of old age. They both are 91.

But their loyalty is sweeter than those sugary pecan logs Stuckey's once rolled out on the edge of town.

They usually travel in tandem, as inseparable in the same sentence as Lewis and Clark.

Because of their physical limitations, they have learned to pool their resources. King has been legally blind since 1992. Jones must endure chronic back and leg injuries he suffered in the war and cannot get around without his "buggy" walker. For the past week, he has been sidelined with a viral infection in an Eastman hospital.

They are a familiar sight around town — Jones moving slowly behind his buggy, and King moving slowly behind Jones with his hands on his shoulders.

It's a slow-moving train, but it gets to where it's going. King does most of the talking. Jones does all the driving.

Sunday mornings, King trails Jones up the handicap ramp at the First United Methodist Church, where they attend the same Sunday School class, eat breakfast and take their regular seats on the fifth pew for the service.

Jones is a widower. His wife, Julia, died in August 1999. King's wife, Bonnie, is disabled. He has learned to familiarize himself with the terrain of the 137 steps from his front door to his mailbox.

In their younger days, they used to go fishing together. They would fill their freezers with their catches of the day, then have a fish fry for senior citizens.

They now get together for lunch several times each week. They discuss everything from politics (Jones was once a city councilman) to the weather to religion to the latest town gossip.

Even though they've already heard each other's war stories, they patiently listen to them again. And again. And again.

King said there are 35 major bridges in Georgia, and he had a part in building 22 of them. "I've been everything from a water boy to time keeper to superintendent," he said.

But the strongest bridge he ever built was the Friendship Bridge, the one that spans 56 years and connects him with Curtis Jones.

They lean on each other.

He ain't heavy. He's my brother.

Curtis Jones, who had been hospitalized, died less than a week after this column appeared.

The Daily Reminders of Rodney Davis
June 7, 2002

Not a day goes by that Ruth Davis doesn't think of her son, Rodney.

He would be 60 now, and a grandfather. For the past 35 years, only his memory has filled the ache in her heart.

Sgt. Rodney Maxwell Davis was a hero. Macon's only Medal of Honor winner died in Vietnam on a September afternoon in 1967. He was 25 years old. He left behind a wife and two young daughters.

It was a week until his family was notified of his death. It was another two years before they learned he had thrown himself on a grenade, saving the lives of the men in his company.

Yes, Ruth Davis will never forget the second-oldest of the six Davis children. Rodney was tall and lanky, a natural leader who took control and was always plotting his next move.

She can't help but be reminded of the son whose image hangs in her living room in a framed photograph of the U.S.S. Rodney Davis, a Navy missile frigate.

Davis was the first black Vietnam veteran to have a ship named in his honor. His name also is enshrined at the Freedom Foundation in Valley Forge, Pa.

His hometown has not forgotten the young man who grew up in Macon's Pleasant Hill neighborhood, where he had a newspaper route. He enlisted in the Marines after finishing Peter G. Appling (now Northeast) High School in 1961.

An ROTC classroom at Northeast was named after Davis. A local public housing project, Davis Homes, also bears his name. Last July, a monument honoring Davis was placed at the new Civic Square in front of City Hall.

"I always try to act like Rodney would act, and step up to do what's right," Ruth Davis said. "This is quite an honor. There's a sadness, too. After all, I am his mother."

She still goes to Linwood, where a memorial to her son is the most prominent feature in the historic black cemetery. A portion of the overgrown graveyard has been cleared so that the memorial, with its large American flag, is visible from I-75.

Still, the upkeep of the 108-year-old cemetery, where the graves of 58 veterans are scattered across the hill where Davis rests, remains an issue in the black community.

"We've been asked if we might move Rodney's grave," said his

sister Debra Ray. "But he would never leave the others behind, so we won't either."

The daily reminders of Rodney remain, too.

Ruth Davis has a 16-month-old great-grandson named Gordon Hays Smith. He reminds family members of the great-uncle he never knew.

"He doesn't want to miss out on a single moment," said Debra Ray. "That was Rodney."

My Father and Vietnam

October 31, 2003

My father has a Vietnam wall.

The "wall" consists of a map in a room at his Macon home. It has been tattered by time and soiled by the elements. It shows the country where he spent a year saving lives and seeing too many deaths. It shows the rise and fall of the land, the rivers along the South China Sea and the mountains and dense jungles where warriors paid the ultimate price.

The map was given to him by a wounded helicopter pilot. He was brought to the Naval Support Activity hospital in DaNang, where my dad was chief of surgery from July 1967 to July 1968.

My father had a special place in his heart for the brave men who flew the daring chopper missions. He could always tell by the sound of their hurried approach if they were bringing in the wounded and the dead.

My dad is one of the most unique two-war veterans I know. At age 17, he had barely started shaving when he went into the Navy for World War II. He missed the Korean War because of medical school.

He went to Vietnam when he was 43 years old, leaving behind a wife and five children.

As a small-town doctor in LaGrange, he was no stranger to death and gruesome injuries. LaGrange was a mill town, and he routinely saw mill workers mangled by the machines. In the emergency room, he saw horrible automobile accident victims and Saturday night stab wounds.

He always tells the sad story of the young boy who went to buy his mother a watch for Christmas. He was crossing the railroad tracks, headed for home. He never saw the train.

But none of that could have prepared my father for the 600-bed hospital in DaNang.

The body bags. The burns and blood. The uniforms sometimes

soaked with Agent Orange. The injured young men brought from the jungles, where the tigers, baboons, insects, snakes and Viet Cong slithered like death.

Nights were never quiet. The sounds of war were always close. He recalls the day a rocket hit some nearby barracks. Within 15 minutes, some 150 casualties were brought in.

My father didn't appreciate the movie (or the television series) M*A*S*H. Although the comedy was set during the Korean War, it was a caustic commentary on Vietnam.

There never was anything funny about the job he did or the sacrifices he made.

On another wall in my father's home hangs the "Legion of Merit" he was awarded for his military service.

But he will never forget another "wall" he has visited twice in Washington, D.C. There are several replicas traveling around the country.

"The real heroes are the ones on that wall," he said. "They gave their lives for their country in an unpopular war. And the families they left behind — the children, wives and parents — have a heavy burden."

My father, who will be 79 years old Saturday, believes everyone who went to Vietnam came back a different person. He has sympathy for the survivors, some whose lives he helped save.

"I feel sorry for what they had to endure when they came back," he said.

They will be among those who will arrive at the traveling replica wall when it comes to Macon — weeping and touching and remembering those who never returned home.

One Day, One Decision, One Fateful Spot

August 11, 2004

DUBLIN — There are times when Reggie Starke opens his eyes to find his hospital bed surrounded by family.

Oh, how he wants to say something. But the words won't come. He must cherish every moment because soon they will have to go, leaving him with doctors, nurses and four walls at the Carl Vinson VA Medical Center.

A Navy man, his eyes sometimes drift like a boat at sea. Still, family members are convinced he senses their presence in the room.

His mother, Betty, runs her hands softly across his face. Reggie may be 36 years old, but he is still her baby, her only child.

His grandmother stands at the foot of the bed and promises to cook him roast and potatoes when he comes home. Reggie has always

believed Ardonia Vinson is the best cook ever to put on an apron.

His father, Napoleon, has been blind since the age of 13. An accomplished musician, his voice is known all over Macon.

In the hospital room, Napoleon sings Reggie a song they wrote together two years ago.

That's when Reggie's wife, Carlis, reaches to wipe tears from the corners of her husband's eyes.

One day.

One decision.

One fateful spot on the earth can unalterably change a life.

The dark clouds moved in on Reggie's world one year ago today on a golf course in St. Mary's, where he was stationed at the U.S. Naval Submarine Base at King's Bay.

Lightning struck him in the forehead. The electric charge surged through his left lung and leg. It shredded the baseball cap he was wearing. It left him partially paralyzed and clutching his vital signs.

He was moved to the VA hospital last October. His family — and the doctors who peer over Reggie's charts daily — can't be certain when, or if, he will ever leave.

"His overall prognosis has been poor since day one," said Carlis, his high school sweetheart. "But we still have faith. We have seen where he has come from. We have seen him respond to touch and breathe on his own again. Anything he does, big or small, is encouraging to us."

In the window of his hospital room are pictures of his two children. Reggie Jr. and Riana. Reggie Jr., 8, has had to learn to understand why his father no longer picks him up from school every afternoon. And 1-year-old Riana, who was born a month before the accident, has started pointing to pictures on the walls at home and saying, "Daddy."

There are cards on the windowsill from Valentine's Day and Father's Day. At his parents' house in the Fort Hill neighborhood in Macon, there are unopened Christmas presents awaiting Reggie's return.

Reggie was a popular student when he attended elementary school at St. Joseph's and high school at Mount de Sales in Macon. After he graduated from Mercer University, he enlisted in the Navy.

No one was surprised. Reggie routinely welcomed challenges. He was adventurous. The Navy was a perfect fit, even for a young man who, as a child, hated taking swimming lessons because he couldn't stand to have water in his face.

He met Carlis in the choir at the New Pleasant Grove Missionary Baptist Church on Maynard Street. They were married in March 1995.

Reggie followed in his musician father's footsteps, learning to

play the piano, guitar and bass. A year before the accident, he co-wrote a gospel song called "Why Did You Choose Me?" and his father recorded it on a CD.

The title is hauntingly prophetic.

A friend had invited him to play a round of golf after work that afternoon. Reggie had only taken up the game a year earlier, but was passionate about it almost as much as his beloved Georgia Bulldogs. He went by his house, changed clothes, grabbed his clubs and hurried out the door.

Carlis talked to him on his cell phone shortly before 6 p.m. It was beginning to storm at the house. Less than an hour later, some friends appeared at her doorstep urging her to get to the hospital quickly. She called her mother, Alice Hollings, in Macon, who drove over to tell Napoleon and Betty Starke.

"We didn't take time to pack. We just threw everything into a sack and drove down there," said Betty. "He was in bad shape. He didn't even look like Reggie."

According to the National Weather Service, there are about 300 documented lightning injuries and 67 deaths in the United States each year. Reggie remained on life support for nearly a month, then moved to the VA facility.

Carlis makes the three-and-a-half hour trip about once a week. Reggie's parents and grandmother drive the 55 miles to Dublin every other day.

"Sometimes, my van acts like it doesn't want to move, but I tell it it has to go anyway," said Betty Starke. "The doctors say family is the best medicine."

Reggie grew up a block down the hill from New Pleasant Grove Baptist on Cowan Street. Betty said she once had a dream she was walking to the church.

She turned around and saw Reggie in the front yard. He told her he had somewhere to go.

"I told him he wasn't able. The next thing I knew, he was gone. ..."

Carlis said the struggles of the past year have drawn her closer to her faith.

"I believe my husband has been given a second chance," she said. "God could have taken him that day, or any day since then. Reggie has a purpose for being here."

Carlis believes maybe that purpose is to share his story with others.

"One day he will stand up and give his testimony at church," she said. "And we're all going to be there to hear it."

A Final Toast

September 18, 2002

There will come a time when the Last Man Club will need a table for one.

It won't be necessary to reserve the banquet room at the Holiday Inn to swap war stories over green beans and peach cobbler.

Families won't be asked to bring members who can't drive at night. Men in the back won't have to turn up their hearing aids. Or help each other into chairs.

No, there will come a time when the Last Man Club — all veterans of the greatest conflict in world history — will hold its annual Sept. 16 meeting for a party of one.

And that solitary old soldier — the last man — will remember his World War II comrades, those bound to him by time and place and duty.

Following orders, he will open the bottle of champagne that has passed through the hands of so many and make a toast to their memory.

That one-table day has yet to arrive.

But the 23 members who attended Monday night's banquet know it will.

At the end of Monday's ceremony, 89-year-old John Terry was entrusted with the champagne bottle and engraved silver cup.

For the first time, he stood before the group as its oldest surviving member. He clutched his walking cane in one hand and ran his other hand across the smooth silver.

Dave Ramey had been last year's recipient. He was in poor health, but he insisted his daughter take him to the banquet.

Ramey died nine months later, just as Arthur Ferguson and Dr. Sam Patton — the previous cup holders — had passed away in preceding years.

Sadly, what has been called the "Greatest Generation" is fading right before our eyes. More than 1,100 World War II veterans are dying in our country every day. The Last Man Club is not immune to the playing of "Taps."

Two of the club's most devoted members, Walter Ashmore and J.D. Lisenby, have died since invitations were mailed out just a few weeks ago.

Lisenby died Sunday, but his family still attended Monday's banquet in his place. His widow, Ann, asked members of the club to sit as a group at today's funeral service at Macon Memorial Park.

Another Monday, 62 years ago, these men's lives changed with the stroke of a pen.

By signing up for military service on the same day, they became brothers in an exclusive fraternity.

Their common ground was taking the oath of enlistment in the 121st Infantry on Sept. 16, 1940.

It was part of the federal mobilization of the National Guard. It came 15 months before the attack on Pearl Harbor signaled the U.S. entry into World War II.

The roots of the 121st go back to the formation of the "Baldwin Blues" in Milledgeville in 1810. During World War I, it was known as the "Gray Bonnet" regiment.

The 121st Infantry was headquartered in Macon as part of the 30th Division.

It was under the command of Maj. Gen. Henry D. Russell, who also was a veteran of World War I and was the first to have his name engraved on the Last Man Club's silver cup.

James M. "Dutch" McLendon, who turned 18 just two weeks before he enlisted, said most of the others shared similar reasons for signing up.

"We all had been to Lanier (High School), which had a great ROTC program," he said. "So we had a liking for the military."

McLendon, now 80, was one of the co-founders of the Last Man Club some 25 years after the war.

Its rolls were limited to those who enlisted in the 121st on Sept. 16. The banquet has been held on that day every year since 1970.

Until last year, only members attended. Now, family and friends are allowed.

The club once had as many as 123 members. About 84 have died since 1970.

Now, only 39 remain on the rolls.

At Monday's meeting, chaplain Jake King read the names of the six men who died in the past year.

In recent years, the club's rolls have spilled over to the obituary page in record numbers.

"I deal with this roster, so I'm always looking at it," said McLendon, sadly thumbing the pages of deceased members.

"I was in Boy Scouts with Walter Ashmore. Ken Keadle was one

of my closest friends. At one time, Arthur Ferguson was the country's No. 1 rifle marksman. ''

All are gone now.

The Last Man Club will not last forever.

To receive the silver cup and become the guardian of the Jacques Bonet champagne bottle is more of an endurance test than a medal to be earned.

"You don't get it for anything you've done," said McLendon. "You're just the oldest. And there is no competition, unless the competition is to be the last one."

At the banquet tables, they sip their coffee and wonder. They are aware that their numbers have thinned on the front line of life.

When will the somber final meeting of the Last Man Club be called?

And who will be there to raise the final toast to the others?

Love Conquers All

You Don't Walk Away from Love
February 10, 2002

WARNER ROBINS — Emily Willeby sat in her living room and talked about love.

It was a special day for her. It was her 32nd wedding anniversary. She and her husband, Wayne, were married Feb. 6, 1970.

"We wanted to get married around Valentine's Day," she said. "February is the month for love."

I asked her where they got married.

She smiled. "Right here," she said, pointing to the exact spot on the living room floor where she and Wayne tied the knot.

It was her parents' house at the time. She lived here when she met Wayne not long after her 18th birthday.

They said traditional wedding vows that day.

For richer, for poorer. In sickness and in health ...

"I meant them then," said Emily. "And I mean them now."

Although Wayne has not spoken a word to her in 10 years, he still tells her he loves her every day.

She can see it on his face. She can read it in his eyes.

He can spell it out through the miracle of a computer program. He cannot move his arms, but he can type by flexing the muscles in his forehead. The cursor scrolls across a keyboard on the screen. He makes the cursor stop when it is positioned on the letter.

I ... L-O-V-E ... Y-O-U! ...

Wayne was diagnosed with Lou Gehrig's disease in 1987. Since 1992, he has been on a ventilator and confined to a bed. At the time, doctors told Emily her husband's life expectancy would be two to five years.

You can do the math. It has been 10 years now. Every day is a gift.

Wayne cannot move his mouth to speak. They have learned to communicate in ways that transcend words.

"People will come to see us, and they'll ask me: 'How did you know what he wanted? How did you know he needed that?' " said Emily. "Well, I just do."

There is another question, too.

Sometimes it is asked. Most of the time it is simply understood. Why does she do it? Why does she so lovingly accept her role of wife and caregiver?

"He is my husband. He is my life," she tells them. "You don't walk away from love."

Wayne will be 54 in a few weeks. Emily celebrated her 50th birthday this past December.

It's easy to understand why their paths never crossed at Northside High School in the 1960s. They lived very different lives. Wayne was a popular athlete. Emily was laid back and unassuming. She was younger, and they didn't walk in the same circles.

They became acquainted after Wayne returned from military service, including 14 months in Vietnam. Their eyes met at an old teenage hangout called the Blind Lemon on Commercial Circle.

He asked her to dance. The band was playing "My Girl." When they held each other in their arms, it was a perfect fit. They dated for one year.

"When he gave me my engagement ring, everybody told me the marriage would never make it," said Emily. "Everyone thought we were too opposite."

But, for all their differences, their matrimony found stability on common ground. They shared many of the same interests. Wayne discovered the girl he married loved to fish and be around the water. She enjoyed auto racing almost as much as he did. When he watched a football game, she would sit down beside him. She knew the difference between illegal procedure and a safety blitz.

They had two sons, Greg and Mike. (They now have four grandsons.) Wayne was a supervisor for the city of Warner Robins water and gas department. Life was good until Lou Gehrig became much more than the name of an old baseball player who wore New York Yankee pinstripes.

Lou Gehrig was the illness that stalked Wayne and crippled him. Amyotrophic lateral sclerosis is an incurable nerve disease that is more widely known as Lou Gehrig's disease. It claimed the life of the popular baseball player in 1941.

It is so rare it afflicts only one in every 10,000 people in the U.S. Among them was the late Morrie Schwartz, the subject of Mitch Albom's touching book and the TV movie, "Tuesdays With Morrie."

Wayne's physical problems began innocently enough. On long trips in the car, his foot would go to sleep. Soon, he became easily fatigued and suffered from uncontrollable twitches in his arm. Emily once handed him a cup of coffee at a youth football practice and it slipped through his grasp.

The next day, he went to see the doctor. Thus began a parade of waiting rooms, clinics and hospital beds from Valdosta to Macon to Augusta. Even after the diagnosis, Wayne vowed to stay on his job as

long as he could. He would come home from work so exhausted he would practically have to crawl in the front door.

"The doctors told me we didn't need to go out and buy a new car or a million-dollar home, but that we needed to get out and do some things together while we still could," said Emily.

For the next three years, they went to a local motel on their anniversary. They didn't want to stray too far from Wayne's doctors. The last time they went, Wayne was too weak to walk to the restaurant in the lobby. Emily knew that might be their last trip together, except to the hospital.

Still, their love is stronger today than it was 32 years ago. Emily cares for Wayne almost around the clock.

Last Tuesday, on the night before their wedding anniversary, they received a special visit from a celebrity.

NASCAR driver Kyle Petty, the son of racing legend Richard Petty, was in town for a banquet appearance before leaving for next week's Daytona 500.

Organizers of the event told Petty about Wayne and Emily and that they were huge racing fans.

"Let's go see them," Petty said.

Emily said the grin still hasn't left Wayne's face. Neither have their feelings for each other.

You don't walk away from love.

Sweet Times in Bolingbroke

February 13, 2000

BOLINGBROKE — Jim Mickle probably would have spotted the car parked at the Varsity anyway.

After all, it was a brand-new burgundy Mercury Comet Cyclone.

But what he mostly noticed was the girl inside the car. She was alone.

She was drinking a Dr. Pepper and eating french fries.

It was October 1965. Somewhere out there, Paul McCartney and The Beatles were singing "Yesterday" on the radio. It was the No. 1 song on the charts.

Yesterday. All my troubles seemed so far away. ...

Those words summed up the way Beverly Wadley felt, too.

"My date had stood me up," she explained.

She was feeling about as low as the ice cubes rolling around in the bottom of her Dr. Pepper. So no one could have blamed her if she

hadn't bothered to see the carload of boys that had arrived at the Varsity in Macon. They stopped beneath the sheltered parking. Her car was facing the street.

But Jim Mickle saw her. He wanted to go talk to her. He was just trying to drum up the courage. His friends decided he needed some assistance.

They pushed him out of the car and locked the doors. He had no choice but to go and introduce himself to her.

"We've been inseparable ever since," said Beverly.

Three months after they met, Jim proposed in the front seat of a '58 Chevy. It was Jan. 28, 1966 — Beverly's 20th birthday. He asked her to open the glove compartment. There was a small box with an engagement ring inside. Five months later, they were married.

Thirty-three years have passed. Sid's Sandwich Shop now occupies the old Varsity property along the bottom of Forsyth Street where curb boys once brought chili dogs and malt shakes right to your car window.

But three decades and change have hardly erased the twinkle in Jim and Beverly Mickle's eyes when they talk about the night they began their life together.

It is one of those magical romantic tales you never grow tired of telling. Or hearing.

Their story now goes beyond those beginnings of two people in love.

It is the story of a deep-rooted love for their community. It is the story of their love for working side-by-side in the old-fashioned restaurant business they started.

And it is the story of their unconditional love for their 29-year-old son, Everingham, who was born with a birth defect and has special needs.

Jim sometimes is known as the "unofficial" mayor of Bolingbroke. That designation comes from his knowing just about everyone in this corner pocket of Monroe County, where life along the kudzu-lined railroad tracks is less frantic than it is to the south in Macon.

Bolingbroke isn't large enough to be considered a town or need a mayor.

But two of his co-workers gave him a white shirt for Christmas with his "mayoral" title stitched across the front. He is plenty satisfied to help stamp out the few political fires Bolingbroke might encounter.

If you smell smoke, you'll be glad he's on your side, too. He's the community's volunteer fire chief.

He is here because of Beverly, though. They both grew up in

Macon. Her father, John Wadley, was the long-time pharmacist at Chichester's. (Her mother, Jane, was the bookkeeper there.)

As a child, Bolingbroke was a second home for Beverly. She would spend her weekends and summers here, staying with her grandmother, aunt and uncles. She was especially fond of her Aunt Sue, who taught her to sew and cook.

Her great-great-grandfather William Wadley, who was president of Central of Georgia Railroad, settled here in the late 1800s. He named the community after Lord Bolingbroke, an 18th-century English statesman and writer.

Jim and Beverly spent the first 18 years of their marriage transferring from city to city with United Parcel Service. By the mid-1980s, Beverly was weary of moving around.

It was time to go "home." This time, "home" meant Bolingbroke.

"She was like Scarlett O'Hara going back to Tara," said Jim. "I learned you don't mess with that family dirt."

So they put down roots in that dirt. Jim got employment restoring old Corvettes. Beverly found part-time work. She adored the "quaintness" of Bolingbroke.

The Mickles always had been fond of collecting "odds and ends." Maybe that's why they were approached about buying an antique soda fountain with a marble top.

Originally, it had been at Wilson's Pharmacy in Atlanta. It was being stored in a warehouse in Macon.

The idea of purchasing it appealed to them, if for no other reason than for the sake of nostalgia. Both had been "soda jerks" in their younger years. Beverly had worked with her family at Chichester's. Jim had been at Balkcom's Pharmacy on Main Street. (Now the site of the Macon Coliseum.)

"We once counted that there were 22 different soda fountains in Macon when we were growing up," said Jim. "There was one on almost every corner. Every department store and drug store had a soda fountain. We always describe those days as pre-McDonald's."

Their dilemma was that they had no idea what they would even do with a soda fountain. One day, Jim answered the phone at the house. It was an offer to sell the soda fountain at a price too irresistible to turn down.

He didn't want to sound too interested or eager. He said he would have to ask Beverly. She wasn't home, but he put down the phone, waited a moment and told the caller: "OK, we'll take it."

They kept it in storage until four years ago, when they came up

with the idea to open "Sweet Sue's Tea Room & Soda Fountain" in a building once owned by Beverly's uncle.

They named it "Sweet Sue's" in honor of Beverly's Aunt Sue. They installed the soda fountain, acquired several stools from a Woolworth's and some tables and chairs from the old Chichester's near Wesleyan College.

Of course, some folks warned they would be lucky to make it. Except for the antique shops and a few scattered businesses around Bolingbroke, they were told there wasn't enough local traffic to sustain a restaurant that was mostly open for lunch and afternoon snacks.

Those same folks now must wonder why there sometimes are as many as 50 people waiting outside to get a table. Sweet Sue's has doubled its seating capacity and tripled its enthusiasm. It likes to refer to itself on the menu as a "step back to the past" along one of the South's most nostalgic routes. (Before nearby I-75 came along, U.S. 41 was the main drag to Florida.)

The walls are covered with bygone signs, old photographs and newspaper clippings. You might expect to see Norman Rockwell in the corner table, dabbling with his paintbrush.

Regulars come for the chicken salad or the nutbread. Others stop by for some old-fashioned phosphates, mixed at the soda fountain by a self-described "fizzician." Still others drop in for ice cream or a cup of afternoon tea.

"It's a lot of work," said Beverly. "But we have fun every day. And we'll keep doing this as long as it's fun."

A lot of their time is devoted to their adult son Everingham, who still lives with them. They have to communicate through sign language. Although he has amazing memory skills in such areas as math and reading comprehension, he has never been able to speak.

Business at Sweet Sue's usually picks up around Valentine's Day. Maybe it's the name. Or maybe it's the sentimentalists who want to stick two straws in an ice cream soda.

But you don't necessarily have to have a sweet tooth.

After all, you'll find some of the stories around here are just as sweet.

A Marriage Still in Focus

September 9, 1998

ROBERTA — She was a farmer's daughter who had gone to town on a Saturday night. She was pretty and shy, and Virgil Olson

sure is glad he and his friend spotted her standing there on the corner with her sister.

His friend made the first move. He asked her to the picture show the following Saturday.

Fate, true love and a horse took over from there.

When his friend's veterinarian father accidentally was kicked by a horse, it was decided that Virgil would go in his buddy's place. His friend slipped him 60 cents to buy two tickets to the movies and two scoops at the ice cream parlor after the show.

The friend never got his date back.

Today, Virgil and Martha Olson are celebrating their 60th wedding anniversary.

It has been a sweet marriage, one that was built on more than just wedding vows. Her first gift to him was a small, metal camera that folded and used a special film. It changed and shaped his life.

"It only cost a dollar, but I had to borrow the money from my mother," Martha said. "It was during the Depression. We didn't have much money."

Martha didn't exactly approve of the first pictures he took. He slipped down to the local swimming pool in Sycamore, Ill., and took snapshots of some bathing beauties.

Later, in his career as a military photographer, Olson took photos of the queen of England, the heads of South American countries and Chuck Yeager, the first pilot to break the sound barrier.

By the time he closed the doors of Olson's Studio Photography in Warner Robins, he had accumulated 18 years of weddings, class pictures and team photographs.

"When we were first married and had two young children, we didn't even have running water in the house, and he set up a darkroom in the pantry," Martha said. "He was in there developing film when they announced on the radio about the Japanese bombing Pearl Harbor. I knocked on the door and told him."

Virgil Olson served his country not only by shooting weapons — he flew 30 missions with the Army Air Corps in Europe — but also by shooting photographs.

In 1948, he took a still-life portrait of his own hands while sewing the insignia of a promotion onto his uniform. The detail is so wonderful you can see the stitches of thread and the pores of his skin. The photo won him the inaugural first prize in an annual worldwide armed forces photo contest that marked its 50th anniversary this year.

His nickname was "One-Shot Olson." The military moved him

around to different states and foreign countries until he landed in Warner Robins in 1961. Olson retired three years later, and he finally put down roots when he opened his own photo studio.

He called in Martha to help him get the motor running. She ended up staying 18 years. His portraits now are captured permanently in high school annuals, wedding albums and scrapbooks from the pages of *The Daily Sun* newspaper in Warner Robins.

He is 82 now, and she will be 79 in a few months. It costs a lot more than 60 cents to go out for ice cream and a movie, but love never has faded from the picture.

Said Martha: "When we got married, it wasn't considered a 'trial' thing like it is now," she said. "I have stood in the backs of the churches waiting for young brides to go down the aisle. I have heard them say: 'I can't imagine having to send all those gifts back!' So many of them just don't think it's going to last. I never had any doubt we would stay married."

Like the some half-million original photographs Virgil and Martha Olson have stored away for posterity, marriage is not a reprint.

One-Shot Olson snapped it right the first time.

The Valentine I Wish I Never Sent

February 13, 2002

I wasn't looking for love in the fifth grade.

I was more interested in finding arrowheads than Cupid's arrows. It never crossed my mind, heart or lips to kiss any girl — except my mama.

Valentine's Day wasn't intended to warm this young boy's heart. It was just another cold day in February.

In grammar school, Feb. 14 arrived with annoying baggage. We were required — and this hasn't changed much during the years — to send valentines to everyone in our class.

That meant sealing envelopes enclosed with preprinted heartfelt messages and delivering them — even to the classmates we despised.

We were forced to be nice to the same kids who would break in line, copy our homework and steal our lunch money. We had to author sweet notes to the same girls against whom we had immunized ourselves with "cootie" shots.

Everyone sent valentines. Everyone received valentines. There was no selectivity, only a code of blanket enforcement.

Naturally, it encouraged every little girl in pigtails.

Hi, Eddie! That sure was a sweet Valentine's card!

Of course, I always wanted the record to clearly show that I did not voluntarily "send" the card. It was a homework assignment, a silly requirement for graduation.

I didn't seal it with a kiss, either. Under orders from a higher authority, I simply dropped it in the grocery sack with flowers painted on it.

I could never remember what I wrote. And, if there was anything mushy in there, I surely didn't mean it.

Yes, Valentine's Day was not a day for flowers and candy. It was a holiday to be endured, not enjoyed. (When St. Patrick's Day arrived, you had an excuse to go around pinching all those girls who weren't wearing green.)

Ruth was a girl in my class. She certainly was not the ugliest or the bossiest. In fact, she might have been the prettiest, smartest and sweetest.

I just didn't know it at the time.

Her only crime against me and my buddies was that she was two heads taller than anyone else. We were intimidated.

She was all arms and legs. She was slam-dunking, sky-scraping tall, at eye level with our teacher, Mrs. White. Her body was several laps ahead of the rest of her.

What I'm about to tell you happened three decades ago and more than three states away. But not a Valentine's Day goes by that I don't remember it with deep regret.

I altered the card I sent to her. I put a "Don't" in front of "Be Mine."

I replaced "Love" with a four-letter word I now don't even allow my own kids to say: "Hate."

It made her cry. Her mother called my mother, and my mother didn't wait for St. Patrick's Day to pinch me.

I was punished. I had to apologize. I don't know why I did it. My parents raised me with a moral compass and an occasional switch from the back yard. I went to Sunday School. I was taught good manners.

I'm now ashamed of writing something so cruel and mean. But it also taught me valuable lessons.

Be kind. Learn to love. And never intentionally hurt somebody's feelings.

Words are powerful. Be careful how you let them go.

Tis the Season

Merry Christmas, Always and Forever
December 9, 2001

It was December 1950, and Bill Meriwether Jr. was busy in his photography studio on Cotton Avenue.

As the calendar edged toward Christmas, customers came by to pick up their holiday orders.

"Merry Christmas!" he greeted them. It made him feel good every time he said it.

Even in the weeks after Dec. 25, that spirit never subsided. Meriwether continued to greet his customers the same way.

"When I told them Merry Christmas, I noticed people were really paying attention," he said. "So I started saying it all the time."

Bill Meriwether is now 82 years old. He retired in 1993 after operating his photography studio for 48 years. He probably has captured and preserved more grins than anyone in Macon history, and he continues to teach photography courses at Macon State College.

"Merry Christmas" became his trademark. He has worn it every day of his life for the past 51 years.

He greets everyone with a handshake or hug and two words: "Merry Christmas."

He answers every phone call with "Merry Christmas."

He and his wife, Betsy, even get mail at their south Macon home addressed to "Merry Christmas." The glee club at Wesleyan College once honored him with a chorus of "We Wish You a Merry Christmas!"

"I now have some people tell me 'Merry Christmas' before I can say it to them," he said, laughing. "It has been such a blessing. It has brought smiles to a lot of faces."

Smiles, yes. You also can imagine the reactions when people are wiping sweat in the middle of July, and a grandfatherly man wishes them a "Merry Christmas."

"Children will come up and tell me: 'It's not Christmas!' " he said. "And I say: 'Well, it's Christmas to me!' "

He insists that the greeting has nothing to do with his last name — Meriwether, as in "merry weather."

"If you don't know him, you might think he's crazy," said his son, Bill Meriwether III, who now runs the family photography studio on Vineville Avenue.

Bill Meriwether III is 49 years old. Merry Christmas is all he has ever known. His sister, Meri Norris, died in 1997. She was never given a middle name, so before she married, she went through life as

Meri Meriwether.

"People always want to know if I am the son of Merry Christmas," said Bill Meriwether III. "And it doesn't just happen in Macon or even Georgia. Because of his photography, my father is known all over the Southeast."

Jeanene Meriwether said her father-in-law's famous greeting is not holiday leftovers. It is genuine. It is heartfelt.

"He always has said he wishes people would act like it was Christmas year-round instead of just the four weeks before Christmas," she said.

Jeanene and Bill Meriwether III have continued that Christmas spirit in their own way. On May 23, 1989, Jeanene gave birth to their second daughter.

Bill III was scheduled to take photographs at Mount de Sales Academy's graduation ceremonies that night. With Jeanene in labor, the elder Meriwether volunteered to cover for his son.

The Meriwethers already had picked out a name for a boy. William Wilson Meriwether IV.

When Jeanene gave birth to a girl, they named her Meri. The decision on a middle name also was unanimous.

Welcome to the world, Meri Christmas Meriwether.

"The lady at the hospital who was filling out the birth certificate called to make sure," Jeanene said.

So what if it was springtime? Bill Meriwether Jr., the proud grandpa, called the florist and had a bouquet of Christmas balloons delivered to the hospital room.

Meri Christmas is 12 now, and she answers to "Christie." She is a seventh-grader at Mount de Sales, where she is a member of the swim team, plays trumpet in the band and is a manager for the boys' basketball "C" team.

Her classmates and teachers sometimes act as if they don't want to believe her when she tells them her full name.

Of course, it can be fun, too. Her family loves it when a cashier tells them to have a Merry Christmas.

"We already do!" her sister, Elizabeth, once said, giggling.

For the Meriwether family, Merry Christmas isn't just a season.

It's a way of life.

Mrs. Santa

December 12, 2001

Joyce Turner can look at her dining room table and tell Christmas is coming.

It is covered with envelopes, stamps, wishes and dreams. The letters arrive in boxes on her front porch. They are addressed to the North Pole.

Some are written in crayon. Children often send school pictures, along with drawings of Christmas trees, angels and candy canes.

Of course, the kids never miss an opportunity to mention their gift requests. And offer instructions.

I'm leaving you some milk and cookies. ...

My cat sleeps by the fireplace. Please don't step on her tail! ...

Could you bring my presents to Grandma's house? It's the green house on the left. ...

Joyce Turner doesn't look anything like Santa Claus. She is a grandmother.

She doesn't live at the North Pole. She grew up in south Macon.

But, this past Monday night, she spent four hours answering 17 of those letters on her dining room table. By Christmas, she will have replied to hundreds for the Macon-based Kids Yule Love program. Many find their way here from other states.

"I can't think of anything that gives me more joy than answering children's letters at Christmas," said Turner, the campus events coordinator at Wesleyan College.

Turner still remembers the Western Union telegram she received from Santa when she was 7 years old. He told her to be good and to go to bed early on Christmas Eve.

Now that she has taken over for Santa, her replies are old-fashioned, too.

The answers are not form letters manufactured on a computer.

They are not cut-and-paste. They are heart-and-hand.

She spends about 15 minutes hand-writing each response. Santa always signs his name in red ink. Parents are sometimes surprised when she phones to check the spelling of names.

She marvels at how tiny hands can produce such long lists. Santa knows never to make promises. Sometimes, her own tears fall on the words of children who share their heartaches and fears.

Turner has volunteered for this assignment every year since 1992. There is no paycheck, simply the satisfaction of bringing joy and

spreading the magic of Christmas.

Joe Allen, the founder and chairman of Kids Yule Love, has offered to enlist help answering the hundreds of letters. But Turner prefers to fly solo on the sleigh. She understands the value of a single voice. Often, she recognizes a name or hometown from a previous year.

The elves and reindeer and I jumped around and waved your letter – we were so excited! Thank you for making it a happy day for us! ... I'm so glad you are helping your mom ... Tell Anna hello. ...

She recently received two notes from the same child in Toomsboro. On the back of the second envelope was a message: "Forget the first letter!"

She also got separate mail from two young brothers in Brunswick. Inside each were three pennies, a gift to the firefighters in New York City.

How much longer does she want to continue answering letters?

"As long as my hand ho-ho-holds out," laughed the lady who loves being Santa.

Man with the Million-Watt Smile

December 13, 2002

Eddie Herron must have the most top-heavy house in Macon.

After all, he keeps his Christmas decorations in the attic.

"By the time I get everything up there, I have about this much space left," he said, holding his hands no wider than a log on the fire.

From January to October, carolers reside in his rafters. The reindeer nest up there and so does at least one animated Santa Claus for every man, woman and child this side of Houston Avenue.

When he brings them all down and plugs them in, the real magic begins. He owns nearly 1,700 animated Christmas characters.

Eddie's face lights up each holiday season, and it's not just the reflection from the nativity scene near his front porch.

Some people call him Santa Claus. He used to wear one of his four jolly-red outfits, but the role took its toll on his knees.

Now he's simply known as the man who pulls the switch on Capitol Avenue.

"I live all year," he said, "just for Christmas."

Eddie may not own stock in Georgia Power, but he is a major glare-holder. He wouldn't tell me what his electric bill runs every December. Let's just say his kilowatts are killer-watts.

There's hardly a square inch in his yard that doesn't glow. In fact, 95 percent of the displays on Capitol Avenue are on loan from Eddie.

Yes, he shares the light.

In his own yard, three wise men simply aren't enough — he has nine.

He has used decorations from his own collection to create impressive displays in the lobby and front yard of The Massee Apartments on College Street, where he works as a maintenance supervisor.

Inside the house at the corner of Capitol and Chatham, where this 60-year-old bachelor lives with his seven dogs, it is even more of a shrine to shine.

There are nearly 300 extension cords. There are so many decorations, he has to put most of his furniture in storage until January.

Retail stores love to see him coming. He once made a trip to Athens and returned with $40,000 worth of Christmas merchandise. It took four truckloads to bring it all home.

"If it's Christmas, I buy it," he said.

In 1982, Eddie made the move to Macon from Louisville, Ky., with Brown & Williamson Tobacco. He brought with him a fascination that dates back to his childhood days in Louisville.

"If we were good, our father used to take us downtown on the bus," he said. "We would look at the lights in all the store windows. Sears had five show windows in its store on Broadway. There were trains and animated dolls.

"You don't see that much any more. I'm trying to give children a little of what I had as a kid."

Twenty years ago, he fathered the tradition of transforming Capitol Avenue — located between Houston Avenue and Broadway — into a festival of lights every Christmas.

In its heyday, Capitol was probably the city's No. 1 luminary attraction.

"Tour buses used to come through. It was that big," he said. "There were nights when traffic was backed up for three blocks, all the way down to Rocky Creek. One night, I had a cop cuss me out. He blamed me for creating such a traffic jam."

Eddie remembers the story of a real estate agent, who was showing a house to a prospective buyer.

"This neighborhood goes a little crazy at Christmas," the agent warned the prospective buyer.

The crowds may not be as large as they once were, but they are steady. Beginning tonight, Eddie will open up his house for free weekend tours through Sunday night. Beginning Friday Dec. 20, Eddie's doors will be open through Christmas. He always keeps up his outdoor display

through New Year's Day.

Sadly, several of Eddie's decorations have been stolen or vandalized in recent years. It's a shame some folks are so mean and thoughtless. Here is a good-hearted man who simply wants to bring joy to others.

"It hurts," said Eddie. "But I don't let it stop me. I just grin and bear it."

When people see his yard, his house or his buggy filled with ornaments down at Wal-Mart, they often question his sanity.

"Are you crazy?" they ask him.

"I love Christmas," says the man with the million-watt smile. "And I love children. So it's all worth it."

Thrill and Chill of a Snow Day

January 3, 2002

Snowflakes across Dixie.

Sleds on Coleman Hill.

For good measure, please throw some salt on Artic Circle over there in East Macon.

Hee. Hee. Hee. Hee. Hee.

It actually snowed in Middle Georgia on Wednesday. Old Man Winter and the New Year huddled on a blind date.

And nothing short of capturing Osama could knock Macon's first measurable snowfall in eight years off the front page this morning.

I'm sure our Yankee transplants are having a nip-roaring chuckle at our rather chilly expense. The carpet-baggers are giggling at our wimpy layer of frozen white carpet.

Hah! You call this a snowstorm? The Weather Channel must have gotten its broadcast signal crossed with The Comedy Channel.

OK, so our flurries might not measure up to those in Buffalo, which got 7 feet of the white stuff last week.

By our standards, though, we have endured a blizzard.

As we ushered in 2002, grocery shelves were being cleared of every slice of Sunbeam bread. Wise men began gathering dry firewood and compiling lists of neighbors with 4-wheel drive.

Kids went to bed Tuesday night, setting their biological alarm clocks to wake up and see if the world had turned white.

No doubt, a few prayers were lifted.

Now I lay me down to sleep.

I pray, dear Lord, my snow will be deep.

Before daylight made an appearance on Wednesday, emergency

management officials were urging folks to extend their holiday vacations and stay home.

Schools and daycare centers were closing at the first hint of a snowflake. Public works and Georgia Power employees were dragging out the heavy equipment, bracing for the advancing armies of a cold front and low-pressure system.

Meanwhile, children used leftover Christmas boxes as makeshift sleds. Grown men playfully tossed snowballs in downtown parking lots. Absolutely nothing can energize and disrupt Southern life at the same time like the forecast of snow.

It's not simply a meteorological event. It's a celebration, a welcome diversion from the routine of winter's wind chill.

Snow is so uncommon in these parts that my youngest son, Jake, who will turn 8 years old next week, had never seen a white blanket on his hometown ground until 24 hours ago.

Of course, old-timers will remember the ice capades of February 9-10, 1973. A bizarre snowstorm dumped a record 16.5 inches on Macon's head, burying the previous mark of 6.9 inches in 1914.

How unusual was that? Well, until now, the city's cumulative snowfall over the past 28 winters had amounted to only slightly more than 24 inches.

Lest we forget that, three days before Christmas, hundreds of people paid $7 a head for 90 minutes of sledding in 60-degree weather at Wesleyan College. More than 50 tons of manufactured ice were used to produce 6,000 square feet of snow in a fund-raiser for the local Make-A-Wish Foundation.

On Wednesday, though, all the snow was free.

Enduring some good-natured Yankee ribbing was a small price to pay for our winter wonderland.

The Day That Holds Time Together

December 25, 2002

Calvin Coolidge may not have gone down in history, like Rudolph and his red nose. But the man did understand something about Christmas.

He said Christmas isn't simply a time or a season. It is a state of mind.

Norman Vincent Peale gave us the power of positive thinking. He also described Christmas as waving its magic wand over the world, making everything "softer and more beautiful."

But my favorite description of this holy day comes from the late Scottish poet, Alexander Smith.

"Christmas," he said, "is the day that holds time together."

Holidays invest our emotions in many ways. Valentine's Day slings arrows at our hearts. Memorial Day and the Fourth of July stir our patriotism. Easter is the only time some folks set foot inside a church. Halloween is a chance to be spooky and kooky. And Thanksgiving is when families gather to count their blessings.

But Christmas is the biggest star on the tree. It reaches out and wraps you up.

Yes, it can be stressful, frantic and expensive. Still, I can think of plenty of reasons why I love it like I love no other day.

It is knowing that, for every Scrooge out there, there are at least a dozen Santa Clauses.

It is watching "It's a Wonderful Life" on Christmas Eve and memorizing every Jimmy Stewart line. It is having a close friend so blessed that he signed his card "George Bailey."

It is caroling with groups from church and having shut-ins tell you: "You have made my Christmas!" You shake your head. "No, you have made mine."

It is kissing that special someone under the mistletoe. (Or thinking of a few you would like to pucker up to under there.)

It is passing the hat for a family you've never met — and may never meet — to make sure children have something under the tree this morning.

It is eating with guilt. It is eating without guilt. It is just eating and eating and eating.

It is happy people wearing Santa caps everywhere. And cashiers at the grocery store donning antlers on their heads.

It is bumping into old friends — and making new ones — while waiting in line at the post office.

It is placing loose change in the Salvation Army kettle. It is having the bell ringer wish you a "Merry Christmas."

It is the small talk of the season. "Got all your shopping done?" "Have you been a good boy this year?"

It is riding through downtown and suburban neighborhoods to view the Christmas lights.

It is the sad reality of the weather report, when we realize we won't have a white Christmas.

It is that wonderful verse from Dr. Seuss.

And he puzzled three hours until his puzzler was sore.

Then the Grinch thought of something he hadn't before.
"Maybe Christmas," he thought, "doesn't come from a store.
Maybe Christmas ... perhaps ... means a little bit more!"
It is wishes and dreams and hope for the world.
Merry Christmas.

A Columnist's Life

A Deal with My Stomach

June 13, 1999

Somewhere around the 12th bite, I made a deal with my stomach.

Get me through this again, buddy, and I'll treat you to some ice cream later.

Call it a bribe. Call it a peace treaty. Call it bunker mentality. But I did survive another chili cook-off.

I think I'll swear off red pepper for a few days, though.

For the third straight year, I was invited/tricked into serving as a judge for the WDEN state championship Chili Cook-Off at Shriner's Park. This event, which annually comes to you straight from the Heartburn of Georgia, is sometimes known as the Pepcid Invitational.

It also is a day of tremendous fun and music, even if your digestive tract does deserve a Purple Heart for its participation. WDEN always does a great job, and it's all for a worthy cause. Still, with so many samples of chili being consumed, the radio station's slogan ("Today's Hot New Country") takes on a whole new meaning.

The state championships have been held in Macon since 1983 and are sanctioned by CASI, the Chili Appreciation Society International. Of course, veteran officials claim the event is governed by Chiligula, the god of chili.

Never met the guy, but he also must moonlight as the god of iron stomachs.

There were 15 judges. Each of us carefully passed around Styrofoam cups marked with the contestant's numbers. Inside was all the chili you would care to eat in one afternoon — or maybe several afternoons.

Judges were asked to grade each cup on five criteria — aroma, color, consistency, taste and aftertaste. That should be easy enough, you say.

But, after about spoonful No. 16, your taste buds have learned a few new words, none of them printable.

"Competition chili is not always good 'eating' chili," said Rex Jones, a CASI official who flies in from Dallas to "referee" these cook-offs. "In fact, you probably couldn't eat a whole bowl of it."

The day began with 43 cooks. Only 21 made it to the final round.

"There is some really good chili out there," said Rick Maxwell, a six-time champion from Macon and a 20-year veteran of chili warfare. "And there is some really bad chili."

Fortunately, most of the really awful recipes never make it to the final round. They are screened, and then eliminated, so that tenderfoot

judges like myself — doctors, lawyers, newscasters and bankers — are spared the goat-gagging stuff.

On Saturday, one of the first-round entries was so dreadful that, based on a 0-10 point system, it managed to collect only a combined three points from a panel of five judges.

No, championship chili hardly resembles the kind you order in the drive-thru at Krystal or tap from a can of Hormel off the shelf at Kroger.

It starts with raw meat, cooked on-site from scratch. Most cooks use beef, although chicken, pork, squirrel and venison are permissible. A few years back, when the event was held at Central City Park, some wise guys thought they could slip a little gator meat into their pot. It didn't work.

Fillers such as beans, macaroni, rice and hominy are also taboo. "Nothing but meat and gravy," said Danny Bullington, from the award-winning Bull's Hotragious team out of Lizella. "Just like Gravy Train dog food."

Thanks for that comparison, Danny, especially right in the middle of my backhand on cup No. 8.

Naturally, some like it hot. Sweat-bead hot. Bernard Reagan and Greg Williams can certainly bring the heat from Norcross. It's called "Chernobyl Chew." It's motto is "Serving Up Toxic Waste."

At their booth, they used to display a banner with a mushroom cloud, but it has since been retired to the archives. The younger crowd doesn't always pick up on the reference to Chernobyl, anyway. The diehards, however, keep coming back for "some of that paint thinner."

"See all that red?" Reagan said, reaching for a bottle of imported hot sauce. "There is no tomato in there. It's all red pepper."

Trust me, there was plenty of fantastic chili to be sampled. Like that from the stove of Rocky Mills of Macon, who won first place Saturday for the second time in the past three years. With the victory comes the proverbial "bragging rights" and a trip to Terlingua, Texas, for the national championships in October.

Me? Well, I'm still feeling the effects of some of those sinus-clearing, palate-popping runners-up. As Maxwell said, some of it was very good, and some of it was pretty bad.

Back home in Dallas, referee Rex Jones is a funeral home director.

Said Bullington: "And, if you make really bad chili, your last visit is to Rex."

Yak of All Trades
October 1, 1999

School can teach you where to go during a fire drill, what button to push on the computer and which bus to catch home in the afternoon.

But nothing can quite prepare you for what to do when a 7-foot-tall Yak appears in the doorway of your classroom.

Do you crawl under your desk or hide behind your teacher?

The "Character Education" curriculum is a wonderful method of teaching moral values, but it doesn't include instructions on dealing with characters.

Especially one so huge and hairy he has been described as a "walking shag rug."

When I saw this tiny first-grader in pigtails out of the corner of my big, Yak eyes, I could tell I must be pretty intimidating.

I extended my giant paw. She gathered the courage to shake it. The smile on her face suddenly warmed the whole room. Her classmates began to giggle with relief once they realized I wasn't going to eat them for lunch.

Yes, I am a gentleman Yak. We played. We danced. We cut up. I rubbed heads, scratched backs, wrote funny things on the blackboard and bumped my head walking in and out of every doorway.

I arrived at Tinsley Elementary on Wednesday, just in time to mingle with the kindergartners as they sat down with their lunch trays. They must think I'm a bit clumsy. I nearly sat on one little fellow.

Oops! I got pudding on my left horn when I leaned down to give another child a hug.

And there was one special little boy. I picked him up, and he accidentally kicked over his milk.

I hope I didn't get him in too much trouble. But I do know when he got home that afternoon, and his mother asked him if anything interesting happened at school, his eyes grew big.

"I got attacked by a Yak," he said.

Since I am a Yak of all trades, I've been known to do a little of everything. *The Macon Telegraph* has invited me here for some guest appearances in the schools to help emphasize the importance of reading the newspaper.

Of course, I spread this important message in my own, non-verbal way.

Yaks don't talk. We are the strong, silent type.

But we do have many outstanding qualities. We're huggable.

And we care deeply about these children and their education.

I would like to thank Diane Rankin and Donna Balser-Smith of the *Telegraph's* Newspaper in Education department for taking me around on my first day in Middle Georgia. They were bodyguards for a widebody.

They had to apologize for stuffing me into the back of a Chevy Blazer (with no Yak restraint) to escort me to three local elementary schools — Winship, Tinsley and Burdell.

They were so nice. They stopped and bought me bottled water at the Citgo on Pio Nono. They rescued me from an afternoon rainstorm, so my hair wouldn't frizz. (I had run out of moose, er, mousse.)

Donna and Diane also took me by a local sandwich shop. I politely refused to go in. I was worried the health department might show up and give demerits for "customer" hygiene.

All the schools have been so much fun. I appreciate the hospitality of teachers, administrators and students. Oh, I've accidentally stepped on a few toes and nearly tripped on some lunch boxes, but I've received more hugs and tugs than just about any Yak in history.

If I didn't make it to your school, maybe we'll try again next time.

Yakety yak. I'll be back.

Ed the Pelvis

June 18, 2001

At times in my life I have been told that I look just like George Will. A guy I barely knew once called me "George" every time he saw me.

It has been said I closely resemble Bill Gates, too. Once, at a festival in North Carolina, some friends and I arrived late to a banquet. There were about 300 people in the room. I had no sooner sat down at the table when a man on stage entertaining the crowd singled me out.

"Hey you in the red shirt!" he hollered. "Yeah, you. Bill Gates. Stand up for a minute."

My face turned as red as my shirt.

I must have been a twin, separated at birth. Folks in my hometown insisted I was the spittin' image of a boy named Calvin, who went to another high school. I learned to answer to Calvin. I regret that I never got to meet him. If he looked like me, I probably should have sent him a sympathy card.

George. Bill. Calvin.

I must admit, though, I've never been mistaken for Elvis. Don't resemble him. Don't sound like him. Can't shake my hips without knowing I have a good chiropractor ready on the speed dial.

I was recently recruited for a show to benefit the Macon Rescue Mission. "An Evening with the Celebrities" will be held at the Grand Opera House.

When Lee Asbell of the Rescue Mission called to ask me to participate, she issued me an assignment and a challenge.

"We think you would make a very nice Elvis," she said.

Me? Blond hair? Wire-rim glasses? So skinny that when you look at me sideways I disappear? A singing voice that has been outlawed in several states?

"Whythankyouverymuch," I said.

I figured if Anita Ponder was already on board as Tina Turner, and Carolyn Crayton was going on stage as Dolly Parton, I could try on some blue suede shoes.

Just call me Ed the Pelvis.

Yep, I've been practicing.

You ain't nothin' but a hound dog, cryin' all the time.

You ain't nothin' but a hound dog, cryin' all the time.

Well, you ain't never caught a rabbit and you ain't no friend of mine.

In addition to the sights and sounds of Elvis, Tina and Dolly, the $10 ticket is an entertainment bargain. Where else can you find Beverly Olson (Dionne Warwick), Randy Bishop (Garth Brooks), Judge Bill Self (Tim McGraw), James Hartley (Merle Haggard) and Bert Bivins (Travis Tritt) on the same bill?

Not to be outdone, Jaime Kaplan is ready to sing as Helen Reddy. Suzanne Lawler and Rob Still will babe up to do Sonny and Cher.

To make it extra special, the audience will be treated to some "real" musical talents — Nikki Woodard and Keith Horton. Cast members from Theatre Macon's upcoming musical "Titanic" will give a sneak preview of several songs.

I'm ready. I'm pumped. We had a rehearsal last week. I pick up my costume from Bill Northenor today.

If I can just learn to twist my mouth like Elvis, maybe I can add some "lip sink" to my "lip sync."

It has been rumored several wild women in the audience are going to attack me. I'm looking forward to that, too.

Long live the King.

If Elected, I Will Serve

October 25, 2004

I am thankful Election Day will be here in eight days, and this ugly, nerve-wracking political season will mercifully come to an end.

I'm also glad I don't have to "run" for my job. I don't think I could hold up during the campaign. I don't think I could sling mud all day.

I have never run for political office, although one brave reader — bless his heart — cast a ballot for me as a write-in candidate for lieutenant governor two years ago.

That vote left me only 1,037,682 votes shy of Mark Taylor, but who's counting?

No, I don't think I could ever run for tax commissioner, school board or water authority. I have no desire to be mayor. I have no aspirations to become a senator.

Besides, politicians have to attend meetings. Lots of meetings. Ask anyone at *The Telegraph.* I have this aversion to meetings. Ask me to come to a meeting, and that's when I really do run — and hide under my desk.

But what if I really had to "run" for columnist? What if I had to seek your vote?

That very prospect prompted me to write down a few of the campaign promises I would include in my platform.

• I will write no column before its time. Writers thrive on deadline pressure. To quote my old buddy Winston Churchill — see, I'm already embellishing like a politician — "nothing is more exhilarating than to be shot at and missed."

• I will never use a big word when an infinitesimal word will do.

• I will not blame the shortage of flu shots on other columnists.

• I will paddle upstream from the "mainstream" media.

• I will exercise objectivity and never show my colors or my allegiance to a particular school.

• Go Dawgs!

• I will never bore you by writing about what I did on vacation.

• I also won't bore you with all the cute things my kids say, although I reserve the right to deliver my annual "state of the family" address in January.

• I will submit editorials in support of giving workers the tools they need to do the job. I want our military personnel to have the weapons they need and teachers to have the supplies they need. I want

every Department of Transportation worker to have a shovel to lean on.

• I will not clutter your yard with clever campaign signs, like "Read Gris!" I will campaign in all neighborhoods and not just the battleground estates.

• I will seek the endorsement of my mom, dad and two dogs. I'm sure my wife also will support me in my campaign, as long as I leave her alone and let her go shopping every other Saturday.

• Being a man of words, I will go after the "letter" vote and get the support of the NAACP, SEC, KFC, AFLAC and ESPN.

• I plan to reach across the rail to both conservatives and liberals, as well as vegetarians, rednecks, tree huggers, brown-baggers, roller hockey moms and trombone players.

• I promise to have quotas. I will be allowed to use the word "I" a maximum of 39 times in any column. (Oops! There goes the deficit again!)

• I pledge to balance my budget with columns that will make you laugh, cry, think, wonder, appreciate and introduce you to some of your neighbors.

That's the true joy of this job.

If elected, I will serve.

If at First You Don't Shuck Seed

June 21, 2002

If there's more than one way to skin a cat and barbecue a pig, there must be more than one way to spit a watermelon seed.

Do you twirl your tongue or clench your jaws? Should you bend your neck?

I've been asking these questions after being invited to participate in today's seed-spitting contest at Third Street Park. It's part of downtown's SunSational Summer Kick-Off Celebration.

Members of the media will square off against community leaders. I've been extremely nervous about this event. Must be "spitter's jitters."

So I've been practicing. I started training earlier this week. (There was a slight setback when my wife returned from the grocery with a seedless watermelon.)

I called Greg Leger in Cordele for some pointers. Greg's family has been in the watermelon business since 1963, and he is president of the National Watermelon Association.

Better yet, he was the 1996 national watermelon seed-spitting champion.

I told him I wanted to spit the way Tiger Woods putts — just the right touch without leaving it hanging on the lip.

Greg's advice was to roll my tongue and place the seed in the center.

Some spitters position the pointed end of the seed toward the front of their mouth, but Greg prefers it to be facing the rear.

It helps with the trajectory, improves the velocity and provides a little more roll. (No, I'm not a switch-spitter.)

A running start is not necessary. Greg recommended the one-step approach to avoid foot faults. It's important to arch your head, he said, "kind of like a rooster."

Greg has a plaque in his office to commemorate spitting a seed 44 feet, 11.5 inches in state competition. That's a tape-measure home run.

He also was on the veranda at the Sheraton Hotel in New Orleans in 1989 when nine-time national champion Jack Dietz of Chicago launched his national record of 66 feet, 11 inches.

"The wind caught it, and it just kept going," Greg said. (New Orleans may be below sea level, but apparently it's not below seed level.)

Other media personalities recruited to spit are *Telegraph* sports columnist Mike Lough, Cheryl Palmer of WMGT-TV (Channel 41), Doug Long and Beth Haynes of Fox 24, Lynn Murphey and Brad Bibb of Cox Cable, James Palmer of *Macon Magazine* and Derek Wright and Philip Black of radio station WMGB-FM (93.7).

The downtown leaders include Milton Heard IV of Hart's Mortuary, Janice Marshall of the Convention and Visitors Bureau, Pat Topping of the Chamber of Commerce and Allen Freeman, Eddie Pruett and Mark Stevens of the Cherry Blossom Festival.

My goal is to be in the media finals against James Palmer, since I've known him the longest. James loves to laugh, so my strategy in the finals would be to tell him a joke. He'll get so tickled he'll swallow the seed and be disqualified, and I will be crowned city champion.

What if I fail?

If at first you don't shuck seed ... try, try again.

I didn't fare so well in my seed-spitting. I finished far back in the pack.

Not a Right-Foot Conspiracy

June 25, 2004

I will not be the keynote clogger when the state clogging

convention taps its way into town.

I'm not disappointed, though. I'm not going to blame it on a right-foot conspiracy.

It's a safety issue. I might step on somebody's toes. Literally.

After all, I only learned a few basic clogging steps this week. So I'm still considered legged and dangerous.

Gail Hardison, local clogger extraordinaire, was gracious enough to offer me some lessons. I met her at her garage studio. She played "Cripple Creek" on the stereo.

She taught me how to do something called the "double-toe step rock step."

It sounds more like a flavor at Baskin-Robbins than a fundamental clogging maneuver.

For a beginner, Gail said I did wonderful. I think she was just being nice.

When the Georgia Clogging Leaders Association brings its annual convention to the City Auditorium this weekend, I would rather just step back and watch them strut their stuff.

How 'Bout Them Clogs!!!

(I've always wanted to say that.)

No, I'm not a complete novice at dancing. I could never be accused of having two left feet. Two right feet, maybe, but not two left.

I took ballroom dancing classes in high school, so I learned the Foxtrot and Charleston. On the dance floors of college life, I could do some semblance of the shag.

Still, I came away from Gail's clogging tutorial with a greater appreciation for this dance form. Later, I learned it began in the Appalachian Mountains as a variation of the foot-tapping folk dances brought to America by European settlers.

It is a lot more refined now. It takes plenty of skill, patience and ... er, legwork to be a proficient clogger.

Gail remembers how people told her she would never stick with it when she began clogging in Atlanta back in the 1970s. That made her even more determined.

In 1982, she formed the local Dixie Doodle Cloggers as part of the BellSouth Pioneers. Since then, her shoes have hit dance floors from Macon to Nashville. Over the years, she has taught clogging to both the young and the young at heart. Saturday, she will be among the judges in the annual state competition.

I asked her about the experience of having hundreds of cloggers all in the same room. I was trying to imagine what it might look like this weekend at the City Auditorium, with all those steel-plated heels and toes tapping against the wooden floor.

"It will sound like thunder," she said. When the routines are choreographed and everyone is in step with the music, she said, "it's the most beautiful sound in the world."

Gail loves the creative expression of clogging, and has invented several steps herself.

She named one step after her dog, Duncan, and another after her daughter, Leslie.

A few months ago, she invented a step in honor of talk show host and comedian Wayne Brady. In January, she appeared on Brady's syndicated national TV show in Los Angeles, where she taught him her own "Wayne Brady Clogging Step."

Maybe one day Gail will name a clogging step after me.

She can call it the Gris Step.

Easy to remember. Rhymes with Misstep.

A Day When the Columnist Thanks You

April 18, 2004

Today is National Columnists Day.

Sure, it doesn't carry the same weight as Easter or Mother's Day. No ham baking in the oven. No big sales at the mall.

Bet it's not even on your calendar. Bet you forgot to get me a card.

That's OK. Newspaper columnists collect their rewards every day. After all, we get to write about the people and places around us and the events that shape our lives. We are invited to sit down at the breakfast table every morning and break bread with our readers.

National Columnists Day is not self-serving. The National Society of Newspaper Columnists simply urges those of us in the profession to "write a column about how great it is to be a columnist."

April 18 is the day we observe because it is the anniversary of the death of Ernie Pyle, considered the patron saint of columnists. Pyle, the famed World War II correspondent, wrote about common folks on the front lines of life trying to make a difference in the world.

On April 18, 1945, he was killed by Japanese machine gun fire on a tiny island in the Pacific. He died with his boots on. He died doing what he loved the most — writing and reporting.

I've never been shot at ... unless you count missing deadline. But I once interviewed former Macon Mayor Ronnie

"Machine Gun" Thompson.

I've never flirted with journalistic danger, except those times when I was asked to serve as a judge at the Chili Cook-Off.

Although I've never been to war, I've written about brave people fighting for their lives in hospital wards. I've been in the trenches with everyday foot soldiers in their battles against bureaucracy and social injustice.

Most of my columns deal with ordinary people. They are the very marrow of life. They are the gumption with which we rise and pour our coffee each morning.

My job has taken me from swamps and hollows to the top floors of buildings. I've hunted down stories in trailer parks, housing projects, pool halls, mill villages, cemeteries and in the shade of oaks. I've found subjects in shotgun houses, halfway houses and outhouses.

It's a job where the assignments not only change by the day, they can change by the hour. One day, you may find yourself dining at the exclusive City Club. The next day, three blocks away, you can be sharing a sandwich with a homeless man.

I've discovered countless heroes in my own back yard. A blind man from Macon who reads his Bible in Braille. A Dodge County family who adopted 21 kids. A double amputee who once came to the aid of a man in a hit-and-run accident. A teenager from Warner Robins who started a free lunch program for underprivileged children.

Over the past six years, I've also learned the delicate balance of writing a newspaper column. It's like holding a bird in your hand. If you squeeze it too tight, you'll crush it. If you grip it too loosely, it will fly away.

No, this is not a day when you're supposed to thank people like me.

It's a day when people like me should thank people like you.

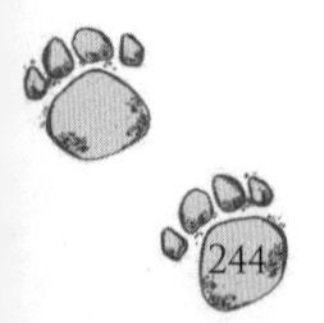